Chronicles of a Slave Girl

1

Chronicles of a Slave Girl

Copyright © 2013 by Bertrand E. Brown

ISBN: 978-1482358568

December 23, 1864

Well, it won't be long now fo' Christmas'll be here which means us slave's gits two whole days off to celebrate... Me, myself, I's has to work mo' harder than I usually does helpin' prepare da food fer all mas'r's kinfolks what'll be comin' in from all ova da county and some from even as fer as Decatur. Still, I don't much mind workin' through Christmas bein' that I gots probably da best job of any a masr'rs slaves and da work ain't nebber ain't whatcha might call hard fo' me bein' that I done been doin' it mos' all my life. And Mas'r John, he always be sayin' dat I's da best cook dis side of New O'leans and bein' dat we here in lower Georgia dat must mean dat I's a purty fair cook. Though Mas'rs' wife, her name, Missy Charlene, she ain't nebber said no such a thing. I believe she might be a might bit jealous is why she don't dish out no compliment even though she knowed da food good.

Missy Charlene ain't nebber took no real likin ta me. And da reason I believe she don't like me much is 'cause she knowed my daddy a white man. Dat right dere make me half-white and half as good as her. Plus, bein' dat I'se of mixed blood, and gots a purty good grade a hair just like her'n, I b'lieves dat right dere bothers her mo' than she willin' ta let on to. But to be sho' dat ain't all what bothers h̶   ̶ b'lieves really bothers her mos' a all is da fact dat Ma

3

up in da kitchen wit' us slaves gals. If ya ast me, dats what really sticks in her craw.

Now, Mas'r John, he a good man. Well, as far as mas'rs go, he a good man. And when we ast him why he all da time be hangin' 'round us womenfolk when he know missy don't 'preciate he jes tell us he like bein' 'round pretty thangs is all. Dat's what he tells us. But me and Aunt Hattie is da only only one's dat be in da kitchen and Aunt Hattie close ta ninety bein' dat she got great grand and dat's why I knows dat when Mas'r John sayin' stuff like dat he mostly be referrin' ta me like da white folks say "indirectly". But what he really be doin' is signifyin'. He always be doin' that. Signifyin' that is. That's what white folk do instead of comin' right out and sayin' what it is dey really want.

Still, me and mas'r 'unnerstans' each other even though we don't say a lot to each other. And ev'rybody will tell you that Miss Mary dat's me, aint never been one ta bite my tongue like most a dese Afreecan niggas roun' dis here plantation. And like I told Mas'r John when he got ta drinkin and just showed up at my door, one night a few years back. I said Mas'r John you is a pretty fair mas'r as far as mas'rs go but I'm durn near fo'ty years old to the best of my recollection and I done seen so much hell in dese here fo'ty years right here on dis plantation dat I know dat I's goin' to a better place so I aint scared a dyin' and dat's exactly what's

4

goin' to happen to one of us if you step one foot inside my quarters wit' dem devilish intentions.

Mas'r ain't say nothin' 'cause he knowed how I was. He jes looked at me then turned and walked away. 'Course I knew I was gonna have ta pay fer dat and da very next day Mas'r John had me whipped like I ain't never been whipped befo' or since. I's still got the scars. But I believe mas'r havin' ta watch 'em whoop me and me bein' his favorite prop'ty hurt him worse than it hurt me. But I unnerstan' him havin' ta have me whipped though. What I said to him that night was what you might call belligerent. And a mas'r can't afford ta have no halfa nigga runnin' roun'thinkin' dey better than ev'rybody else just 'cause they half-white, wit' good hair and fortunate enough tta be allowed tt work alongside a him and his family in da big house. He jes cain't have dat. Say it don't provide a good image for da other slaves. And I knows dat's true. But sometimes I think I forgets that I'm just a niggra slave because of all this white blood I got in me. But mas'r he don't never forget to remind me of who I is or how blessed I am to be one of his slaves and I guess I am in a way though I ain't rightly figured out how but still I knows things could be worse. I's could be in da fields all day croppin' tobaccy or pickin' cotton so maybe I is blessed in a way.

Well, gotta get some sleep and some rest, as I's powerfully tired. Ain't young as I useta be and I gotta gits up and like I sayed I gots ta git up early and git Christmas dinner started. Tomorrow's Christmas and yall ain't never seen a place mo' busier than dis here Marshall Plantation 'round da holidays.

December 24, 1864

Today is December the 24th and jes like I expected, mas'r and missy gots niggras runnin and jumpin' and ev'rybody jest a bumpin' into each other tryin to stay outta mas'rs hair and offen his bad side which aint usually hard to do but today it is 'cause he gots all dese impotent folk comin' in and he want ev'rything to be just right so's he looks good in front of his guests. Makes it hard on a niggra though 'cause we aint useta all these extra special specifications he want us ta adhere to. But for me and Aunt Hattie it ain't nearly so hard bein' that we been doin the same for Lord knows how long.

Far as I know I's somewhere 'round fo'ty or fo'ty-one years old. Least dat's what I figger 'cause Mas'r John say he buyed me in New O'leans for his daughter when I's jest a small fry. Say the trader who sold me told him that I was near abouts four or five give-or-take a year and bein' that I been here on da Marshall Plantation here for the last thirty-five years, that would make me somewhere's around fo'ty. I's spect, lessin my math ain't too good.

6

Still, and all, I's been here long enough to know the goin's and comin's and how ta get along wit' out too much in da way of problems. And dat ain't necessarily easy for a niggra ta do. But sees I's figgered da easiest way ta avoid problems is ta keep ta yo'self. So dat's mainly what I do. I keeps ta myself even when it comes ta da men folks dat be houndin' me alla da time. So, while mas'r and missy runnin' roun' screamin' and hollerin' they knows ta leave Mary, that's me, and Aunt Hattie alone 'cause we's gots all bizness in da kitchen purty much under control. But meanwhile dey gots everybody else jes' a runnin' and a jumpin' dis way and dat tryna stay outta dey way and that poor excuse for an ovaseer, ol' Sam who can't hardly stand no niggras whippin' heads ev'ry chance he gits.

But mostly everybody seem purty happy about da Christmas and havin' a day off and all but ain't nobody happier than me. You see I's got a secret dat I ain't tol' not nary a soul, not even Mas'r John but I's gittin' married on da Christmas day. Well, da real reason I ain't tryin' ta let nobody know is 'cause mos' niggras is always lookin' for any excuse at all to git all likkerd up and start jumpin' up and down just like the apes they comes from and I don't want missy or Mas'r John ta think that I's like dem fool niggras one bit. Ya see I works extremely hard ta stay separate and keep a certain air of sophistication and class about myself. I figger jes 'cause I's a niggra don't mean I's caint be no lady.

7

Plus, the onliest one's that I really talks to aside from Aunt Hattie on dis' here plantation is mas'r and he surely wouldn't be int'rested in coming to no nigga wedding. Besides Auntie Hattie know a whole hell of a lot about white folk bein' that she been sold five or six times and she knows how they think and she say that mas'r might not take too kindly to his most favorite slave giving her stuff away to some Afreecan nigga before he got a chance to try it out fer hisself. She also say that when two niggras from different plantations gits married and git da craving and need to see each other caint nobody or nothing stop 'em. So, dat's another reason da owner's don't want no slave marriages. Dey gits ta thinkin' about runnin' jes so as dey can be together. So, I figgers to keep it quiet 'til Joseph can buy us ar freedoms but 'til then me and hims gonna do all da stuff I hear married peoples do.

My Joseph aint much like me. Everyday he be a slave he gets mo' and mo' bad-tempered. I could see if he was an ev'ryday field hand but Joseph's no ord'nary field hand. No suh! My Joseph got a trade. He a blacksmith and he aint jes' no ordinary blacksmith. Joseph the best blacksmith in all a de Savannah County. All de white folks from near and far always be requestin' Joseph but his Mas'r Reynolds aint like my Mas'r John. He aint no fair man nor no good man and even though he let Joseph keeps a portion of what he earn, Joseph don't think it's hardly

8

enough and he say we be old and gray before he ever have enough ta buy us ar freedom and that's why he hate Mas'r Reynolds and all de rest of dem white folk so much.

Me, on da otha hand, I tells Joseph to be patient and put his hopes and dreamins' in the Lord's hands and things will work dem selves out. I always tells him to just have a little patience and have faith in de Lord and I think he's learning to 'cause he no longer spend all his time talkin' about runnin' away to freedom.

When I first met Joseph it was 'cause someone tol' him about a slave gal dat could read and writ'. And so he come to see me hoping that I would write him a pass to get him past the slave catchers on his way to Florida but I refused. Tol' him to think about it for a week then come back and see me 'cause I could see he was mo' than a little upset about the way Mas'r Reynold's been treatin' him. But dat all he talk about. Runnin' and freedom. And I's was scairt I was gonna lose him befo' I had him good. He useta sayed to me alla da time dat Mas'r Reynolds da worstest mas'r a slave could ever be owned by and from his accounts he knowed many a slaveowner in his time.

Anyways, Joseph put off all notion of runnin' away for a spell, took my advice and come back ta see me afta he had a chance to set upon the idea for a spell. And since I had dat talk wit' him, he been back ev'ry Friday and Saturday night since.

'Ventually, I said yes to his plan which he commenced ta bug me about ev'ry time we was togetha but afta I spoke to Aunt Hattie to make sure I agreed but I hadda make sho' I wasn't doing the wrong thing fo' I give him a answer. Funny thing though, Joseph knew what I was goin' to say befo' I even sayed anything. And I can remember it like it was yesterday wit' him standing dere all tall and black and shiny wit' all dem big, fine, muscles and dem shiny white teeth. Ya see, my Joseph was pure Afreecan as I ever did see. And 'bout da only one dat I could stand. And Aunt Hattie she sayed my Joseph was da biggest man she'd ever laid eyes on. Sayed she'd never seen no man with no hands and no feet that big. And tonight I'm gonna see what all else goes along with dem feet and dem hands and jes hope I can accommodate my Joseph.

December 25th 1864

I'se in tears. And jes cain't stop cryin'. I don't know what happened but my Joseph ain't nebber show up. It ain't like my Joseph ta jes not show up. It jes ain't like him. 'Specially on our wedding night. I don't know if da slavers done picked him up or that mean ol' mas'r a his done sent him

10

somewhere's but I's so worried dat I can't hardly think a nothin' but my

Joseph. I's so worried I jes wanna go up t mas'r and ast him but iffen

Mas'r Reynolds done sold him all he gonna do is git ta wonderin' what

me and Joseph's connection be befo' hollerin' and telllin' me ta stop

meddlin' in white folks affairs so all I's can do is sit and wait 'til I git some

word.

Ev'ry Christmas since I been here Mas'r John always makes sure he

gives us slaves somethin' special. Mos' a the time, it don't 'mount ta

much more than a ham and a bottle a corn likker but it's mo' 'n what we

had and ev'rybody grateful and fo' mos' a us slaves it was a joyful

occasion but fer me it was one a da most saddest occasions a my life up

'til then.

Dat evening bein' dat it was Christmas I made my way from da quarters.

Dat's what us niggra's called ar lil' vllage of shacks lined up in a row.

Dere was rows and rows of shacks in da quarters all lined up in a row

some bigger than othas but all but none a dem bigger than da smallest

room in mas'rs house. Mos' a dem had dirt floors and almost none a

dem had a stove or fireplace ta do dere cookin' but mas'r made sho'

mine had a pot bellied stove and a fireplace, both so I could practice

cooking and making new dishes. Plus he made sho' I had a reg'lar wood

flo. I believes mos' a da otha niggras was jealous a me and Aunt Hattie

'cause a da way mas'r treated us and da way he bestowed stuff on us

11

but I's didn't care. Iffen dey hadn't been so lazy and shiftless he mighta done betta by them but all I heared him say was how lazy and shiftless and connivin' dey was most a da time and so dat's what dey got fo' dey efforts. Nothin'! Me, on da otha hand, was up here at da crack a day headin' up ta da big house ta clean up afta da white folk from da night befo. I woulda done it las' night but mas'r sayed he didn't knowed what time his guests be leavin' and he didn't want me ta have ta wait roun' all night; it bein' Christmas and all. Didn't much matter ta me though long as I's didn't have ta sit in my shack all alone on Christmas which I's ended up doin' anyway. At da time I thought about moseyin' on down ta Aunt Hattie's. I knew it would be a purty festive occasion down dere in da lower forty. Ya see da quarters was divided inta da upper quarters where mos' a da niggra's dat been wit' mas'r fer quite a spell lived and den dere was dat part—da lower forty we called 'em where mos' a da Afreecans dat jes arrived off da boat lived. Mos' a da lower forty was made up a da field hands and Aunt Hattie chose ta live down dere as 'pposed ta livin' in da upper quarters. She sayed she seed enough a da white folk and when she ain't have ta she wanted ta be as far away from 'em as possible. Plus she liked bein' 'round her own kind; referring ta da Afreecans. I tol' her dat as long as she been wit' mas'r dat she ain't hardly no Afreecan but she a niggra jes like me tryna make her feel good even though I knowed dat she was pure Afreecan and ain't had no white blood in her like me and mos' us niggras in da upper quarters but I loved

12

dat ol' woman and so I's tried ta make her feel equal but I b'lieved she knowed dat she waon't quite like da rest a us dat stayed up dere and jest felt more comfortable wit' her own kind. Plus dey needed her when ta translate or when one a 'em gots sick or was wit' child.

Anyways, I's in such low spirits dat I didn't see goin' down ta da lower forty to Aunt Hattie's wit' da long face so I jes stayed in and thought about my Joseph 'til it was time ta go up ta da big house and clean up. Well, when I gits dere, dere's a whole new group a white folk, mos'ly gentlemen's like mas'r—ya know—slaveowner's and bizness mens sittin' in da parlor takin' brandy and I hears Mas'r John and Mas'r Reynolds talkin'. And I's cain't help but overheared dem bein' dat I had ta bring mo' brandy and clean glasses and straighten up 'round dem. Dat's when I heared Mas'r Reynolds sayed how he was feelin so troubled but could find no otha alternative. Mas'r weren't in da room at da time and I wished he had been but he won't. Anyway, I heared Mas'r Reynolds sayed dat he was in sech a bad financial bind dat he jes couldn't find no alternative to 'lleviatiin' all da pressure and debt he was in 'ceptin' by sellin' off some a his mos' prime hands. But one thing in p'ticular caught my ear and dat's when I's heared him sayed dat he even hadda ta git rid a nigga Joe da best blacksmith in da whole goddamn county.

13

Now I's not sho how I gots back ta da quarters but I do r'memba seein' mas'r and missy standin' o'er me. I ain't even sho' how many days had passed but I ken tell you dis. No one rushed me back ta my chores.

When I did go back, some time later—I don't know how much time passed—missy telled me dat I done had what dey called da nervous breakdown. She sayed dat I had been talkin' outta my head wit' da fever. She sayed I was sayin' all kinda stuff 'bout da white folk bein' evil ta da core and some kin ta da devil. Sayed she and mas'r didn't know iffen it was safe to have me in da house wit' dem dere kinda thoughts wit' Nate Turner and so many slave revolts goin' on right through here.

I's knowed it won't nobody but missy talkin' and fabricatin' and feedin' mas'r all dem lies as I ain't nebber sayed nothin' what you might call derogatory 'bout mas'r or none a dem white folk good as dey been ta me. I's knowed it was her but I's didn'y say nothin' 'cause right through here I didn't rightly care 'bout nothin' but findin' out what all happened ta my Joseph and bein' free a dem ol' devilish white folk.

When she proceeded to tell me dat Aunt Hattie's grand baby would be takin' my place in da kitchen a da big house and she won't even half a woman yet 'cause she was a betta cook I wonted ta rip dat ol' white heifer's head right offa her shoulders, fer da simple fact dat I knowed dat

14

what she was doin' ain't had nothing' ta do wit' my cookin' or me havin'

no nervous breakdown spell. Inside I knowed da real reasons and I's

wondered why mas'r ain't had da brain ta see what it was she was doin'.

I knowed it was cause I was half-white and had good hair jes like hers.

And I knowed it was fer alla dem times missy caught Mas'r John in dat

kitchen oglin' us womens folk when she figgered he should been settin'

somewhere lookin' at her ol' ugly, shriveled up white ass.

January 4th

I guess missy thought she was bein' nice by givin' me some time off fer

me ta git betta from my nervous breakdown. Eitha dat or she was tryna

convince mas'r dat I was really sick. I's don't riightlly know at dis point

but I ain't mind da time off and I knowed dat won't nothin' ailin' me but da

fact dat dey done stole my Joseph 'way from me. 'Sides dat won't

nothin' wrong wit' me. Ya see, I ain't nebber been one ta fret ova things I

cain't fix. Plus, I's one who don't b'lieves in lettin' anotha human be dey

niggra or white, git unda my skin so I took dat time off ta freshen up my

quarters and do some work in my garden. In fact I's was plantin' some

collards and some turnips one day. It was early evenin' when dat ol'

nasty ova 'seer come by ta tell me dat I be startin' in da fields dat next

mo'nin'.

15

I kinda figgered dis day was comin since I had dat talk wit' missy so I's won't too upset 'bout it and iffen I's had been—like I sayed—I's wouldn't a let it show. Well' I's wasn't too upset 'bout it ceptin' fer da fact dat afta all de years I spent slavin' in dat white woman's kitchen and makin' sho dat ev'rything was done ta mas'r and missy's 'zact specifications and settin' dere listenin' ta mas'r go on-and-on 'bout he done made a mistake marryin' da most' evilest and unhappiest woman ta ever walk da face a da earth he let her set me out in da fields wit' da common fiel' hands.

Afta all dat listenin' and tryna regulate his drinkin' and all dem nights havin' ta help Aunt Hattie drag his drunken self off a da buckboard when ol' Ben bringed him home from his nights out in Savannah. Afta all dem nights tryna drag hm up dat long and windin' staircase and undressin' him whilst he tried ta grab ev'rything wit' in his reach no matta if it was me or Aunt hattie and tellin' us how we was da purtiest women's in all dem parts—purtier dan mos' white womens in dem parts—I jes had a hard time b'lievin' he would allow 'em ta stick me out in da fields like a common fiel' hand is all wit' out even comin ta tell me hisself.

It was 'bout dis time afta I done heared da news 'bout my Joseph from Mas'r Reynolds' own lips and den afta mas'r let missy have me put ta work out in da fields dat I's got ta thinkin' dat maybe my Joseph was right 'bout dere not bein' no difference between a Afreecan slave and a

16

niggra. Joseph useta say dat a slave is jes a slave. Make no difference ta white folk where he from. A niggra is jes a niggra and a slave is jest a slave—nothin mo' than a good buckboard or a right strong plow hoss ta be used til all its useful ness been spent or white folk growed tired of it den he sell 'em or jes toss it away. Dat's what my Joseph telled me jes a few nights befo' dey selled him down da river. Dat's what he telled me. He sayed a Afreecan ain't no mo' than a tool. Dat's what my Joseph telled me lyin' dere in my arms. I's didn't unnerstan' then but I's beginnin' ta b'lieve dere's somethin' ta what he had ta say.

Still, I's couldn't unnerstan' how my own mas'r could jes up n put me out dere in da fields wit' da otha hands. 'Specially since dere was nothin' dere but Afreecans—jes common field hands—and I's was da best cook in alla Savannah County. Mas'r had said so hisself. Plus, I learnt ta sew on my own and was purty fair at dat as well. Even mo' impotent was da fact dat I's won't made fo' field work wit' no hot Georgia sun beamin' down on my head. Too long out dere in dat hot sun and I would sho'lly faint dead away. And soon I's be lookin' like dem Afreecans and be all black and shiny and glistenin'. I jes wont made fer da fields. Maybe Mas'r John was fergettin' dat me bein' high yalla I couldn't take no heat. Maybe he was fergittin' dat I's only a half a nigga and wont meant fer dat sorta thing.

17

I's ain't hadda chance ta talk ta him since I's fell ill wit' da grief a findin' out my Joseph been sol't away but he mos' sho'ly gwine find out and dat's gwine be da end a da fields fo dis ol' gal.

January 5th

It's a wonder a Afreecan don't jes lose his mind. Spent all day out dere in dat hot sun diggin' potatoes. Da ova'seer—him go by the name of Samuel Bush. Anyways, he say he gonna take it light on me bein' that it's my first day and all but he gonna be keepin' an eye on me though and he sho' enuff did that. Ev'ry time I be bending ova he eitha standin' right behind me on that big ol' black bay of his or he be sittin' up high and standin' right next to me lookin' down my blouse tryna see what he can see. I thought about wearin' mo' in da way a petticoats t'morrow but it be so dang hot out dere dat I's already overdressed. But I gots ta find a way ta makes him stop 'cause he got da reputation fo' makin' cabin calls in da middle of the night and done had every wench on da place 'ceptin' me and Aunt Hattie and dat's only 'cause Aunt Hattie too ol' and I's always in da kitchen unda Mas'r John's watchful eye. But now dat I's unda his care and a'thority I figures it's only a matter of time fo' he come a callin' on me.

18

And rights now I ain't gots no time for no trouble wit' no ova'seer and nobody else fer dat matta. I gots otha plans a fillin' my mind. Rights now I just wants to git healthy and gain some of da weight I lost back so's I can git about da business at hand.

Bein' out dere in da fields today, did one thing for me though. It gived me a new 'ppreciation for dem black Afreecans dat mas'r all da time callin' lazy and no good. To tell you da God's honest truth, I ain't witness not nar' lazy one yet. Fer da mos' part dey jes goes 'bout dere business of pickin' cotton like dey was born to do it—all methodical like—jes a pickin'and all da while a singin'like dey was at a jamboree. And all da time dat mean ol' overseer wit' da shifty eyes be ridin' up-n-down da rows on dat big, black bay horse a his crackin' dat dere ridin' crop on dere backs hollerin' and yellin' and cussin' at 'em tellin' 'em how dey ain't no good and how he had a betta hound dog and rushin' 'em ta all da time speed it up. And Lord knows dey couldn't wo'k no faster than dey was already wo'kin unda dat sun and dem conditions. But nebber—not once—did dey look up or utter a word a disrespect at dat mean ol' overseer. Dey jes keeped right on singin' and wo'kin' hard in spite of ev'rything Sam, da overseer, threw dere way.

19

I 'spect I kinda unnerstan what Joseph been tryna tell me a might betta now bout da hardships and all a bein' a common ev'ryday field hand unda a mean mas'r but I was sho' Mas'r John woulda nebber let this go on had he knowed it was happenin'.

Den ag'in I spoze that's just da price of bein' bo'n a heathen Afreecan. Dats why I's so glad da Lord done blessed me wit' bein' half-white and a Christian. Truth is half da reason dey gets treated da way they do is 'cause dey Black and ugly and sinners and don't believes in nothin' cept getting' likker'd up and dancin' and hollerin' and singin' dem ol' crazy Afreecan jibberish songs dat don't make no sense.

When dey git smart and start actin' mo' white and mo proper den I 'spects things will start pickin' up for dem. But da first thing dey gotta do is stop all dat laughin' and dancin' and carryin' on and start tryin' ta appear mo' civilized and s'phisticated.

I knows what I's talkin' bout too. Much as I's been 'round white folk, I should. Not only dat but I can tell you dis as well. Auntie Hattie useta be a heathen Afreecan like dem dere niggras out in da fields but she seed dere was no future in dat and got tired of bein' whipped alla da time so she got da religion and started actin' civilized like da white folk and fer you knowed it she won't out dere bakin' and getting' blacker than she already was in dat Georgia sun. No sir, once she got her mind right and starts actin' mo white, and fo' she knowed it, she right up dere in da big house next to me.

Well, anyways it tain't enough room in da big house for all dem niggas no way and bein' dat dey Afreecans it really ain't no concern of mine no way. I says, da hell wit 'em and dere heathen ways. Ain't none of 'em out dere like my Joseph or Auntie Hattie. Dem two is what Mas'r John call da 'ception ta da rule which means dey jes diff'rent from da rest.

Anyways, I done spent too much time thinkin' bout dem no account field hands when I's got mo' impotent things ta consider like how I'm a gonna find my Joseph . 'Sides I gots ta be up by da crack a dawn and Lord knows I needs my rest since I don't what that mean ol' overseer gots in store for me t'morrow.

January the 6th

Lord knows I's don't know what I's done ta deserve dis. I swears fo' God I don't know. My hands what useta be so soft and purty is raw and bloody and hu't so bad dat when ol' Sam da ova'seer give us a water break, I poured da water ova my head ta hide da tears. And my back aches liked it ain't nebber ached befo' –even worser than when I's got whipped fo' bein' b'lligerent and dey throwed dat salt on dem open sores

21

ta make it heal proper and ta make me r'member so's I's won't be b'lligerent no mo'. Dat dere hurt worser than anything—well—up 'til now dat is.

Dis here is a new kinda pain and I's don't recollect ever comin' across anything dis bad in my life. Dey says it's from bendin' ova ta pick da cotton from cain't see in da mornin' ta cain't see at night. And I'll tell ya. Ain't no way, no human bein', not nary one a God's children s'pozed ta be subjected ta nothin' like what I's experienced dese last few days. Jes ain't human iffen ya ast me, p'sonally. I useta heared Mas'r John says dat's why da good Lord created da Afreecan but much as I's dislike dem I's cain't see nobody bein' subjected ta dat. 'Course, mas'r say dat da Afreecan jes natur'lly designed ta pick cotton and rice and tobaccy whereas white folk is jes not designed dat way. Dey designed to lead whereas Afreecans is meant ta follow. He say it in da Good Book. Dat's what he says but I's read da Good Book through and through, and I's cain''t find dat dere passage nowheres in my 'ttempts ta be a betta Christian.

On da otha hand, it jes might be something' ta what mas'r be sayin' 'cause aiin't a one a dem heathen Afreecans come outta da fields dis evenin' lookin' like or feelin' like I do. Leastways, can't nobody tell da way dey alla da time jes a grinnin' and a laughin'.

From what I seed dey laughs and jokes mo' n da white folks and I swears I b'lieves dey ain't no mo' animals like chimpanzees or apes in makeup and 'lil childrens in dey minds da way dey wo'k and den tells jokes afta' wards like dey ain't got a care in da world. It jes seem funny dat white folk got all da money and da big houses but you hardly ever sees 'em laugh and frolic da way dese simple fools do.

But enough about dem fool Afreecans. I jes wishes somebody would tell me what I done did ta be in dis here predicament. Iffen I had my druthers I's b'lieve I'd ruther be whipped than ta have endure dis pain in m'back. Lord knows I ain't nebber been one ta complain or be foul in anyway but I b'lieve I's gonna sleep wit' my shoes and clothes on t'night it hurts so much. But what hurts even worser is dat Mas'r John jes gonna 'llow ol' Sam da ova'seer ta jes put me smack dab in da middle in da midst a all dese heathen knowin' full well dat I ain't jes no common field hand. Why, iffen he ain't recognize it, I's half white and gots skills and a trade besides. He jes gonna stick me in dere and 'spect me to work wit' dem ol' heathen Afreecans afta servin' in his kitchen fer durn near thirty-fi' years. By now, he must a knowed I's gone; lesin he's on a bizness trip to Savannah or somethin'. I sho do he hopes he come back soon though, so he can sees what his lil missy done gone and did dis time.

Out here workin' wit' da Afreecans when I done made it plain on mo' than one occasion ta mas'r, jes in case he didn't know, dat I's a Christian woman and don't be hangin' 'round no heathen Afreecans. Onliest thang I do is nod my head in passin'. Mos' of 'em thinks I's too high falutin— which I guess I is 'cause a m'birthright and bein' from New O'leans and all. Mos' of 'em thinks I's white anyway and Aunt Hattie says dey thinks I's high falutin' 'cause a da way I carries m'self wit' m' head in da air when I's down in da quarters amongst them. Iffen you wanna know da truth of da matta though, it's dat I jes don't wanna be 'sociated wit nobodody blacka than tar runnin' 'round here like dey's still in da jungle, naked wit' no religion and believin' in witch doctors and da voodoo and all dat otha kinda ol' crazy nonsense. Dat's da real truth of da matter if ya really wants ta know. Dey don't hardly seem like dey even wanna be civilized. And now dey done throwed me right smack dab in da middle of 'em. And if ya ain't recognized it yet, I ain't all dat tickled about da proposition.

Still, I gots ta admit dat despite all dey sho'tcomins mos of 'em is right friendly and a couple of da womens even showed me how ta wrap m'hands so dem dem cotton stickers don't cut what's left of 'em ta threads.

Well, it seems dat da tallow in m'candle 'bout gone so's I's gonna rest
dese ol' weary bones and munch on some a Aunt Hattie's homemade
biscuits she had one a her grands drop off earlier.

I sho do miss Aunt Hattie's cookin' and all dat good food up at da big
house but I's sho don't miss Miss missy runnin' 'round screamin' and
hollerin' all a de time. Now dat's one thing I sho don't miss.

January 7th

Lord chile, I gots ta go somewheres outta this hell dey call slavery...

I couldn't hardly wo'k today I was so sore. Back kept feelin' like it was
goin' ta give out any second. Couldn't hardly bend and m'fingas was so
sore and swoll, I couldn't hardly grasp da cotton and Lord knows dat ain't
hardly da worst of it. Fell off ta sleep last night and heared dis noise a
comin' from right outside m'cabin. At first, I figgered it was Aunt Hattie
tellin' me dat da lil' Afreecan gal so big in da way a motherhood was
'bout ready ta drop dat youngun a hers. And since I always served as a
midwife along wit' Aunt Hattie I jes naturall figgered dat's what all da
commotion was about. Ya see it ain't a lot a niggra gots ta be thankful
fo' but when a youngun comes along it's like dat right dere is anotha
chance for a savior ta be born in our midst ta save us from dis ol'
wretched existence. At least dat's what Auntie Hattie sayed when I ast

25

her why niggra's gits all excited when a baby's born. Seem funny ta me dat dey'd want a youngun ta come inta dis ol' world knowin' dat chances is good he gonna be sol' away from 'em. Lord da mo' I gits ta thinkin' da mo' and mo' I gits ta soundin' like Aunt Hattie and m'Joe. Aunt Hattie say dat it ain't no mo' than da experience in da fields makin' me finally see da light but I believe dat all dat sunlight startin' ta blur m'vision. Eitha dat or I's been 'round dem Afreecans a might too long and am starttin' ta pick up some a dem fool ideas a deres.

But anyways, I hear da noise mo' clearly now and recognize da sound of hoof and dey was ridin' strong and hard da way da drovers and slave catchers do when dey hot on a niggra's tail or dey tryna frighten us. But mas'r he don't 'llow them ta come 'round here no mo' so I knowed it won't dem even though that's how hard and fast dey was ridin'. Den I figger it must be mas'r comin' in from business ta tell me dat it had all been a mistake and how how God awful sorry he was for lettin' dem put me wit'dem field hands. Only trouble was mas'r nebba but nebba come down ta da quarters alone and from what I heared it won't but one horse. And dat's when it dawned on me dat da only otha person I knowed brave enough ta ride down inta da quarters dis late at night was none otha than m'Joseph who feared no man Afreecan or white.

Well, just thinkin' about dat big ol' black shiny, Mandingo warrior comin' ta see me got my heart just a flutterin' and da butterflies started ta join right in and I jes don't know what I was feelin' but I thought I's was goin' ta burst wide open thinkin' 'bout how m'baby come back. Ya see, m'Joseph da only niggra I knowed dat rode a hoss, he bein' a blacksmith and all, it wan't uncommon fer him ta come a ridin' up at dis time of night ta tickle m'fancy. So's I jes knowed it was m'baby and I leapt up offa dat dere bunk, bad back and all and went a runnin' ta unhook da latch half-expectin' ta see m'Joseph but won't a soul out dere as far as I could see wit' it bein' dark as hell. Den outta da blackness I seed him a comin' in m'direction from 'round da side a da house. Only it won't m'Joseph. It won't nobody but dat mean ol' Sam da ovaseer and lookin' at him as he growed closer it won't hard ta tell what he come fer even though he nebba sayed a word to me. No suh, he jes pushed me back in da cabin in spite a me tryna resist him wit' out seeming belligerent. But he was too strong and when he got inside dere he jes stand dere a grinnin' fo' no apparent reason. Iffen he hadda knowed what I was thinkin' at that very moment I doubt if ol' Sam woulda been smilin' atall. But he ain't know so he jes stood dere grinnin' wit' all dem cracked up, rotten teef a his and like I sayed, I knowed right away what he wanted from me but iffen I had anything ta do wit' it I's was gonna stand my ground and won't gonna give him nothin' even if it meant me dying ta keep what was mine and keep him froom it. In all m'fo'ty years on dis here earth nobody ever got

27

near m'stuff but m'Joseph and dat's only 'cause I had a mind to let him. And I b'lieve if was ta ast him he'd tell ya dat it took a might longer fer me ta let him than even he knowed I was feelin' him..

Now, I ain't nebber been one ta boast and 'specially 'bout somethin' like this here what I's 'bout ta tell ya cause Lord knows da Lord ast us all ta be humble when it come ta ar good fortune but mos ev'ry mans, from white gentleman to da blackest a Afreecans done tried and nobody but m'Joseph done got near ta it and like I sayed dats' only 'cause I let him. And I gots ta admit that even though at first I didn't p'ticularly like him lyin' on top a me and sweatin' and groanin' and actin' like a crippled bull I did 'llow him to scratch his itch. It didn't help—him bein' so big and all down dere but afta awhile I guess my body jes got used ta him and right before he got sol' off I was jes getting' ta da point where I's was startin' ta enjoy dat time a the night when we was all alone and da candle burned dim. Dat's 'bout da time when m'Joseph took it away and sayed ta me dat wouldn't be no mo' activity unda da moonlight 'til we gits ta sweet freedom. Sayed he don't wonts ta have no chiddrin born inta dis here world a slavery.

Da onliest otha man I even considered letin' git close ta me in dat way was Mas'r John and I won't p'ticularly fond a de idea but I ain't no nothin' 'bout it and what it all consisted of. But I jes got so tired a his beggin' me

28

fer it and I jes figgered dat iffen he really wonted to he could jes make me give it ta him anyway and at least if I gived it ta him I wouldn't a had ta have him whip me and be mad at me. Still, he ain't really nebber pursued it no mo' than jest ta tease me and make idle chatter and dat was mos'ly when he be drankin' a lot.

I was much younger den and when I finally did tell him no 'cause I git tired a his beggin alla da time ya know what mas'r did? He lookt at me and seed jes how serious I's was and he jes walked away and it won't long afta dat dat he had me whipped fer somethin' else altogetha diff'rent but I knowed it was fer me tellin' him no when it come ta dat. I knowed it was fer dat 'cause he ain't nebber approached me around dat again. Dat right dere was it.

Well, up 'til now dat is. And ain't nobody nebber tried ta actually force demselves on me but I's could see dat dat was 'xactlty what ol' Sam in mind right through here and iffen my nose didn't deceib me, I's quite sho' I smelt alcohol on his breath. Now I's got a right peculiar sense a smell and I could tell ya 'jes what kind a likker he been driankin' jes from da smell. Dat's how good m'nose was 'bout pickin' up stuff like dat and I could tell ya Sam had a variety fo' him ta come ta see me. One thing was fo' sho though dat corn likker was outweighing dem othas by a heap and I knowed dat dat corn ain't nuttin' ta be played wit'. Shoot, I seed niggras had a lil' too much and got ta walkin' right up ta big house ta tell mas'r jes what dey thinks a him. Took two r three right-sized bucks ta hol' 'em down and save them from da whip. So's I know what dat corn can do ta a man's courage. Mek him feel like he a kin ta da gods. Dat's why I knew it won't gonna be easy tryin' ta persuade ol' Sam dat his tryin' ta bed me down might not be in his or my best int'rest. But years bein' roun' white folks, plus da fact dat I's only half niggra makes a purty smart and connivin' wench. And Lord knowed I's was sho' nuff thinkin' and connivin' right through there.

Anyways, I seed him jes a standin' dere grinnin' wit' all dem rotten yalla and brown half-broked teeth lookin' like I's somethin' good ta eat and fo I gits a chance ta say anything, he says ta me, 'Gal take dem dere britches offa ya fat ass and tu'n around so I ain't gotta look atcha nigga face.'

I jes lookt at him and wondered where all dat hatred come from. I ain't nebber in my life done nothin' ta nobody ta have 'em hates or dislike me and yet dis man gots mo' hatred in his heart for me den any man I's ever seed and yet he wanna stick me in my private places so he ken bring me some a his pain and bring hisself some happiness at da same time. Lord, I swears, I jes cain't unnerstan' dese people. But still, it sho won't no time to try and start thinkin' 'bout da why's and why nots a white white

30

folk so I jes stood dere and lookt him in da eye. Truth was, I could hardly

even talk but somehow da Lord give me da strength ta let him know how

plumb tuckered out I's was from all de work he done made me do dem

past few days. Ya see, white folk likes it when dey hears how hard dey

works dere niggras. Den I telled him dat afta alla dat wo'k he done

heaped upon dese po' tired ol' bones, I had ta accomadate Mas'r John

and his pleasures right befo' he rode up, (which was a bold-faced lie),

dat I hoped would turn him astray. I was hopin' dat he wouldn't wanna

mess wit' none a mas'rs' stuff. But he jes stand dere griinin' and showin'

me all dem bad teef ag'in and say dat he done jes left Mas'r John.

Sayed he and da mas'r done jes got finished sippin' some brandy and

Mint Juleps. Well, now I knowed he's gonna whoop my tail fer sho fer

lyin'ta him but he jes laughed and telled me ta turn around and put my

hands on top a dat potbellied stove what set right dere in da middle a da

room and spread m'legs which I did right quick so as not ta suffer his

wrath.

All dis time, da wheels is turnin' and I's thinkin' ta m'self. I says, 'self

ain't nebber no man ever tookt you wit' out you wantin' dem to and it sho

ain't gonna happen now. So, I gits ta lookin' fer anything ta smash dat

peckerwood upside his head wit cause I knowed wit' him drinkin' and all,

he ain't hardly heariin' me and den I telled him dat, I's really been hopin'

fer dis day fer some time now but wi' me alla time workin' in da big house

31

and not really knowin' him I's didn't know how he'd take it iffen I jes approached him and offered it ta him. I wasn't sho iffen he was a bible totin' God fearin' man dat didn't b'lieve in some healthy fornicatin' or iffen he had a wife and chiddrin at home dat had him all tied up or iffen I's jes didn't appeal ta him like dem black Afreecan gals dey say he was so useta takin' up wit'. But I tells him dat I's sho was hopin', mightily dat he would come ta see da light and how much I's willin' ta be his concubine iffen he was of a min' ta have me as such.

Well, he seem purty durn tickled ta hear dat. So, I added dat I hoped he didn't mind da fact dat I was on my menstruation and things could be a tad messy but if he favored ketchup on his sausage den won't no need ta delay no longer. Lord knowed my mind was racin' and I's done jes 'bout run out a all da figgerin' and connivin' I's got in me so I did what come nat'chal ta someone in my p'ticular situation. I grabbed da iron lid dat covered da burners on dat ol' stove top and I gripped it as tight as I could and I jes set dere and waited fer him ta make da next move. I waited patient like ta see jes what it was he planned ta do now. I's was hopin' I wasn't gonna haveta kill dis here piece a po' white hillbilly trash but I won't sho 'bout nothing at dis point 'ceptin dat he wasn't gonna have me. In my heart though, I really and truly was hopin' dat I wasn't gonna have ta kill dis here man fer him tryin' ta soil me. Still, iffen it come down ta dat then I guess dat's jes what I's gonna have ta do and I's jes gonna

32

have ta put my plan inta action a llil' sooner than I had a min' to.

By dis time he already had m'petticoats up roun' m'waist and I's standin' dere wit m'butt out 'cause I ain't had no britches on fer da fact dat it was jes too durn hot ta be wearin' britches out dere in dem fields wit alla dat mos cumbersome binding jes a squeezin' on m'innards. So, fer comfort sake, I jes stopped wearin' alla dat which in turn gave ol' Sam even easier access ta da prize. Anyways, he's 'bout dere now and I's jes about ta crown him a good one and be on my way when he dropped my petticoat, turnt me around and said, 'You let me know when dat well a yours runs dry, ya hear?'

Well, I ain't nebber been dat happy in all m'life, (though I sho didn't let him knowed it), but ever if dere is a God I knowed he was wit' me right den. I's mo' happy fer Sam though than I was fer even me 'cause he don't know how close he come ta meetin' his maker dat dere night. Still, I jes dropped m'eyes ta da flo' like I's real sad 'bout him changin' his mind and all and nodded befo' I eased dat top back down on da stove top.

'Sho nuff will,' I telled him. 'I jes cain't wait suh.' But what I's really couldn't wait fer was ta git da hell away from him. Den I watched as he made his way out da do' but I didn't move, well 'cept ta git dat heavy iron

33

poker from next ta da fireplace jes in case he saw fit ta come back. When I think back, I cain't remember movin' 'til long afta I heared da sound of his hosses hoofs in da distance. Lord knows I cain't remember bein' dat scairt in all m' days but what I's was really scairt of was m'self. I didn't wont ta have no man's death on my conscience and on m'record when it come time fer me ta ante up.

"Course I's don't rightly know what's worser nowadays. I don't know iffen it's worser ta work da fields wit' dat man alla da time lookin' fer ways ta git up under m'petticoats or losin' m'Joseph. None of it is all too good right through her. Too be sho none of it look too promisin' and I know it won't do a bit a good fer me ta tell mas'r 'cause he got so much on his mind right now wit' dis years crop doin' as bad as it is and all dis mumbo jumbo talk about war. But I's jes gots ta do somthin' about ol' Sam 'cause I fears da next time he get all likkerd up it gonna be mighty hard ta dissuade him from havin' his way and den I'm gonna haveta kill him fo' sho. Ya would think wit' half a dese snotty-nosed lil' pickaninnies runnin' roun' here already favorin' him he would slow down a might but it seem like he tryna see how many seeds he can plant in da garden and out. One things fo' sho though, I ain't, by no means, tryna help him add ta da list.

34

And with all da otha things that was on my mind wit' m'Joseph bein' sol' off like dat and me, bein' stuck down in dese fields and ol' Sam gittin' all likkerd up wit' da idea a havin' his way wit'me. Wit' all dat dat I had goin' on at da time der was also da fact dat I ain't had m'cycle in months. I won't sho what it meant fo' a woman a my years but eitha way I's couldn't be too sho. I thought 'bout tellin' Joeseph on dere wediin' night even though I won't 'xactly sho' how he was goin' ta take it but if I was with child, God forbid, there won't nothin' he could do about it now but accept it.

Anyway, it was all too much to think about right through here and my plan whichI made it a point to work on ev'rynight was a distant plan dat Sam had made urgent even though I couldn't think about it or nothin' else that night.

January 11th

From my accounts I'ts been two days I reckon since I had a chance ta correspond wit' you 'cause I's been so sick wit da fever I don't know what ta do. Da first day out in da fields followin' Sam da ova'seer droppin' by dat night and I gots ta throwin' up so bad dat two a dem ol' black, hard Mandingo's picked me up and toted me back ta m'cabin. Dey say ol' Sam called Aunt Hattie from up at da big house ta see what all was ailin'

35

me and from her accounts it won't 'til a day later when I comes ta m'senses dat I sees her standin' ova me jes a grinnin' and carryin' on like dere's some call fer a celebration or somethin'. I lookt at her grinnin' at me like dat and holdin' m'head in dem ol' big swolled up hands a hers and I said Lord here anotha one dat done jes lost her mind and then I got ta thinkin' and hopin' I ain't sayed nothin' else outta m'head cause Lord knows where dey gonna put me dis' time. Aunt Hattie sayed mas'r rode down his self to see what all was ailin' me and ta see iffen I had anotha one a dem nervous breakdowns.

But earlier dat night, Auntie Hattie say she heared mas'r and missy talkin' ova dinner sayin' how I wasn't much of a field hand accordin' ta Sam and wit me havin' dese nervous breakdowns all da time combined wit' m'faintin' spells dat it might be best if dey jes sol' me as a cook and a breeder. But befo' he done dat he was first gonna have me matched up wit' a few a dem big ol' strappin' bucks ta see iffen I can still produce despite m'age.

Seems like dats when missy telled Mas'r John he betta hurry 'cause mos a my prime breedin' years is well behind me and she was mos' certain dat dat dere was a waste a time. Sayed I lookted every bit a sixty iffen I look a day. To which mas'r jes smiled knowing full well dat wont nothin' but a jealous woman talkin' dere wit' all da mens both white and niggra

36

always lookin' ta purchase me jes so's dey could bed me down. And Aunt Hattie laughed and sayed ain't too many menfolk lookin' ta bed down no sixty year ol' woman. Anyways, accordin' ta Aunt Hattie missy ain't quit dere. She jes keept on proddin'mas'r ta sell me while he could still git a fairly good price.

And den a funny thing happened. Aunt Hattie, (who I has always considered my oldsest and dearest friend), gots ta laughin' so hard when she git through tellin' me dis dat tears commenced ta rollin' down her face. Dat's when I's had ta start wonderin' iffen she won't da one havin' a nervous breakdown or iffen dis jes her way of cryin' and lettin' off steam since all da time I's done knowed her I ain't nebber seed her cry once.

So, I lookt up ta her and I sayed, 'Aunt Hattie is you alright? I mean dey tryna sell me afta thirty-fi' years a wo'kin' and slavin' in dere kitchen and doin' dere biddin'. And nebber, not once, in dat thirty-fi' years did I cause mas'r or dat needle-nosed, mouse faced, squint-eyed missy a his a bit a problems and you sittin' here like you da one dey done drove stir crazy. Tell me da truth Aunt Hattie. Has dey got to you too?'

Aunt Hattie laughed again. "No, chile. Dey ain't made white folk yet dat can git ta Hattie Mae. Jes like dey cain't nebber git ta you unless you let 'em. And yo' mind's like mine. It jes too strong ta let 'em effect you no matta what dey do or how hard dey try.

Ya see, Mary, dats da problem. You so so strikingly, fine-looking and add ta dat da fact dat you smart dat you done jes about drove dat po' ol' white woman crazy outta pure jealousy.

Ya can lissen ta dem iffen ya wants to chile but I's done been on dis here earth a might longer than you has and I's learnt one thang if I ain't learnt nothin' else. I's learned ta b'lieve nothin' they tells ya. Nothin' whatsoever. Dese here white folk is da closest thing ta da devil you'll see this side a hell. They'll tell ya one thing and do anotha jes as sho as my name is Hattie Mae. And I ain't even sure dat's my real name since dey da one's tol me it is. But I's don't say nothin' ta 'em or give 'em a second thought 'cause I's sees how dey treat each otha. Besides, long as I's gots da good Lord Jesus on my side da devil don't stand a chance in hell.'

'I hears you auntie, but you still ain't tell me what you thinkin' and why you grinnin' like a slave who jes got ta da Promised Land.

'I's laughin' cause you thankin' these white folks concerned 'bout yo welfare. And I's here ta tell yoa that there ain't no diff'rence between you and dat dere Afrieecan dat mas'r bought and brung here taday. I don't care iffen ya from da bustlin' streets a New Orleans or da quietest plains a Africa you still ain't nothin' but a slave in da eyes a da white folk. So,

38

ain't no need havin' alla dem crazy, mixed-up, notions 'bout bein' betta

than somebody cause you half a nigga or from New O'leans. 'cause da

truth is half a dem niggras you out dere wo'kin' wit' now down in dem

dere fields is da sons and daughters a queens and kings from cities and

dynasties dat go back ta long befo' da time a yo' Jesus. and dey out

dere in da same fields as you lookin' at you like you's a fool fo' thinkin'

mas'r care mo' fo' you than he do fer dem when ev'rybody 'ceptin' you

know dat mas'r—well, Mary—he don't care fer none a us too much mo'

than what he can git outta us.

I guess dat's why yo' passin' out and him talkin' bout sellin' ya struck me

as funny. It won't so much dat. It jes da way you took it, da 'spression

on yo face like it must all be some kinda mistake.

Ya see gal, you come up ta da big house wit' all ya high falutin' talk and

all ya high falutin' ways 'bout bein' betta n' us po' ol' Guinea slaves

'cause dey done teached you ta read and right and dressed ya all up in

Miss Irene's lil' hand me downs and ya fo'got you was a niggra jes like

da rest a us. Fact is ya got so uppity dat you even started scarin' da

white folk. Ya see, Mary, mos' a da white folk you so intent on impressin'

ain't nothin' but po' white trash dats gots us niggra's 'round ta make 'em

look good. Dey walkin' 'round here putting' on airs 'bout how much land

and money dey got and how fine dey house is and how many acres dey gonna bring in come harvest time and dey ain't lifted a finger ta do any a dem things dey talked about yet. Only finger dey lifted was ta whip us inta doin' somethin' faster. Don'tcha see gal? We da one's r'sponsible for alla dis here. But you ain't seed dat. You's runnin' 'round here thinkin' you part a da family. You thinkin' you right along wit' da aristocracy. And chile you done got so's uppity and high falutin' dat you outdoes even da white folk some a da time. Dat's why mas'r had you stuck out in da fields, gal. You done got so dey had ta bring ya down a peg or two or you be wontin' ta take missy's place fo' long. Dat's why I gots ta laughin' so hard.'

I had ta chuckle when Aunt Hattie telled me dis even though I knew there was mo' truth in her words than I cared ta admit. You know Missy Charlene ain't nothin' but a backwoods country gal in a pretty dress dat found out Mas'r John had a big ol' plantation den waited 'til he come roun' to gittin' on one of his drunken binges and laid up wit' him 'til she came to be in a childlike manner and forced him to marry her. Hell, chile that gal ain't no more-n-a backwoods country hillbilly. This here plantation her first exposure to da world and here you is dis beautiful quadroon from da New Orleans and ev'rybody who comes by womens and mens alike is alla da time time talkin' about how beautiful da cook is and hardly payin' missy no mind in her own house. Den ta make de

40

matters worse her own husband spend mo' time staring at chou den he do his own missus.

You shoulda seen it comin' chile."

"And dats funny auntie?"

"No, chile dats sad. What's funny is dat you believes anyt'ing da white folk tell ya, like Jesus hisself done said it. I tell you child I's was right dere da whole time when you first passed out up dere in da big house. It was jes me and missy tryna nurse ya back up on yo' feet again. Well, at least I was and you nebba said a peep. Missy saw a chance to get rid of ya so she made up all dem lies 'bout you talkin' that rebellious talk like da one dey call Nat Turner who mu'dered all dem white folk and plantation owners up North a few months back. Ev'rybody still talkin' about dat. Leastways, white folk is. Dat Nat Turner really scared dem whitefolk so missy jes made up all dat rebellious talk and sayed you said it. Then she telled 'em you was out yo' brain and had de nervousness breakdown. Missy made all dat stuff up 'cause she ain't know how else ta get Mas'r John ta stop payin' so much attention to you. Funny t'ing is he still don't pay her no mind. And she figger now dat when he sneakin' off it ta see you but it tain't. He really goin' ta see Mas'r Reynold's wife but ol' missy still hung up on you, chile. Telled him just last night he need to breed you, then sayed he need to sell you 'cause you was way past your breeding prime. Anyt'ing she can find ta get rid a you is fine as far as missys concerned."

41

"And that's funny, auntie."

" No, but I's kinda suspected what was ailin' ya when ya passed up at da big house and it won't no nervousness breakdown like missed sayed it was and now I's sure it aint no matter what dat lil pinched-faced heifer sayed."

"Well, if it ain't da breakdown that ails me what is it dat ails me so auntie," I ast de ol' woman chewin' on da empty corn cob pipe sittin' at the foot of my bed still smilin' wit dat ornery grin.

"Iffen it ain't da nervousness breakdowns then what is it that ails me so, auntie? Why I keep havin' dese pass out spells?" I ast again.

"Well, chile I'll tell you. And won't ol' missy be surprised when I tell her that you ain't pass the breedin' stage yet," the old woman laughed.

"What you sayin', auntie," I repeated, hoping what I was hearing won't true.

"Why ain't nothin' wrong wit you ceptin' that you wit' child and yo body is jes plumb wore out. You jes need some rest is all chile. And I's gonna tell Mas'r John and Missy Charlotte first thing t'morrow mornin' so's he can getcha way from ol' Sam and offen yo feet as much as possible."

My heart sank when da old woman tol' me da news. I's had a feelin' for sometime now but didn't wanna think 'bout havin' no chile in dis ol' crazy mixed up world a slavery and sellin' folks and wit' out my Joseph but dere was nothin' I could do now and it sho wouldn't be easy tryna make

42

no plan work wit' no youngun hangin' on but I could feel myself smilin' inside.

Anyways, dere was a goodside. Leastways, now I ain't had ta worry 'bout ol' Sam bangin' on my cabin door. Not dat pregnant wenches got any special treatment but Mas'r John always keeped his pregnant wenches close ta da big house helpin' out wit da laundry or somethin' easy so he could keep a close eye on his 'vestment. See a nigga baby, 'specially a boy meant mo' money fo' Mas'r John at the auction should he decide ta sell 'em but that was six months away 'ccordin' ta Aunt Hattie and plenty of stuff could happen in six months. And Aunt Hattie was right, I sho didn't know nothin' 'bout how whitefolk think.

January 15th, 1850

A rider came in today from over da Reynold's place and jes like I figgered massa had a boy come down ta move my little bit of b'longins' up ta da temp'rary quarters next ta da big house so auntie could keep a mindful eye on me whilst I was pregnant.

That meant he was considerin' selling my baby and maybe both of us when the time came. Sent auntie's granddaughter back down ta da field's and had me placed on da laundry detail jes like auntie predicted which was fine wit' me 'cause it didn't do nothin' but keep me closer ta da news.

43

And like I sayed, no sooner than I gots my belongins in place than a rider came in at a gallop which always meant somethin' was a brewin'. When I heared he was a colored boy ridin' in I knowed right den and dere dat somethin' was stirrin'.

Now if I had been up in da big house. I's sho I would had knowed everyt'ing but all I could do now was wait like da rest of da hands 'til Aunt Hattie could let us know da big news and iffen it had something to do wit' us slaves.

Me, myself useta have dat job too but now dat I wasn't in da house and so I is pretty much in da dark myself. 'Course I really won't carin' what happened o'er at da Reynold's place unless it was somethin' bad. Lord, forgive my wicked thoughts but I prayed fo' somethin' bad, like da plague of da locusts, like what's in de bible ta reigndown on those Reynold's for takin' my precious Joseph from me.

Iffen it was good news I's won't interested. What I wonted mo' 'n anyt'ing was to get to dat rider, whoever he be and find out where dey done took my Joseph too. And I knowed he would a knowed too 'cause anytime a slave mas'r let one a his hands ride a horse from one place ta anotha it mainly be because he got truss in dat dere slave. And iffen he got truss in him den dat dere slave usually gots a heap a knowledge about da

44

goins on on dat p'ticular place. So, I figger dat maybe I could find somet'in about my Joseph from dis man iffen I could get close enough to him. I's also asked Aunt Hattie ta see if she could find out anyt'ing since all da nigga couriers had da come inta big house past auntie and state their bizness wit' her first befo' dey was permitted an audience wit' Mas'r John. I only hoped auntie ain't forgit ta find out.

Tried to git close up ta rider but soon as I gits wit' in de close proximity. Mas'r John commence to come walkin' up. Now I ain't and you know what he sayed to me his mos' favorite outta all de hands and servants he got on de place. He say, "Gal, what you s'pozed to be doin'? Ain't ya on da laundry detail? Gal, iffen you don't git yo little skinny a-s-s back where you belongs I'll have yo nigga ass back down in da lower fo'ty quicker than you can say Brer Rabbit." Always pokin' round some nigga buck. That's why yo ass is pokin'out now."

And ta tell ya da truth, I's was plumb taken back. In thirty-five years a dedicated service Mas'r John ain't nebba uttered a mean word in my direction. Now dat ain't ta say I ain't heard him say mean spirited t'ings but in all da time I can remember it was alla da time justified and always but always di-rected at dem mos' deservin' of a harsh word which was mos' all de time dem lazy Afreecan niggras and field hands. But he ain't nebba spoked ta me like dat and I ain't nebba ebba heared him cuss fo' no reason even when he been drunked up off da corn likker.

It was like I didn't know dis man and he didn't know me. And I wondered what I done did ta make mas'r treat me no betta than a common field niggra and disrespectin' me in front a ev'rybody.

Guess Aunt Hattie was right. I sho didn't unnerstan' white folk. But I had ta wonder iffen maybe one a those dere Afreecan niggras always practicin' dat dere voodoo on po' ol' mas'r ta have him actin' dis way towards me his favorite.
They was always a chantin' and drummion' and tossin' chicken bones tryin' ta fo'see da future and well, I didn't believe in all dat dere witchcraft but seem like too many folk includin' Aunt Hattie did so it was hard to say fo' sho but I knowed dere somethin' ailin' mas'r cause he didn't even look at me da way he useta. Jes kinda looked right thru me like I's won't even standin' there I hated dem Afreecans fo' doin' dat ta my mas'r and best friend but made my leave anyway so as not to incur anymore of his wrath and ta save myself de embarrassment.

Thinkin' about it, later that day as I hung the laundry ta dry it dawned on me dat if da Afreecan voodoo was dat powerful den chances are dey would have thrown off da yoke of slavery a long time ago. Derefo' it could be only one t'ing troublin' Mas'r John in such a way and dat had ta

46

be da news from dat courier from da Reynold's Place. And since it won't no way fo' me to find out. I commenced ta goin' about my chores in a mos' professional manner so as ta set a good example fo' dem young wenches out dere lollygaggin' and makin' it bad for alla us good niggras. 'Sides dat, it's impotent dat we keeped our Mas'r cleaned and pressed and all da time lookin' good. Dats what a good slave gal on da laundry detail s'pozed ta do.

Spent da rest a day doin' jes dat and felt pretty good fer da first time in a long while.

January 16ᵗʰ 1850

Lord chile, I cain't talk today. Ev'ryt'ing's in a uproar round here. Us slaves, Afreecans and ev'rybody been forced ta stay in dere cabins ta night and ev'ry few minutes da paddy rollas is stickin' dey heads in da door ta count and make sho I's in my rightful place seems like two niggras done escaped from da Reynold's place jes yesterday and t'ree mo' from here last night or dis mo'nin.

Hattie sayed all de big white owners from miles 'round done had slaves escape o'er da last two ta t'ree days. All total 'bout fifty and dey t'ink dey be conspirin' whatever dat means, but what dey rally scairt of 'cordin' ta

47

Aunt Hattie is dat da niggras, mos' of whoms Afreecan is gatherin' in da mountains ta have a uprisin' and do a Nate Turner and kill all de white folk.

Aunt Hattie sayed da white folks say dem niggras is maybe armed and done gone plumb crazy.
White folk is scairt to death so she telled me not to write nothin' 'cause dey maybe t'inkin' I's writin' em travelin' passes so she telled me ta jes blow da candle out and go ta sleep and wait 'til da whole t'ing blow ova, which is jes what I's intendin' ta do.

Leastways, now I's ken unnerstan' why Mas'r John was so awful powerful upset and I's jes glad it won't nothin' I did intentional ta upset ol' Mas'r John. Despite ev'ryt'ing he a purty good man and a fair mas'r iffen niggas behave and stop alla time tryna run off ta freedom.

January 17th 18

T'ings a lil better today but Aunt Hattie say I don't need ta write nothin' and seein' Mas'r John totin' dem guns 'roun' all day and whippin' niggras fo' no reason I think Aunt Hattie may jes be right bout my writin' bein' dat a niggra really ain't s'pozed to. None of dis woulda happened t'ough if dem fool niggras would jes stayed put and knowed dere place.

February 11th,

Took alla dis time fer things ta finally git back ta normal. Lord knows, I's seen a lot in my day but nebba has I's seen white folks as scairt and jumpy as I's seed em dese past few weeks. Shootin' dere guns at anyt'ing movin' and thinkin all of us is plottin' ta kill 'em. I swear I don't know what's gotten into 'em but I's certainly tired a walkin' 'round here feelin' like I done did somethin' wrong.

Walkin' up da road yesterday mo'nin' same as I always does paddy rollas came out da bushes guns drawed, rifles cocked only ta find a pregnant woman wit' a basket a dirty laundry. Talk 'bout disappointed.

When I ast Aunt Hattie what all da fuss was truly about since all dese white folk wit' all dese guns cain't possibly be a scairt of a handful of escaped slaves, she got dat ornery smile again like she got when she told me I's pregnant and bein' dat I ain't nebba seen her smile befo' or since dat day I's got ta wonderin' if maybe I was havin' twins. So, I repeated da question ta make sho she heared me correct-like 'cause I's sho couldn't afford to have no twins. So, I says ta her again, "Aunt Hattie tell me wat really got dese white folk so scairt and upset that dey done took ta totin' guns and wantin' ta shoot a niggra on sight who ain't da

49

nothin' but serve his mas'r ta da best a his ability and Aunt Hattie jes

stare at me and smile and say, "Chile, Jesus ain't nebba see fit ta carry

no gun but de devil sho as hell do."

Ta tell da truth I ain't nebba could unnerstan' Aunt Hattie when she git ta

talkin' like dat. B'lieve it's da Afreecan in her comin' out. I ain't rightly

sho'. But Aunt Hattie do say some crazy things from time-ta-time.

February 13th

Well, it's been nary a month since dem niggras done escaped from

here at da Marshall Place and we is jes now gittin' da word on what

drove dem white folk all crazy in da head. "Cordin' ta Aunt Hattie who

got da news from ol' Ben da butler who was servin' Mas'r John and Mas'r

Reynolds dey drinks on da veranda yestaday; Mas'r Reynold's say dem

dere escaped slaves set fire ta his barn and da big house to cover dere

escape.

Missy Reynold's jes happened ta be in da house so it lookted like dey

was tryna kill her too and dats when da white folk sayed it was a slave

insurrection but we slaves already knew da real deal 'cause Mas'r

Reynold's cook, Minnie and Aunt Hattie is good friends bein' dat dey

useta be on da same plantation up in Carolina somewhere's to Mas'r

50

Reynold's bought em both. Seems he got inta debt ta Mas'r John and had to let Hattie go ta pay part a his debt but still owes him a heap a money and really truly hates Mas'r John but dat's anotha story altagetha.

Anyways, Minnie got word ta Aunt Hattie dat Mas'r Reynold's was s'pozed to go away one weekend but decided not ta go bein' that he was suspicious 'bout somethin' or another so he slips inta da guest house and sits and watches and waits and lo and behold who should come a ridin' up not long afta but Mas'r John. And Mas'r set right dere and watched ev'ryt'ing dem two commenced to do.

'Bout drove Mas'r Reynold's crazy him seein' his missy in bed wit' yo Mas'r John. Say ain't nobody he hate worse despite him bein' neighborly and all. Anyways, dat mo'nin' as I was comin' in ta prepare breakfast I's notices Mas'r John's horse still dere and dis 'bout fo' thirty in da mo'nin'. Now, I's pretty much useta yo' mas'r stoppin' by but he ain't nebba but nebba spent de whole entire night. And if any night he shouldn't have it was dis p'ticular night wit' Mas'r Reynolds spyin' on 'em from right dere in da guest house but he ain't know. And I sho won't gonna be da one ta tell 'em fond as I am a missy. Anyway, Mas'r Reynolds come in for breakfast jes as cool as a peacock fan on a hot August day and missy sittin' dere all prim and proper and I says ta myself, Mas'r Reynold's right here at da breakfast table right here in front a me but he ain't do nothin'.

51

Do you hear me? Dat man sat right dere at da breakfast table and ain't do nothin' but talk dat small talk da way whitefolk do so good and Mas'r Reynold's he act like he ain't nothin' happenat all. And ev'rything went on peaceable like 'til I got ta da point dat I sayed to myself. Minnie, you old fool, you's jes havin' one a ya spells again. But den dat night when I was cleanin' up I sees Mas'r Reynolds get them dere two gallon cans a kerosene and pour it all da way around da house wit missy in it. See now I's suttin' on my front po'ch and got a plain view of ev'ryt'ing. So's not ta disturb anything I's real quiet but I goes and gets me a fresh ear of corn and a big ol' glass a lemonade and set down on my front porch and watched Mas'r Reynold's light his own house on fire wit' missy upstairs in da bedroom sleepin' like a baby. Well, I don't rightly knowed how missy got da hell outta dere but she did and I gotta admit it tickled me a bit ta see miss prissy jes a screamain' and a hollerin' bloomers on fire. Makes my eyes water jes t'inkin' about it. She made quite a site.

But let no one tell ya different. Dat's what happened. Ol' Mas'r Reynold's caught his missy cheatin' and tried to kill her. When it ain't work out he done like mos' white folks do. He lost his mind. Mas'r Reynold's done what mos' white folk do. He blamed it on dem niggas dat was smart enough to run when dey saw a good opportunity.

White folks sho is somethin'.

52

February 14th,

Days is goin' by mighty quick now and I's gittin' bigger each day. Had ta

take some laundry up ta big house and bumped inta Mas'r John who

seemed ta be in good spirits. Made it a point not to do no mo' than nod

but he commenced ta grabbin' the laundry basket from my arms.

"How ya been doin' Mary?" he asked.

"Fair to middlin', I reckon all t'ings considered," I replied knowing it won't

no good to be seen talkin' ta da mas'r fo' any length of time in public.

Niggras t'ink you be tellin' on 'em or his concubine and iffen missy see

she probably have a hissy fit and Lord knows where she stick me.

Probably have me balin' hay or shoe'n horses so I eased my way 'round

ta back door and inta da kitchen and outta site. "Been meanin' ta talk ta

ya Mary but I's been so busy wit' ev'rything I aint nebba git a chance to

but I's been so busy wit' da harvest but I been keeping tabs on you," he

said before reading the old woman on the other side of the kitchen,

"keepin' tabs on you da way I do all my slaves," he added for decorum.

"Yassuh," I muttered

"But nobody tol'me you was getting' big as a house," he laughed, before

turning to Aunt Hattie. "Why didn't you tell me Mary was gittin' big as a

house?"

"Suh?" The old woman replied pretending not to hear the conversation.

"Lord, why y'all do that I'll never know. You know you heard ev'ry word."

"No suh. Mind musta been preoccupied wit'…"

"Wit' what Hattie? You ain't got but half a mind and it's empty mos' a da time. And where you pick up dem big words like pre-occupied, anyway?"

"Dunno, suh probably from being around all you 'telligent white folk suh," the old woman replied.

Mary grinned at the old woman's feistiness but Mas'r John saw little humor in it.

"That's enough sass outta you, Hattie," he said, pretending to be angry.

"Yassuh," the old woman replied before continuing with her version of the old Negro spitual of Lord I's Ready to Join You, Please Just Call My Name.

"So, how many months along is you, Mary," he asked trying to sound concerned.

"Aunt Hattie say I'm well into my fourth month, suh," I answered.

"What Aunt Hattie know? Big as you is you gotta be well, into yo' sixth month."

"Aunt Hattie knowed enough ta bring both yo' chiddrin' into this world," the old woman said not even botherin' to look up.

"Thought you wasn't listenin' you meddlesome ol' woman."

"You telled me to, suh," she answered grinning now.

54

"You know you aint too old for me to have ya whipped," Mas'r John said good humoredly.

"Won't be da first time, suh," she replied under her breath.

"That mouth's gonna be the death of you, Hattie Mae," Mas'r John said his voice changin' indicating he was tired of the game. "Yassuh," Aunt Hattie replied before bursting into a rousing chorus of Lord, Please Take Me Now, which Mas'r John recognized immediately but chose to ignore.

"So, Hattie says you're in your fourth month does she?" He inquired returnin' his attention ta me.

"Yassuh."

"Well, much as I hate to admit Hattie-Mae's a pretty good judge of things like that."

"Yassuh," the ol' woman replied.

"Hush gal," he said turnin' his attention back to the ol' woman.

"Sorry suh, heard m'name thought you was talkin' ta me suh," she grinned.

"No, I was not talking to you I was making a reference to you is all."

"Yassuh, I unnerstan'. Won't hear no mo' from Hattie Mae today but iffen you needs ta refer to her or use her as a reference for anyt'ing else today that'll be fine by me suh," she grinned.

"Well, Mary this was all quite a shock to me. In all the time you been with me I've never seen you shown any interest in any man. Do you recollect you know who the father is?"

"Why of course I knows who da father is, suh. We was supposed to git married last Christmas."

"And what happened? Did the nigga get cold feet and run off on you?"

"No, suh, it weren't nothin' like dat dere, sir."

"Well, what happened then, Mary."

"Not exactly sho suh but from mah unnerstannin' it seems like Mas'r Reynold's sol' him off, suh."

"Why, that can't be Mary. The last slave Thomas Reynolds sold was that one over there pretending to be a cook. Anytime, he decides he gonna sell off any of his slaves I get first choice 'cause the man owes me more money than I can discuss or either of you gals would ever understand," the man they knew as Mas'r John stood their laughin'.

"Now, tell me the boys name that got my favorite gal all swolled up and lookin' like she's gonna burst and I'll see what I can find out for you."

"His name be Joseph. He useta be Mas'r Reynold's blacksmith and stable boy. Dat be my Joseph. Dey say he da best horseman and blacksmith in dese here parts and Mas'r Reynolds up 'n sol' him on da day we was ta be married," Mary said grabbing the butcher block table which stood in the middle of the kitchen.

The ol' woman realizin' what was about to transpire rushed to the younger woman's side and grabbed her under her armpits just as her legs were about to give way. Mas'r John, not about to let anything happen to one of his more valued pieces of property cleared the butcher

56

block table of the crates of tomatoes and bushel baskets of corn and other assorted food stuffs in one fell swoop then grabbed the slave woman from the older woman who was now struggling beneath the weight of the pregnant woman and laid her out on the table then turned to the older woman for direction.

"Whadda ya need, Hattie?" He asked concern and panic showing in his face and his voice.

"Need some cold water and some fresh towels, suh. I believe she brought some fresh linen in; in dat dere basket," the old woman said gesturing towards the basket of clean clothes by the door.

"She gonna be alright?" the slave owner asked his calm slowly returning as he watched the ol' woman loosen Mary's clothing in a cool methodical manner.

"Yassuh, I believe she gonna be fine. Some womens jes has a harder time than others in childbirth is all. Dat and da fact dat Mary ain't no spring chicken, suh."

"Well, have her come back in da kitchen with you, Hattie and have your grand daughter replace her with da laundry, ya hear?" the elderly gentleman shouted from outside at the well. Bringing in the bucket of water in and pouring it in the wash basin he turned to the old woman who was now applying cold compresses to the younger woman's head.

"Say, Hattie."

"Yassuh?"

"Is there anything to what Missy Charlene says about Mary having a nervous breakdown and being out of her mind?"

"Well, suh I'll tell you da truth if I can be so blunt as ta speak my mind," the woman replied.

"Ain't never seemed to stop you before," the man said smiling as he watched the woman wipe the beads of sweat from the pregnant woman's nose and forehead.

"Well, Mas'r John what I's got to say might not seem appropriate."

"Just say what's on yo' mind Hattie Mae. Hell, you too ornery too whip and too old to sell so I guess we're stuck with each other."

"I was kinda figgerin' on dat too, suh. But about what you asked me befo' suh. I believe what ails Mary here ain't got nothin' to do wit' no nervous breakdown. Unless n' a nervous breakdown means you done lost da only man dat you ever really truly loved. Ev'rytime dat gal starts ta thinkin' and lamentin' o'er Joseph this here is what happens but she strong. But you know as well as I do Mas'r John dat dat ain't what dis is all about. Sho, she hurt 'bout her Joseph bein' sold but she don't unnerstan' why she bein' treated so bad and sent down to da lower fo'ty after workin' so hard fo' you. But truthfully speaking, if I may sir, you and I both know that missy jes don't want her aroun' 'cause you looks at her mo' n u looks at yo' own wife. And ain't no white woman gonna be upstaged by no mulatto or niggra slave."

"That's quite enough out of you, Hattie Mae."

"Well, you ast me ta be honest, suh," the elderly woman replied.

"And you know that don't mean talkin' badly 'bout no white woman. I believe you's f'getting your place old woman."

"Yassuh."

She had made him angry, she knew. The truth sometimes did that. She knew that, too but the time for caring about his feelins had long passed.

"Let me tell you something old woman. I run the Marshall plantation and before me it was my daddy and before me my grandpappy. Ain't no niggra wench or no white woman tell me John Jay Marshall what to do or how to run things around here. Do you understand me?"

"Yassuh," Hattie Mae replied.

No sooner than Mas'r John finished reciting the history and hierarchy of the Marshall Plantation to a less than enthusiastic Aunt Hattie Missy Charlene, the volatile matriarch entered the kitchen her permanently furrowed brow suddenly giving way to the horrifying thought of that woman lying prone acress her kitchen table.

"What is that nigga wench doin' in my house—in my kitchen—on my table," she screamed her already contorted face twisting even further until her eyes bulged making her face appear as a grotesque gargoyle.

"She sick, missy," the old woman replied ringing outa towel and replacing the now warm compress with a cold one.

"I won't talkin' to you, you fat black bitch. Mind your goodamn business."

"Charlene! That's not called for. There's no need for that and I will neither have you speak that way to my niggras nor will I have you use such language in this house. This a God-fearing house." Mas'r John was visibly upset but the woman who had worked so hard to have Mary driven from not only her house but from her life refused to concede. "Can't you see, she'sick and with child?" He asked turning to face his wife. "Have you no compassion?"

"No, I have no compassion for your nigga whores. If it's not enough that you spend more time in her bed than you do ours you have the nerve to parade your prize mulatto in front of our guests and keep her in my kitchen to remind me that you were forced to marry me. But no more. Do you hear me John Marshall? I want her out of here and off of this plantation by Monday. That gives you the weekend to say your goodbyes. Then, I want her gone. Natchez or New Orleans. I don't care where you go but you take her pregnant ass away from here and you sell her or I'll get rid of her. And right now I ain't much interested in what she'll bring at the market. Now, do you hear me, John Marshall? Either she goes or I go. Do you hear me?"

And then Master John did something Aunt Hattie hadn't seen her mas'r do in years. He turned, faced his wife and smiled. And then taking both of his hands in hers and spoke softly.

"Funny, I was just tellin' Aunt Hattie how my daddy and my granddaddy built this place to be what it is today. And never once did they allow a woman to take part in the decision-making process of this here plantation and we have always prospered. And we will continue to do so. Now how long do you need before I have Ben bring the carriage around? I take it, you will be returning to your father's house so I will have your belongings sent there as soon as I have them gathered together."

The woman not used to her husband's chastisement stood stunned before turning abruptly and storming from the room.

John Marshall then turned to the old woman tending to Mary and asked, "How is she?"

"B'lieve she'll be fine, mas'r suh," the old woman replied. "Iffen it's alright wit' you suh, I's gonna git a coupla a da hands to carry on down ta her cabin. B'lieve she'll rest mo' comf'table dere suh."

"Do as they you see fit, Hattie. Just make sure she pulls through okay. And keep her on light duty 'til she recovers fully. Do you unnerstan'? I'm countin' on you, Hattie."

"Yassuh. I unnerstan', suh."

"Good, then get on wit' it."

"Yassuh, right away, suh. Suh?"

"What is it now, Hattie Mae?"

"Suh, can I ast you a question, suh?"

"No, no mo' questions, Hattie."

"Yassuh."

"Oh, go ahead and ast me, Hattie Mae."

"Well, suh I's was jes wonderin' iffen you was only int'rested in this here gal well so's you can sell her baby.?"

The man turned and faced the old woman and smiled.

"Always thinkin' 'bout the angles ain'tcha, Hattie?" he said his smile broadening. "If this were a different world I think you woulda made me a purty fair missus, Hattie or at the very least a helluva business partner; betta than John Reynolds anyway", he said laughing.

"I don't unnerstan' suh."

"Oh, I think you unnerstan' quite well," he replied.

"Is she any better?" he asked.

"Hard to tell 'til she comes around, suh, the old woman said lifting Mary's head and squeezing drops of water onto her now parched lips.

"You think perchancedat I could have a spot of whiskey or brandy, suh?"

"Not a problem. Will half a glass do?"

"That should do quite fine, suh." The old woman replied.

A minute or so later, he was back with with a little more than half a glass ofhis finest Tennessee whiskey.

"Need me to hold her nose while you pour it down?" he asked still troubled by Mary's condition.

"No suh. No need fer dat. You know Mary don't touch no spirits a any kind," she said taking the glass then tilting it up up to her own mouth until not a drop remained.

The man stood there amazed but found himself once again grinning deeply.

"You are truly a mess, Hattie Mae."

"You is truly right dere sir. My nerves is truly a mess afta all dat commotion between you and da missus but dat brandy should settle 'em down nicely. Now suh befo' I be on my way wit' dis child is you gonna answer my question like you promised, suh?"

Two strapping young men stepped thru the door nodded at Mas'r John then turned to Aunt Hattie and said, "M'am?"

"Won't you two boys to load Miss Mary up in da buck board and take her down ta my cabin. Be careful wit' her. She's wit' child so drive slowly and put somethin' under her head and when you git dere tell Lulabelle ta look afta her 'til I gits dere. Ya hear?"

"Yes, m'am," they replied in unison.

Once they were gone she turned back to Mas'r John.

"Yes, Hattie?"

"Well, suh is you just gittin' her well so's you can sell her youngun'?" she asked again.

"You know I don't have to answer your question?"

"Yassuh."

"Truth is Hattie I don't know. I ain't thought about it. If that youngun favors his momma it'll bring a handsome price at any market and I'm gittin' up dere in age where if I keeps him I'll probably be long gone

63

before he's old enough to make a good field hand so I just don't know.
Guess we'll just have to cross that bridge when we come to it."
"It would probably kill her if you did suh and I believe she too old ta go
through da whole affair again and specially wit' no man ta consummate
wit, suh." "Thanks for letting me know that Hattie. I'll take that into
consideration and let me know when she's up and on her feet again.
Now git on outta here. Don't you think you've caused me enough pain for
one day?"
"Yassuh. Goodnight suh."
"G'nite Hattie."

February 15

Aunt Hattie told me all about what went on afta I feinted yestiddy. 'Bout
how Mas'r John stood up fo' me las' night wit' missy and we's all still
waitin' to see how long it gonna be fo' she git her t'ings in order and
leaves. So, far it's been a day and it don't seem like she in no big hurry
to go back up in da mountains wit' her daddy but it don't seem like mas'r
done changed his mind one bit 'bout what he tol' her 'bout leavin' and
who runnin' t'ings round here 'cause he still got ol' Ben perched up on
Missy's carriage waitin' to fetch her home and it been dern near two
days.

64

Sayed Ben still wonderin' iffen he spozed to go but he don't wanna ast Mas'r John and git his ire up 'cause he knowed a man-wife t'ing is a might touchy sitchiation so he jes commenced ta sittin' dere. But afta sittin' perched up on dat carriage all night dat first night, he got ta wonderin' iffen maybe mas'r and missy done commenced ta work t'ings out and jes plain forgot 'bout him so he make it a point when it time for de mas'r ta git up ta ask him iffen it's alright fer him ta git down ta relieve hisself. That way he still bein' 'spectful wit' out signifyin' or pryin' in da mas'rs private affairs. When mas'r tell ol' Ben ta go ahead and den say Missy Charlene will be 'long directly we all felt good again and is keepin' our hopes up.

Aunt Hattie also told me about what mas'r sayed 'bout sellin' my baby. But much as I's cares fo' mas'r and would nebba 'liberately t'ink about pu'posely disrespectin' or disobeyin' him he ain't nebba gwon git a chance ta sell my youngun'. I kill em befo' I let him come up in dis system. Dat's what my Joseph would say do and he half Joseph's too even iffen he ain't here. Yassuh, I kill 'em befo' I spends my ev'ry wakin' hour wonderin' if and when mas'r gonna sell him ta pay fo' some note he cain't pay or some bet he done made drinkin' I's seen dat first hand but I's swears to da good Lord above dat won't happen to know son of Mary and Joseph.

February 17th

Jes like Christmas roun' here. Two mo' a mas'rs runaway last night but dat dere ain't nebba been no reason for celebratin'. See ev'rytime mas'r loses prop'ty he say he lose money—thousan's of dollars and den he be in da foulest a moods and he take it out on us good slaves what stayed and still be doin' his biddin' but he still be cross 'cause he gotta go inta Savannah and put up a reward and lose valuable man hours gittin' otha slaves ta go out wit' ol' Sam da ovaseer and chase 'em down. Den it seems

□□

□□

□□

□□rice fer de crops and travelin' ta New O'leans and Savannah ta pick up some new hands so's he can break ground on anotha hundred acres dat he cain't keep a mindful eye on da slaves he got already.

Mas'r say dem Spanish in Florida is da real problem da way dey openin' da borders and allowin' slaves da sanctuary. He say da Spanish don't like us dats why dey allowin' slaves ta jes come ta de Florida and be free to farm and own dere own land but I t'ink maybe the Spanish ain't too

66

bad if dey allow slaves to be free. I t'ink dat maybe dey jes ain't too fond a Mas'r John. Mebbe dey caught him on a bad day like today or see-ed him afta he had too much ta drank.

Anyways, even though he upset 'bout losin' dem slaves and fit ta be tied and ev'rybody walkin' roun' on pins and needles it still feel like Christmas 'round here. Dere's a quiet calm in da air and ev'ry slave dat been here awhile greets you wit' a nod a da head and a easy grin. News travels fas' 'roun here and befo' a field took ta da fields and even befo' Aunt Hattie made her way up ta da big house ta prepare breakfast we got da news. I dunno who brought da news and right now an it don't even matter. All dat matters is dat ol' Ben – ol' beautiful Ben wit' all dat grey hair who must be dose to eighty and who mas'r loves and trust-es and who stands right behind me—left befo' da break a dawn ta fetch Missy Charlene back ta her daddy's house somewhere in da mountains a Tennessee.

Oh, God is so good.

February 19th

Been two days since missy left and it like pure heaven 'round here now. I's back in da kitchen where I's belong and feels good workin' long side a Aunt Hattie again even though she's soundin' mo' n' mo' Afreecan ev'ryday.

67

Jes this mo'nin' fo' instance I mentioned da fact dat iffen dem Afreecans dat run had waited jes one mo' day til missy be gone dey probably wouldn't a hada problem in da world. Dat's all I sayed. And she tu'ned and looked at me and sayed, "Gal, hush. Dem dere Afreecan's is smarta than you'll ever be and got somethin' you'll nebba have."

I jes stood dere and looked at her. Dey say when you gits older yo' mind kinda floats in and out but Aunt Hattie alla time was sayin' t'ings dat had two meanin's and made ya stop and t'ink about what it really was she was tryin' ta say. Da Afreecans did dat a lot. Dey say one t'ing or tell you a story. And in dat story dere would be a whole 'notha story wit' a whole notha meanin'. Like in da bible. I believe dey call 'em parables. So, I went back ta choppin' up dem green peppers and tomatoes fer my ghoulash what Mas'r John so fond of and I's gots ta t'inkin' 'bout what Aunt Hattie sayed and I's swear fo' God I's couldn't make heads or tails outta what she sayed.

First of all, she gonna say dat dey gots somet'in I'll nebba have and I just don't know how dat's possible. Here I's Mas'r John mos' favorite and I ain't nebba been no concubine. My daddy be a white man and from what I hears my momma was a French, nigga who men useta pay high dolla' jes ta be in her company. Mas'r John say she was da most beautifullest mulatto in alla New O'leans French Quarters.

Plus Mas'r John tell me dat da French and white in me knocked out da bad blood and all da Afreecan influence. And ev'rybody 'cludin' Missy

Charlotte hadda admit dat my bein' fair-skinned and havin' a good grade a hair and all sho nuff makes me a cut above a Afreecan wit' dat kinky nappy hair dey got on top a dey heads. Half da time dey don't even tries ta comb it 'cause dey ain't got no pride in demselves.

Anotha t'ing is dey steady gittin' whipped fer always tryna speak dat Afreecan gibberish, 'stead a tryna learnin' proper English like I's be speakin'. Why dey so resistant to lettin' go of all dat Afreecan mumbo-jumbo and dem Afreecan ways I'll never rightly unnerstan'.

How Aunt Hattie can see somethin' good in gittin' whipped jes ta speak some crazy ol' gibberish or ta go out inta da woods at night fo' da sake a practicin' Afreecan rit'chals dat ain't even considered no real religion is beyond me. And so I's don't see how Aunt Hattie could say dat dey smarta or better'n me. Dem few t'ings I's mentioned right dere tells you dat a Afreecan cain't be too smart. Plus, (and I's gonna ast Aunt Hattie about dis one soon's I's sees her), but iffen an Afreecan is betta and smarta than me why dey always runnin' away from Mas'r John and takin' a chance escapin' wit' da dogs and da paddy rollas alla da time intent on catchin' and whippin' em and stringin' 'em up? Why dey gonna take a chance runnin' and tryin' ta escape ta Florida when dey ain't maybe nebba seen no Florida—not even on no map. Florida wit' all dem swamps, and snakes, alley-gators and crocodiles and spiders and scorpions and red ants dey say is almost da size of a two mont' ol' baby. And I's see-ed dem Seminoles—you know dem Indians dat be so friendly welcomin' runaways. See-ed 'em come t'ru here when Gen'ral Andrew Jackson sat way up top dat big ol' white horse lookin' so strong and handsome-like. And dem raggedy ol' Seminoles was followin' along behind Gen'ral Jackson's troops all chained and shackled lookin' poorer and worser than any niggra slave I's ever see-ed. And even den I ast myself why, would anyone in dey right mind wanna runaway to join dem lookin' worse than you do. Well, I guess dat dey does has a good grade a hair is a plus but jes why a nigga gonna go speculatin' and give up alla dis fer somethin' he don't know nothin' 'bout is beyond me. Right dere dat don't seem to smart ta me. And now dat I's given da whole subject some complete thought and believe fer sho after considerin' ev'ryt'ing dat Aunt Hattie may be da one goin' sof' in da head but I's gonna bring da matta back up t'morrow and see what she gonna say den but right now I's cain't hardly keep my eyes open. Good nite.

February 20th

Lord knows I's had plenty a time ta think and I's was where I's always stands to wait fer Aunt Hattie ta walk up ta da house tagether likes we always does.

Aunt Hattie stay farther down in da quarters 'mongst da Afreecans whilst I's stays closer ta da big house. She could stay up where I stay wit' mos' a da ol' niggras and mullatoes and dem dat's jes been wit' Mas'r John da

70

longest. Mos' us is da cream a da crop and mos' us has small gardens and even a flower bed or two.

Me and ol' Ben even got fireplaces and a wood floor. But Aunt Hattie say she pr'fer ta stay down farther even though it's a longer walk fer her and dem shacks ain't quite as nice and ain't one of 'em got nothin' but a dirt floor and a hole in da roof ta let da smoke go out and nothin' to stop da rain from comin' in. But she say she dey first gits here. Plus, she helps ta tend ta da sick. But what I t'inks she like mos' is speakin' dat gibberish wit' dem ones dat come from near her village in da Africa.

Anyways, I's chompin' at da bit t'inkin' about dat conversation we had yest'rday and so's when I's sees her I rush up to her and starts tellin' her what I's been t'inkin' 'bout what she sayed 'bout Afreecans bein' better and smarter than me when I noticed all de niggra and Afreecan field hands headin' towards da big house 'stead of da fields which is da custom. And den I see-ed ol' Sam da ovaseer driving 'em wit' his ridin' crop like dey plow horses and I drop my head so he don't notice or remember me and he hits me across my head and yells at me ta shut up and move along. Hit me so hard I thought I was gonna fall out right dere but I did what he sayed to do and I keeps on movin' 'til we gits ta da big oak and I's notice a whole lotta mo' slaves than jes ars. Lord knows I ain't nebba see-ed dat many niggras in one place at no one time in my life. Mas'r Reynolds slaves was dere and Mas'r Johnson's from da next county ova was all gathered dere in front of da big oak. Aunt Hattie

71

sayed it was mo'n t'ree t'ousand. Bein' dat I's never learnt ta count past a hunnerd it was hard fer me ta say whether she was right or wrong but one t'ing I's can say. It was a lotta property dere dat day.

Anyways, ol' Sam da ova'seer brings da buckboard from da barn. And I notices dats it's da very same buckboard dat Afreecan Jesse and Young Saul put me in and toted me ta Aunt Hattie's shack in when I's had my passin' out spell in missy's kitchen dat day. And in da back of dat buckboard, britches torn and ragged, looking half-starved laid Afreecan Jesse and Young Saul. Both of 'em had treated me mo'n kind and stayed wit' me when dey couldn't find Aunt Hattie's granddaughter, LulaBelle. They'd fetched me water and cold compresses and hunted and cooked me a rabbit and dey didn't even hardly know me.

Now here dey was 'bout ta be whipped ta wit' in a inch of dere heathen Afreecan lives 'cause dey didn't have sense enough ta stay put where dey belonged and act civilized. Now dey was goin' ta be whipped and made example of fo'anyone else who had any notions about runnin'. And ta me it just didn't make no sense. Ev'ryt'ing was real quiet—always is when a niggra 'bout ta be whipped 'cause every niggra knowed dat dat could very well be him. It's a sad time in da life of a slave but I felt I's just had ta ask Aunt Hattie now more den any other time what made dem two niggras smarter dan me.

72

Lord knows, I won't up dere 'bout ta bein' skinned alive. Didn't care what she said I was smarter than dat. But befo' I ast her anyt'ing I looked aroun' ta make sho da coast was clear and ol' Sam da ovaseer won't nowhere in sight cause my ear was still bleedin' and my whole head was ringin' from where he done cracked me upside m'head. When it first happened Aunt Hattie grabbed me in time so da second blow missed. But later on while we was walkin' she got ta grinnin' dat little ornery grin she been smilin' so much lately. When I ast her what was so funny she said she remembered gittin' hit like dat ev'ryday when she was in da fields—sometimes two or three times a day 'til dere was somedays she wish-ed she was dead so she wouldn't have to endure anotha day of treatment like dat.

Anyways, since Ol' Sam da ovaseer had his hands full wit' dem dere two boys in da back of da buckboard I tu'ned ta Aunt Hattie and ast her, plain and simple like, ta please tell me how dem two Afreecans is mo' betta and mo' smarta than me right now.

And Aunt Hattie jes turnt ta me and said, 'In time you'll come to unnerstan' chile. In time, chile. But fer now jes watch and listen. And dat's exactly what I did. I watched Mas'r John as he got up dere atop dat dere buckboard and waved us all in closer so we could heared

73

what it was he had ta say dat was so impotent. Then he commenced ta

sayin' how he wanted us ta listen closely ta what he was sayin,

"Most of y'all been wit me for years and know I've always been a fair

man if not a firm man. Most, if not all my niggas know that when you

work for me and do what you're s'pozed to do then there's no problem. I

paid good money for you and I own you and I expect for you to do as

you're told. When you decide to run or try to escape then you have to be

punished. In recent months, I have had seven slaves leave. Mas'r

Reynolds has lost four and Mas'r Johnson a total of nine. That's close to

twenty-thousand dollars in property combined and that is too big a loss to

take.

These gentlemen and I believe that these slaves who are running in

increasing numbers are not doing this on their own and are being

encouraged by northern abolitionists who are against the southern

planter and the Spanish in Florida who do not like the United States or its

policies concerning slavery. If I find, however, that any of my niggras are

working with the abolitionists or the Spanish or the Seminoles who have

been raiding and pillaging along the Georgia coast this is what I will do to

them.

And with that said, he took bout whip and riding crop from ol' Sam, the

ova'seer and began lashing Afreecan Jesse who was now tied to the tree. With each stroke Afreecan Jesse screamed out in obvious pain as the rawhide from the whip sliced through his flesh like a machete through sugar cane. After thirty lashes, Mas'r John turned and looked out over the crowd but said nothing.

He then turned back to Afreecan Jesse who was now on his knees, the tree and the rope the only thing keeping him up. Cutting the rope binding his hands around the tree Jesse fell to the ground face first.

"Git up nigga," ol' Sam yelled before kicking the young Afreecan in the head with the toe of his riding boot.

"Git up and face yo master, nigga."

When Jesse did not move the oversser laid a boot to the young man's ribs and repeated the command.

At the same time, Aunt Hattie began moving forward but the pregnant woman who stood beside her grabbed the old woman's shoulder with all the strength she could muster and held her firmly. Aunt Hattie turned to Mary and watched as the tears began to well in both their eyes. The two women hugged hoping to find solace and comfort in the warmth of each others arms. They were not alone. Men and women alike held hands, crying and praying for Jesus and Allah to relieve them of their burdens and to help them find their way home. It was like a church revival to some, standing on the doorstep to Calvary for others and through it all cam Master John's voice.

75

Afreecan Jesse had Young Saul holding him now so Sam couldn't kick him anymore and Aunt Hattie sensing the end was near and knowing she would soon be tending both mens wounds beckoned a young girl of about fifteen and sent her back to the quarters to boil a tub of salt water to clean their wounds when ol' Sam turned his head.

From deep below the murmur of the crowd rose a voice and Mary who had suddenly gone deaf rather than hear anymore of the young man's cries heard warmth of her master's voice.

"Now tell them, Jesse. Was runnin' from this fine plantation worth thirty lashes, son?" he asked, quite certain he'd made his point.

But there was no answer.

"I asked you if running away is worth thirty lashes." "Mas"r John repeated.

"I am no slave. I am Yoruba. I must be free. I will run until I find freedom." The young man said.

Aunt Hattie squeezed Mary's hand and Mary felt a chill go through her. She wondered if Afreecan Jesse understood what he was conceding but the fine young man who had taken such good care of her when she was having her spells soon cleared up any doubts she may have had about his understanding his plight.

"You run, you will die. It's that simple." Master John said facing the man. "Is that what you want?"

"I am no slave. I must be free. I will run unitl I reach freedom."

76

"Then you must die," Master John said.

"Then at least I will be free," Afreecan Jesse replied.

And although Mary could not understand why she felt a feelin' she'd never quite known before and this time she found herself squeezing Aunt Hattie's hand. And no longer did she feel sad or remorseful or wonder if Afreecan Jesse understood. She knew he did when he'd withstood that whipping then stood right before Master John and all his slaves and all his property and looked him straight in the eye not as a slave or a piece of property but as a Yoruba warrior, an Afreecan, a man accepting— no—welcoming his plight gladly even if it were death.

Master John certainly hadn't gotten the response he wanted. Instead of fear there was a sense of pride among the Afreecan slaves. The tears gone replaced by pride and the grim, resolve that this might be their fate but never would they ever embrace it or accept it or make it theirs because master said so.

And as ol' Sam da ovaseer, dropped the noose over Afreecan Jesse's head and tied the rope securely tightly round the lower portion of the big oak tree before slapping that old move to pull that buckboard from under Jesse's barefoot. Afreecan Jesse smiled a smile as big as any Mary and shouted something in Afreecan that brought about a loud response from every Afreecan slave in attendance and a smile from Aunt Hattie.

"What'd he say? What'd he say?" Mary asked. "He said, Finally I's free," said Aunt Harriet as she brushed a tear from one eye.

77

It was Young Saul's turn now. But Afreecan Jesse whose lifeless body still swung slowly to and fro in the brisk February wind words were still alive and resonating loudly. And recognizing he had neither gotten the affect or response he'd wanted Master John hoped that he would have better luck with Young Saul who though tall and muscular couldn't have been more than fifteen or sixteen.

Master John was counting on his youth and love for life to show him the much needed fear required to keep his slaves in check but when he whipped him even more soundly than he had Afreecan Jesse then asked if he would run again or accept the fate of his friend.

Young Saul replied. "I too am Yoruma so I guess I too will swing with my fried with a smile if that is the only way for me to achieve my freedom." This he said in the most perfect English but instead of a hush or a tear a loud but brief yell went up and Mary felt her own voice rise above all the others.

Master John accepted the young man's decision and bid Sam bring the buckboard once again as he headed for his horse at the edge of the walnut grove.

Mary unable to watch another young man hang and thinking of her own plan let Aunt Hattie's hand drop made her way through the crowd not worried about who saw her now and headed for her master;

"Suh, may I have a word?"

"Yes, Mary. What is it?"

78

"Well suh, if I may speak freely…"

"Yes, but be quick. I've wasted far too much time with you niggas already."

"Well, suh, I was thinkin' how much you done got invested in dat dere boy and how dem dere Afreecans has been reactin' ta Afreecan Jesse's hangin'. It's almost like you done made him a martyr or a hero by hangin' him and all dem boys really need is someone ta get dere minds right and well you see-ed how respectful dey is when dey come up ta da house ta fetch me dat day. Well, Aunt Hattie, can git dat young boy to do jes 'bout anything we need done and wit'out. Afreecan Jesse to do a lot a da chores we's gonna be powerfullyso'thanded.

"Well, what would you suggest Mary?"

He asked knowing there was a catch.

"Well, suh. A good strong young buck like Young Saul can fetch ya upwards of twenty-five hunnerd. I gives ya my word suh that I will have him ready for next years market, suh."

"But you still haven't tol' me what it is you want."

"Suh, twenty-five hunnerd and a year in da field from a top hand adds up to a whole lot mo' than what you can git from a baby still on its momma's titty."

"Got a point there, gal. O'kay tell ol' Sam I said to cut him down but you're responsible. He stays in your cabin till I get one built next to yours for him. And when he ain't in da fields with Sam I expect for you to be keeping a close eye on him. Do you hear? I get one bad report I'm

selling him and your'n in New Orleans come next year. Is that

undersood?"

"Perfectly, sir."

"Now tell ol' Sam to look here so I can get him cut down and get on with

my business."

"Yas suh. Thank you, suh."

Lord, chile I don't know what's goin' on wit' da world Jes' seems like

ev'ryt'ing done gone topsy turvy or somethin'. I really don't know but

Mas'r John been walkin' roun' here da last few days like he a woman on

his cycle—all evil and ready to snap o'er any ol' t'ing.

Aunt Hattie say it's because he jes now feelin' da loss of missy and even

though dey didn't all da time seed eye-to-eye wasn't no need to see

when da tallow burned down at night in da bedroom. She say mas'r, he

missin' missy's inner warmth. And I' say, she mus' be her inner warmth

alright 'cause she sho' won't warm no where's else."

Aunt Hattie say when a man gits 'customed to somethin' it jes plain hard

for him ta let it go. She say dat's why he been so cross wi' ev'rybody in

da last few days and he might jes come a knockin one a dese nights

'cause I's always been de apple a his eye. Plus, when he really git ta

missin ol' twitch face, missy he gonna be lookin' for somebody ta blame

and don't be surprised iffen it be me. And Lord if dat be da case I's don't know what I's gonna do ta keep him off a me but I's done it dis long and I's jes prays I ken keep doin' it.

Other than dat, t'ings is mo quiet than I's ken remember dem bein' in quite a spell. But dat's always da way it is after a hangin'. Folks jes sorta keeps ta demselves and goes 'bout dey daily tasks and tries ta git closer to day God I 'spect.

But what's mo unusual than anyt'ing is da way alla da slaves and 'specially da Afreecans be lookin' at me now and ev'ry night when I's returns ta my cabin dere always be a special treat atop my windowsill. At first, I thought da Afreecans placed 'em dere fer Young Saul since he be stayin' wit' me til' his own shack finished bein' built next ta mine. But it always be too much for Young Saul. When I told Aunt Hattie about it she jes smiled and ast me iffen I's noticed any sign'ficant change when it come ta da way da field hands used ta look at me and da way dey look at me now? And I's 'spect I has in a way. Seem ta me like ev'rybody jes mo' friendly-like—always wantin' ta do somethin' fer me— whether it be carry my load or fetch me my water from down at da creek each nigh fer my daily wash up. Now, ev'rytime I's step outside my cabin, dere's a youngun' I ain't nebba laid eyes on before waitin' ta fetch me dis or fetch me dat.

And Aunt Hattie telled me dat alla dat food bein' let' on my windowsill ev'ry night ain't fer Young Saul at all, It be fer me. She say de Afreecans is jes sayin' t anks da onliest way dey knowed how fer savin' Young

81

Saul's life. Dat what she sayed. And she sayed dat one act right dere made up fer ev'ry notion dey eva had a me up 'til den. She sayed dat dat one act right dere made me one a dem far as dey was concerned. Kinda like a hero. But I's don't care what dey sayed 'bout what I's did. I's still won't no Afreecan.

Young Saul a real good boy and from what I's can see when I walks down to take ol' Sam his lunch vittles ev'ry afternoon he a fairly good hand in da field too.
And b'lieve you, me afta I telled him 'bout my plan he ain't even give runnin' a second thought.
And I's ain't got to worry none even made it plain 'bout lyin unda da same roof wit' him even though he bigger and mo muscular than mos' a da menfolks on da place. I's let him knowed right off dat I's 'spected he was ol' enough to take a wife and might even be gittin da itch but dat I's was no heathen. I's be a Christian woman and I's therefo' onliest committed to one man inna lifetime and dat be no otha than my Joseph, who dey done sol' away from me. Still, I knowed in ma heart dat one day me and Joseph would be reconciled whether it be on dis here earth or in da kingdom ta come. That I knowed and I telled Young Saul jes dat so's he wouldn't git no p'culiar notion 'bout why I save his neck from da rope and I's purty sho' he unnerstood 'cause he jes smiled and sayed 'yes ma'am', like dat he da farthest thought from his min.'

82

Neva da less I thought dat be da best way ta go about it. Jes make it plain from da start. But I's don't 'ink dat boy got no mo' notion when it come ta mountin' me than a man on da moon. And iffen anybody be tryin' ta get a quick peek, it be me recollectin' but only 'cause I's be memberin' how Joseph useta make me feel when he git to takin'off his shirt right befo' he commenced to rubbin' me down da right way. But soon as I's feels my innards git ta twitchin' I grabs me a cupful a water or runs down ta stream and takes a cold swim.

Still, he be very he'pful and be mindful a ev'ryt'ing I say and I's jes hopes my boy grow up ta be a strong, respectful man like Young Saul.

February 25

Mas'r John he say to me today dat he def'initely seed a change in Young Saul and I believes dat's a good t'ing

February 26

Aunt Hattie say Mas'r John git a letter today. Seems mas'r write to missy inquirin' 'bout ol' Ben since he shoulda been back close ta a week ago and bein' that ol' Ben is jes dat; old and mas'r's otha fav'rite 'sides me, he worried. Ben to ol' to run and havin' a touch of da rheumastism and all, so I believes he seriously concerned 'bout his whereabouts and hopin' dat da highwaymens ain't rob him fer da buckboard and hosses.

But de slaves know. Da slaves always knows and da word in da quarters is dat Ben sayed dis be his last trip and he either gwine ta freedom or ta Zion, but he sho as hell won't gwine ta be no slave no mo."

Mas'r John don't know all dat. And therefo' he jes patiently awaitin' ol' Ben's return

What's mo' fascinatin' though was da fact dat missy beggin' da mas'r ta takes her back in dat very same letter amd mas'r he sayed ta Aunt Hattie dat dat don't even warrant no response.

Rider come in from Mas'r Reynold's ta day with' news dat Missy Reynold's sick. Well, she always been what ya might call sickly and I's guess I be too iffen I was married ta dat ol' mean husband a hers. But when Mas'r John hear-ed dis you could jes see how da news upset him. I's do believe, he truly love dat woman and I's cain't much blame him for feelin' dat way. She one a da mos' nicest misses you ever wanna come across. And I guess dat 'cause she always been so sickly and so skinny. Ain't nothin' mo' than skin and bones ta her. And she bein' all quiet and timid like; it jes hard not to like her. Den when ya think 'bout her bein' married to the meanest man in Georgia well ya jest kinda feel sorry for her. Anyway, I's does p'sonally.

84

Neither her nor Mas'r John like what Mas'r Reynolds done b'come ov'er da years and iffen you ast me I's trly b'lieve dat's exactly what bringed dem two t'gether.

Well, you could seed dat Mas'r John was powerful shook by da whole state-of-affairs but he jes couldn't go paradin' o'er dere ta Miss Reynold's 'cause dat in itself wouldn't be correct or gentlemanly.

Iffen missy was here she woulda benda one ta go, but she ain't and 'sides Mas'r Reynold's won't lookin'fer no sympathy he was mainly lookin' fer someone ta come o'er ta wait on her and make sho' she was looked afta til she recovered her strength.

And bein' dat I's was gittin' bigger ta da point I's wasn't much help doin' anyt'ing round da place. Mas'r John sent me ov'er ta da Reynold's so's I's could tend ta missy 'til she was back on her feets again. He also sent Young Saul to 'company me and run down de stairs ta fetch t'ings as was necessary since I's wasn't in too good a shape m'self and dis I much appreciated. But mos'ly I knowed he wanted me ta keep a close watch on Young Saul and you could jes see how ev'rytime he look at dat boy how he was a calculatin' how much a big, strong young buck like Saul would bring him at da market raight prior ta plantin' season.

Anyways, mas'r sent word by dat dere rider dat he be sending some help since he knew Mas'r Reynold's ain't had a hand ta spare wit' plantin' season right roun' da corner and him bein' not jes shorthanded but in ev'rybody's debt as well. Mas'r John say he jes a bad financia' manager

85

but I's for one is of da impression dat he jes don't know how ta calculate too good.

Well, anyways me and Young Saul gwine pack a few belongins and head on o'er ta Mas'r Reynold's fer it gits late. Ain't but a few miles and we mighta been dere fer long but bein dat ol' Ben ain't brang da buckboard back Mas'r John ain't right p'ticular 'bout letting no mo buckboard's go out so's we gots to git a move on fo'da paddy rollas and slave catchers come out.

I done heared mas'r say on mo' than one occasion dat you gots ta be mo' afraid a da slavas than you does da abolitionist. And it be a knowed fact dat da slave catchers and paddy rollas along wit' da highwaymen dat be roamin' round at night is mo' of a threat ta kidnap us po' devils than a us 'scapin' on ar own. And dat be sayed I's got ta rustle up Young Saul so's we can be on our way befo' night falls.

Mas'r Reynolds da meanest man I ever did see. He treat missy like she no better than a slave. Even though she sick wit' da pneumonia he don't hardly pay her no mind 'cept to yell 'bout her bein well enough ta keep his books even though she be burnin'up wit' de fever.

Me. I jes did da best I could—bathin' her down—and feedin' her 'cause she too weak to feed herself. Den when she ast me to read to her from da bible and so I did. And dat's why I say he da meanest man I's ever seed. My first day dere missy ast me to read ta her from da bible which I was doin' when he walked in and slapped da good book from m'hand

86

and slapped me upside da head so hard I felled off da stool at da end a da bed and seed stars but I rolled up in a ball and covered my baby jes befo' dat mean ol' Mas'r Reynolds kick me and hit me wit; his riding crop. Missy was screamin' all da while but he won't listenin' My head was spinnin' but I balled up and covered my stomach so he couldn't harm my baby and all I's keep hearin' him say was who taught you to read gal. Dat's when I heared da door open and seed Young Saul movin' towards Mas'r Reynolds and I knew right den and dere from da look in Saul's eyes dat he meant ta kill dat white man when he saw me lyin' dere on dat dere flo' wit' Mas'r Reynold's standin' o'er me wit' dat dere ridin' crop but I grabbed his leg so's he could do anyt'ing and held on with both arms 'til he couldn't move t'wards Mas'r Reynolds. Mas'r Reynolds musta knowed what Young Saul intended 'cause he moved away from me and eased out da door but I hearded him ast one a his niggras who dat big buck was and I's was glad dey sayed he b'longed to Mas'r John and was bein' loaned ta help me out else I's sho Mas'r Reynolds woulda had him whipped—iffen he didn't have him stringed up fo lookin' b'lligerent.

By da next day me and Young Saul was shipped back ta da Marshall Plantation and missy sho won't feelin no better.

March 1st

87

Lord knows I's always hearin' niggra's complainin'. Always talkin'how bad t'ings be and I always be quick ta tell 'em dat t'ings can be worser. But mos' da time dey jes don't unnerstan' I's tries ta tell 'em dat mas'r a good mas'r but dey don't see dat. Mos' of 'em ain't been wit' no other mas'r so dey don't know. But I know I's goes ta Mas'r Reynold's fer one day and he wanna whip me fer somethin'. Mas'r John 'lowed me to do. Read.

Well, spite Mas'r Reynold's I's still glad I gots to go o'er ta da Reynold's Place. Missy was mo' dan helpful when I tol' her about my Joseph and even went so far as ta tell me where he been sold and who buyed him. And though I's nebba heared of de Natchez, in da Mississippi I sho aims ta find it.

Mas'r John tried not to let nobody know but Aunt Hattie heared dem white gentlemen's in da parlor when dey come ta bring Mas'r John da news.

Seems dey found some niggra old man 'bout eighty up in da mountains, lyin' long side some ditch. Say da nigga still had mas'r's travelin' pass in his pocket. Don't know who or why they kilt him but da pass sayed his name was Ben, gave his age as eighty, but could easily pass for sixty, and sayed that belongin' to a Mas'r John Marshall of Savannah County. There was no buckboard and no hosses and dey sayed Ben was beaten so badly dat when dey found him his face was— how did Aunt Hattie say dat word—oh, yeah unrecognizable. Dey was lookin' fo a reward cordin' to Aunt Hattie but she say all Mas'r John do is slan his fist down so hard on da parlor or table it shattered. Den he turned and asked dem dere gentelmens wit' tear in his eyes, Gentlemens have you any idea how much I payed for them two mares and that buckboard?

March 3

Everyday now I's beginning ta unnerstan' Joseph and Aunt Hattie and da Afreecans mo' and mo' I cried like I ain't nebba cried befo' when I heared da news 'bout Ben. To me Ben was da closest t'ing to a fatha' figger I's ever knowed.

When I was jes a lil' gal I useta sit and watch and jes stare while mas'r bounced his lil ones up and down on his knees on da front porch. Lil missy be jest a laughin' and gigglin' and da like she be lookin' like she was havin' so much fun dat I wanted ta jes run up ta mas'r and ast him ta bounce me up and down too, but even den I knowed my place. But ol' Uncle Ben would see da wander-lust in my eye and take me in da kitchen wit' Aunt Hattie and bounce me up and down on his knee da same way mas'r would do his lil' missy.

Otha times when he seed me starin' at missy whilst she played wit' da dolls mas'r would bring back from New O'leans and Savannah, ol' Uncle Ben would grab my hand, lead me away from watchin' lil' missy.

Though 'til dis day I's aint nebba figger'd out why. But a week or so later Uncle Ben would stop by Aunt Hattie's or takes me out ta barn when we both could git away and have me look unda dat ol' hoss blanket and lo and behold I declare iffen dat man ain't seed fit ta find da time ta whittle me a whole fam'ly a dolls all brand new and painted and shiny. And he say dese befo' me and told me not to show 'em ta nobody. And da one time I did 'cause I's so proud of 'em missy went ta cryin' ta her pa, Mas'r John about my dolls bein' betta dan hers which dey was and den mas'r sayed, 'Ben, I want you to make a set of dolls for my missy the same way you did for Mary! And he did. But dey wasn't no way as good as mine 'cause he put time and love and tendaness in mines 'cause he truly loved me like a fatha loves a daughta. And now he gone. And all mas'r concerned 'bout is his hosses and his ol'buckboard.

March 19th

Well, plantin' season done started so it seem like all da work done doubled and mas'r don't do nothin' but pick up supplies in town den stay out in da field 'til almost midnight rotatin' da crops and givin' orders ta ol' Sam so he can give 'em ta da hands but bein' dat Sam ain't too bright mas'r usually end up hollerin' at Sam and commence ta givin' em ta da hands hisself when Sam don't carry em out right.

Seem ta me like he could jes tell da hands what it is he wont
done and 'leviate all dat extry conversation. If you ask me, White folk sho
got a funny way a doing t'angs.

March 20

I's big as a house and tired all de time. I ain't sho if it's dis baby
or da fact dat mas'r stays up ta all times a da night workin' on his books
and paperwork, which mean eitha me or Aunt Hattie gots ta be 'round ta
fetch him dis and dat as he see fit.

P'sonally, I's don't see what he be doin' when he say he keepin'
da books, so's me, bein' of a curious nature I ast him. I jes come right
out and ast him one night. I walked right up ta him and sayed, Mas'r
what is it dat you be doin' wit' dem books and papers ev'rynight?"
And mas'r tu'ned ta me and laughed and jes telled md dat I's wouldn't
unnerstan' but I sayed to him.
'Please 'splain it ta me Mas'r John. I swear I's don't wanna be a dumb
nigga all my life. And mas'r say ta me, "No, I guess you don't wanna be
in the dark your whole life.
Den mas'r he git ta tellin' me 'bout how he gots ta balance da books so's
he ken see how much he spendin' on and how much he puttin' out on
stuff like dat. So he know how much profit he be makin' when he harvest
and sell ev'ryt'ing in da fall.

91

He say it very impotent dat he stay on top of things so he don't wind up in debt and losin' ev'ryt'ing like Mas'r Reynolds.

And I t'ink about how Mas'r John been stayin' on top of Missy Reynold's da last few months and da way I figger it Mas'r Reynold's betta git ta work on his books fo' mas'r take ev'ryt'ing he own, 'cludin' Missy Reynolds.

But Lord knows I don't rightly know why it's so impotent. Da way I see it mas'r ain't really buyin' nothin'. All he doin' is usin' last years seeds along wit' dis years crop a niggas and ain't neitha one a 'em costin' him a dime.

March 27

E'er time I see dat rider come in from o'er Mas'r Reynold's place I jes gets a bad thought. I t'ink a ma Joseph and how dat ol' mean Mas'r Reynold's tried to stomp my baby. I t'ink about how Mas'r Reynolds be behind Afreecan Jesse bein' whipped and hanged. Den I t'ink 'bout dat po' woman lyin' dere sick wit'dat ol' evil man. So, ev'rytime a rider come up from the Reynold's Place might find out dat he ain't stupid and maybe he been put here to be more than jes a slave. Aunt Hattie truly believe dat too. She say dat she jes bein' held in bondage 'til Moses come ferth ta carry her home.

Like I's said befo' I truly b'lieves dat age is startin' ta show itself where Aunt Hattie's concerned. She startin' ta speak real freely ta be Mas'r John's property. As good a man as Mas'r Reynold's is he still ain't gonna allow no slave to jes talk any ol' kinda a way. And ol' as Aunt Hattie is she s'pozed to knowed dat by now. And I know she do 'cause she useta stop me when I wasa youngun and gots to sowin' my oats and would f'gits my place. But now it's like she knowed but she jes don't care 'bout t'ings no mo'. Like jes dis mornin' when I tells her ta hush up 'cause mas'r ain't fond of his slaves talkin' like dat and she tell me dat she ain't nobody's slave and she freer than he is. Well, dat's when I knowed the wheelbarrow won't entirely full but I's says to her anyway dat she a slave jes like da rest of us and she gits a right nasty attitude and says ta me dat she ain't no slave and ain't nebba in her life been no slave. Dat's when I's tu'ned ta her and says, 'Now Aunt Hattie, you been Mas'r John's prop'ty fer mo' than seventy years and now you's sayin'' you ain't no slave.

And Aunt Hattie, tu'n ta me right den and dere and say ta me dat she been bought and held against her will but mas'r John and no otha man could ever enslave her unless she 'lowed dem too.

Dat's when I jes let it go 'cause I knew mas'r owned alla us slaves and ev'rybody else knowed it too includin' Aunt Hattie and I figgered she was gittin' closer ta her time and didn't want ta see herself dat way no mo'.

93

Still, she had me kinda worried but later on when I telled Young Saul what Aunt Hattie sayed he jes laugh. I telled him right den and dere not to laugh at Aunt Hattie 'cause dat would be disrespectful and he telled me dat he ain't laughin' at Aunt Hattie. He laughin' at me. And when I's ast him why, he jes keeped right on laughin'. Well, I ain't nebba like ta be made fun of and he could seed I's was gittin' a little riled so he commenced ta stop laughin'.

Den he jes looks at me in a mos' curious fashion and says 'Miss Mary , you really don't unnerstan' dat when peoples git old dey minds start ta actin' funny but Lord knows I's nebba 'spected nothin' like dis ta happen to Aunt Hattie 'cause she so strong."

And do you knowed what Young Saul telled me den? He telled me dat dere ain't not a t'ing da matter wit' Aunt Hattie mind. He sayed Aunt Hattie one a da few on dis here place dat knowed from day one who she be and no matta what da white folk t'row her way she nebba gwine be no slave 'cause she always been free in her mind. And I's jes lets him knowed dat free as she is in her mind she still a slave in Mas'r John's kitchen.

Dat's when Young Saul lookt-ed at me grinned and jest shooked his head like I's was da one wit' da feeble mind and not Aunt Hattie.

But I ain't say nothin' 'cause I knowed dat Saul loved auntie much as I did. Plus dem Afreecans stick together and has funny ideas

94

when it come to slavery and admittin' dey was slaves. So, I jes let da whole t'ing go.

Anyways, mas'r come by dis evenin' ta tell me dat he been informed dat Missy Reynolds won't farin' ta well and he wonted me ta ride over and look in on her til she feelin' betta. Sayed I's needed to stay wit' her till she up-n-about so I's should bring somet'ings and be quick about it.

I begged him to send somebody else 'cause Mas'r Reynolds don't like me. But he sayed it won't me Mas'r Reynolds a dislikin' fer. He sayed Mas'r Reynolds jes peculiar is all and really don't like nobody 'cause truth-be-tol Mas'r Reynolds don't like hisself. I's don't rightly know what dat dere means 'cause sometimes he gots a down right funny way of 'spressin' hisself, but I begged him ta git somebody else ta take my place. But he won't havin' it so I telled him dat I's scared bein' short wit' da baby's comin' and all.

And he look at me all strange-like and sayed. "Mary tain't no reason ta be scared a Tom Reynolds. That's what he sayed to me. Sayed, I've known Tom Reynolds my whole life and he ain't nothin' to be afraid of.

So, I says, "Well maybe not for you suh but maybe fer a slave I's different."

And he jes looks at me and sayed, "Mary, is there something you're not telling me?

Well, I's been a slave and a nigga fa'as long as I's can remember and certain things I knows. It's like dey jes comes nat'chal ta a slave like you was born wit' certain things you know dat you ain't s'posed to tell on no white folk. So, when Mas'r John ast me if it was somethin' I's wasn't sayin' I knowed right den and dere dat iffen I's tol' him, I may as well have tied m'self ta da big oak and put da whip in his hand. But I's figgered dat still would be betta dan taken a chance and lettin' Mas'r Reynolds kill me and m'baby so I sayed, Mas'r da last time I's o'er da Reynolds Place, Mas'r Reynolds beat me bad. Dat's all I sayed. And den I watched his face git all red like a beet and he say.

"Why dat low-down dirty bastard. And is he the one who give you that there shiner?"

I nodded and when I seed dat he won't gonna hit me fer tellin' on his friend, I tells him ev'rything 'bout how Mas'r Reynolds stomped and kicked me fer readin' da bible like missy ast. Fo' I thought 'bout it good, ev'rything jes come a rollin' out.

 And I swear fo' God, I ain't nebba seed mas'r git so mad in all da time I been wit' him. All he sayed was fer me ta git m'belongins and ta git ready ta go. Den he sayed dat he ain't got time fer all dis here nigga foolishness and added dat when I git back da Reynolds Place he was gonna deal wit' m'lyin' Black ass.

Well, I knowed I's was in fer it den and da tears jes started a flowin' when Young Saul come in ta see what all da ruckus was about. Dat's

96

when I telled him dat I be back in a few days jes as soon as Missy
Reynolds be back up n' around and dat's when he start puttin' his stuff in
a sack. Mas'r john jes look at him and say, "Boy, where you think you
goin'?" ta which Saul replied.
"Mas'r I thought I's s'pozed ta stay by Miss Mary's side like you telled
me, suh."
And mas'r, him jes ignored Saul and sayed. "No, boy dis here is
somethin' Mary don't need no he'p doin'"
But instead a Saul jes noddin his head and sayin' 'yassuh' as he shoulda
done dat Afreecan come out and he sayed, "Beg your pardon, mas'r, but
you cain't send Miss mary o'er da Reynold's Place suh. Iffeen you does,
why mas'r Reynolds mos' likely gonna kill her, suh."
Mas'r jes lookt at Saul and den sayed, "What you talkin' bout boy?"
And when he tell mas'r da same 'zact story what I jes telled him, mas'r
ain't sayed nothin'. He jes stand dere fo' what seemed like fo'ever. Den
he tell us both ta git in da carriage.
Lord knows when Mas'r John git ta da Reynolds I's scared fo' both me
and Saul and da whole way dere nobody sayed nothing.
Well, when we git dere Mas'r John still ain't sayed a word. He jes leave
us settin' dere and walk right up to da house wit' his ridin' crop in his
hand and da next thing I knowe Mas'r Reynold's come a rollin' down da
steps a da big house da same 'zact way I did when he was tryna kick
me. He was doin' his bes' right through dere ta cova his head and all but

97

won't nothin' he could do and I feared Mas'r John was gonna kill him. But won't nothin' I could do, pregnant and in da condition I was in and ta tell da truth I was scairt dat angry as he was he jes might jump on me and say da whole affair was m'fault. But even despite what Mas'r Reynolds did ta me I couldn't he'p but feel sorry fer him at dat point and I was halfway sad I sayed anything 'bout it atall. But not Young Saul. He jes stand dere tryin' not ta grin too much. And fer da first time since I knowed him, he refused ta lissen ta me when I telled him ta pull Mas'r John offa mas'r Reynolds befo' he killt him.

Now as you very well, knows, I ain't nebba had no love fer dat dere man lyin' face down, in da dirt face all bloodied and to' up but I prides m'self on bein' a Christian woman iffen I ain't nothin' else and I know da good Lord would not 'preciate da way Mas'r John was actin' now. Besides Mas'r John was a Christian too and right now it was purty obvious dat da devil had got ahol' a him in a big way and won't gonna let go wit'out somebody interferin' directly. Sides dat bein' dat dis here whole account was on my account I knowed dat I's gonna haveta git out da carriage and stop mas'r or have dat dere killin' on m'conscience and I jes won't sho I could live wit'dat.

By dis time, ev'ry nigga on da Reynold's Place was dere by now jes a standin' dere lookin' on like dey was at a cock fight or something'. But ain't a one a dem try ta step in and he'p dey mas'r out. And I wondered iffen dat had been Mas'r John in da same position would hissen Negroes

98

have come ta his aid even though I's purty sho dey would have. But not

here. And I had ta think ta m'self dat dis here must be one, purty evil

man fer nobody ta want ta he'p him not even his own ova'seer.

Still and all, I feel like it was m'fault and like I sayed I didn't wont

nobody's murda on m'head. So I gits down from da carriage and walks

o'er ta mas'r who by dis time has got down on one knee and is liftin'

Mas'r Reynolds's head outta da dirt and den slammin' it back down wit

all his might. And lookin' at dat man's face all covered wit blood and

leaves wit' bruises and cuts all ova it I knowed it was my duty as a

Christian woman ta stand up 'gainst da odds despite what dat man had

did ta me and aid him in his time a distress. And so I climbed down

froom m'perch on da carriage and went o'er ta Mas'r John much

expectin' fer him ta turn 'round and give me some a what he was givin'

Mas'r Reynolds but it ain't much matta I still knowed I had ta do my part.

Like I sayed I knowed by now dat nobody else was gonna he'p dat man

and so I went o'er ta Mas'r John and bent down o'er him and whispered

inta his ear those same exact words Aunt Hattie been tellin' me alla m'life

when someone do somethin' cruel ta me. I sayed, "Mas'r John,

vengeance is mine sayed da Lord," and den I backed up some and

braced m'self and waited fer him ta turn around and slap me fer causin'

alla dis his here ruckus and den turnin' right aroun' and tellin' him he ain't

handlin' things like a proper soldier in da good Lord's army. But instead,

a turnin' and swingin' out at me, he jes stopped. I'm sayin' jes like dat he stopped as if da good Lord hisself come down and tol' him he won't actin' like da good Christian we all knew he was.

Me, I felt real relieved dat he ain't kill dat man and I knowed dat I won't gonna haveta worry 'bout him botherin' me no time soon even iffen he had a notion to he won't in no shape afta dat whoopin' mas'r jes disposed on him. But a funny thing occurred right afta I git mas'r up offa him. When I turnt ta head back ta da carriage ta git m'belongins I noticed dat dem very same Negroes dat seed me save Young Saul afta dey hanged Afreecan Jesse was watchin' den and praisin' me silently den was sho nuff da same ones dat was cussin'me now fo' not lettin' mas'r kill dat man. And I was quite sho by dis time dat dey wouldn't a minded iffen I hadda let mas'r whoop on him jes a little mo but I don't care how bad a man aim ta be it don't warrant anotha man killin' him and den have ta walk aroun' an shoulder dat burden da rest a his days. 'Specially on m'account. So I stopped it and was content wit' mas'r jes lettin' him know dat he would finish da job iffen he ever laid a hand on any his prop'ty again. Den mas'r git ta talkin' 'bout how he gonna pull all his notes iffen Mas'r Reynolds doin' any such a thing ag'in. Mas'r say it loud enough fer ev'rybody ta hear dat he da sole and rightful owner of da Reynold's Place anyway considerin' how much he was owed and iffen he didn't b'lieve it den all he had ta do was let him hear about him layin' his hands on anotha niggra what ain't belong ta him. And I ain't nebber been so proud a mas'r as I was dat day. Ta tell da truth I could hardly speak and I do b'lieve I's even felt a tear roll down m'cheek.

Den somethin' I heared catched my 'tention and I's eased up right close so as not ta miss a word and heared mas'r telled him how he made it plain ta him dat befo' he sold da blacksmith, (da blacksmith bein' my Joseph). Anyway, mas'r sayed he tol' him he wanted my Joseph and would buy him at da market price and Mas'r Reynold's bein' stubborn and mean sprited sol' him anyway. He say, he jes betta be glad dat deys daddy's useta be friends. When I heaared dat I wisht I hadda let mas'r whip him some mo'.

And Mas'r Reynolds, lyin' dere wit'in a inch a kingdom come and still mean as a backwoods black snake turnt and lookt up at Mas'r John his face all bloody and swolled up and sayed, "I'll be damned if you'll own ev'rything John Marshall. He sayed, "You already own damn near all of Savannah County and if that's not enough you want my wife too. How much is enough, you greedy bastard?"

By dis time Missy Reynolds who'd somehow found the strength to make it downstairs and to the front door stepped onto the front porch when Mas'r Reynolds, his back ta her made his last remark before Mas'r John put that size twelve boot to his temple and quieted him for da remainda a dat day.

Now, I's not too sho iffen dat po' woman who been through I's don't know how much wit' damn man was jes too weak dat she stumbled or if fen

101

she fainted from havin' her mos' intimate business made public, (though we all knowed she and mas'r was beddin' down together long in advance a Mas'r Reynolds informin' us). But anyways, she heared dat dere remark and come down dem steps in almos' da same fashion her husband did only a short while earlier.

Well, me and Saul bein' da closest ta her and da only one's who looked like we was willin' ta he'p dat po' woman rushed ta her side whilst like I sayed mos' a her very own hands acted as iffen dey didn't even see and Lord knowed when she fell it was in plain view a ev'rybody. But den soon as me and Saul gots her up on her feet I knowed why nobody stepped in ta he'p. Young Saul seein'dat da weight was too much fer me in m'condition and alla da time tryna he'p me in some fashion or anotha jes nat'chally grabbed missy up in his arms like she won't nothin' mo' n' a sack a potatoes. Den he proceeded ta take her inside 'cordin' ta m'directions when Mas'r Reynolds yelled, "Boy, if you don't take your hands offa that white woman I'll whip the black off yo' ass."

Saul lookt at me but I couldn't say anything and Mas'r John grabbed missy from Saul and pushed his way past me and took her inta da house and up ta her room and tol' missy dat I's be stayin' wit' fer jes as long as she needed me.

April 1st

Fo' I left Aunt Hattie warnt me 'bout readin' and writin' whilst I's at da

Reynolds. Sayed Mas'r Reynolds don't take kindly ta no niggra doin' no

readin' and writin' 'cause he won't p'ticularly good at it hisself and won't

p'ticularly disposed ta havin' neither no smart nor uppity niggras 'round

him. She sayed it make him feel inferio'. She sayed he don't wont no

niggras who ken see jes what he doin' bbut a niggra ain't gots ta be book

smart ta know dat Mas'r Reynolds is one evil man.

April 3rd

I stays in a empty shack right in da middle a da quarters even though

missy gots a empty bedroom next ta hers and ast Mas'r Reynolds iffen I

could stay dere in case she feel bad in da middle a da night. Dat way I

ken go and fetch her her medicine but he say no. Say he don't truss no

nigga livin' unda da same roof wit' him. Boy dat man sho do gots

problems. And ta tell da truth I don't see why dat would bother him much

since he always down in da quarters at night anyway. Funny ta me dat

as much as dat man hates niggras he sho do love stayin' down dere in

da quarters.

April 5th

I ain't s'pozed ta be writin' but long as I stays up in da big house I ken write all I wont 'cause Mas'r Reynolds ain't nebba ever here. Like I sayhe spend mos' a his nights down dere wit' his niggras goin' from shack ta shack.. I declare I ain't nebba seen nothion' like him and I swear he worser 'bout dat than ol' Sam and I ain't think nobody could be worser than ol' Sam. Ta tell da truth, I don't think he care nothin' at all 'bout missy and she know it too. I think dat's why she ain't gittin' no betta. It's like she don't even wont ta and it almos' seem like she done lost all her fight and da will ta live. Guess she jes figger since no one love her den what da use. And da man what s'pozed ta truly love her, (dat bein' m'mas'r), well—he married hisself and bein' dat she married to, well—it jes ain't no hope. Now see dat wouldn't be no niggra. But white folk so worried 'bout keepin' up a air a respectability dat dey is all unhappy. I tells ya it's all a pur' d mess. And I cain't he'p but think a alla da people runnin' 'round talkin' bout jes how bad dey has got it. Dese here white folk sho nuff ain't got it easy eitha if ya ast me.

Dis woman wit' dis big ol' fine house, wit servants and da like is da mos' unhappiest person I's ever had da pleasure a meetin'. And here I is jes a plain slave gal who would simply die fer somethin' like dis and here she is fadin' away 'cause da man she choosed don't love her and da man she done come ta love she cain't see fit ta be wit'.

I s'poze mas'r too embarrassed afta what Mas'r Reynolds sayed 'bout him wontn' ta own ev'rything includin' missy ta come aroun' but I ain't seen him since I been here. Still, he doin' ev'rything else he ken do ta make sho' she git betta. He done sent fer doctors from as fer away as Beaufort and New O'leans ta tend ta missy and fin' out what be ailin' her. But dey all jes shakes dere heads and say dere ain't nothin' dey ken do fo' da fact dat what ails her ain't no medical remedy for. Doctors say it's far worse. And right through here she done stopped eatin' almos' completely.

April 7th

Sent fer mas't taday. He need ta see missy iffen he care anything 'bout her cause I's ken see she sufferin' from da same affliction dat had da grip on me not too long ago when dey sol' m'Joseph. Iffen mas'r, come, spend some time tell missy he love her and wanna marry her den I's almos sho' she be jes fine.

April 8th

Mas'r ain't see fit ta come. I guess he don't figger m'request is serious enough ta warrant no c'sideration or otha wise he jes don't care. I's really beginnin' ta see anotha side a mas'r since I been away but anyway he send Aunt Hattie and Saul in his stead. He sent word dat his comin' would not be appropriate c'siderin' what Mas'r Reynolds sayed 'bout him and him bein' a respectable gentemen and all in da plantas community. I jes shaked m'head when Aunt Hattie telled me dis.

I swear. White folk always worried 'bout how somethin' gonna appear. Here a woman lyin' here 'bout ta die and dey worried 'bout how itgonna appear iffen dey come ta see her. Lord, have mercy on dey mixed up souls. And dey calls us dumb. He send Aunt Hattie wit' a couple a apple pies, some soup and some orange marmalade and I guess dats s'pozed ta cure a broken heart.

Well, I swear I cain't take no mo'. Here he got me doin' his job and settin' here waitin' fer dis good woman ta die and I guess it was mo than I could take. So, I jumpt right on da back a dat dere buckboard and rides back o'er dere ta see mas'r and telled him dat it won't nothin' wrong wit missy 'ceptin' dat she outta her head wit' grief from missin' him so much and she done lost da will ta live. Well, it was him dat was alla da time tellin' me dat da truth would set me free when he wonted ta know somethin' what was goin' on 'round da place so I knowed dat he won't goin' ta have no touble wit' da truth now. And I was glad ta see dat he was deeply troubled when I telled him dis piece a info'mation and it

106

occurred dat he ain't changed atall and dat dere was still a good

Christian man in dere. He was jes troubled was all.

Now, I was glad I come ta tell him even though Aunt Hattie telled me ta

stay outta white folks business. She say, "Mary you needs ta stay outta

white folks affairs a da heart', but standin' dere in front a mas'r right den,

I's was sho'lly glad I hgadn't followed her advice dis time. Mas'r lookt so

sad. And I gotta tell ya. Dis was da fi'st time in all da years dat I knowed

dat man dat he really and truly lookt like he was about ta shed a tear.

Den he turnt ta away form me and so's I couldn't see him cry and but

when he turn't back ta face me I feel like I was lookin' inta da face a da

devil hisself. Lookt jes like Lucifer hisself had taken o'er Masr John.

Dat's when he turn't ta me and said.

"Gal, I don't know where you get the audacity to come here with the idea

in that nigga head a yours ta approach me, a white man, thinkin' you can

advise me on how to run my goddamn affairs but if you dou don't get

your fat black ass out of my sight immediately so help me God I'll have

your pregnant ass whipped to within an inch of your life. I ain't sure now

if Tom Reynolds wasn't right in whippin' your ass. I'm of a right mind to

do it myself right now. I swear I don't rightly know what's gotten into you,

gal. He jes might be right about all that book learnin' goin' to your head

either. All that book learnin' do is make a nigga dumber than he already

is. Make 'em uppity and think they as good as white folk, make 'em think

they can talk to white folk any kind a way. Well, I'm here ta tell ya that ya can't and if you ever approach me and tell me how to run my affairs or give me yo' opinion without me askin' for it first, I'll sell yo' high yalla ass down the river before you can sing the first stanza of Oh Susannah. Now git on away from here.'

Den mas'r did somethin' he ain't nebba done in da whole entire time I's been unda his care. He grabbt m'neck and threw me up against da parlor wall jes as hard as he could almos' like I was jes a common fiel' hand or somethin'. M'head hit dat wall so hard I's sho he done jarred somethin' loose and all I seed was spots. Thought fo' sho' I's goin' ta faint but I grabbed da corner a da fireplace and held on as da tears jes burst out from da pain. I tried ta gather m'self and make m'way outta da room but m'legs acted like dey didn't wanna hold me and 'fo I I knowed it I's was on da flo' and feelin' dis bu'nin' sensation in my my side right above m'hip where mas'r kicked me and was windin' up ta kick me ag'in. And all da while he jes a rantin' and a ravin' bout me bein' one upiity nigga and not knowin' m'place and I knowed right den and dere dat what ever it was dat was botherin' him at dat moment ain't had nothin' ta do wit' me but dat thought ain't he'p dat burnin' in m'side and it was den dat I realized dat mas'r ain't cared no mo' about me than Mas'r Reynolds. Onliest difference dis time was dat won't nobody dere ta stop him or pull him offa me. He still rantin' and ravin' and cussin' 'bout how all da niggas in da world ain't measure upta po' white trash and how he wisht now he had followed his daddy's advice and been a lawyer instead a bein' in da nigga business. Sayed he wisht he could jes sell da whole lot a us no account, meddlin', shiftless, niggas and be done wit' us once and fer all. And 'specially me fer makin' him lose his wife and his best friend. Dat's what mas'r say and all da time tryin' ta find da strength ta lay his boot inta me ag'in. He sayed soon as dat baby a mine was bo'n he was gonna sell both a us jes as fer away as he could. Talk 'bout bein' shocked. I's couldn't b'lieve m'own ears. Dis mas'r dat I's done served so faithfully all dese years sayed he was gonna sell both me and m'baby fer away from da onliest home I's ever knowed jes like I's one a dem common fiel' hands what constantly runnin and 'causin' him so much problems. Dis da very same man dat give me his word. And now he jes gonna go back on it. And fer da fi'st time in m'entire life, I wisht dat dat man and all those like him would feel da wrath a da Lord and da Lord would send down a plague a locust or a bolt a thunder and strike 'em all dead.

It was at dat very moment dat I unnerstood why none a dem slave hands, at da Reynold's Place, went ta helps Mas'r Reynolds when Mas'r John was so set on sendin' him ta Zion. Guess Aunt Hattie knowed what she was talkin' 'bout when she telled me 'bout not meddlin' in white folks affairs.

I's begged fer mercy and I ain't rightly sho iffen mas'r heared or he jes git tired or iffen it won't da good Lord who stepped in and stopped him from killin' me but he stopped kickin'me and jes went o'er, fetched hisself

some brandy and set down and steered at me befo' tellin' me ta git m'ass
up outta dere and carry m'self back ta da Reynolds.

I won't sho' dat I could walk but I got up outta dere da best way I knowed
how which meant crawlin'on my hands and knees 'til I got outta his sight
and den I checked ta see how bad I 's was hu't. Bein' dat I ain't feelin'
nothin' feel like it was broke I jes prayed dat he ain't hurt m'baby. Da
whole time I tried ta keep m'stomach covered and balled up inta da
tightest little ball I could and den I prayed. And I's says ta m'self. Iffen
dis here youngun' survives dis here he gonna be one strong man.

Dat night as I walkt dem seven or eight miles back ta da Reynolds, I
prayed. I mean I prayed da whole entire way. I prayed fer m'baby and I
prayed dat da Lord would kill Mas'r John and iffen he couldn't see fit ta
do it den he jes give me da power ta do it m'self. Dats what I prays fo'. I
prays dat he let me kill dat man befo' he has a chance ta sell m'baby
away from me, his mama like dey sellt me. I prays fo' a end ta alla dis
slavery and meanspiritedness but mos' a all I prayed dat he ain't die a
nat'chall death but death by m'hand. Dat's when it come ta me. Den as
I finally come inta view a da Reynold's Place and afta comin' up wit' a
sho fire way ta kill mas'r it come ta me dat whoever takes mas'r's place
was jes as likely ta be even worse and dey probably would sell
ev'rybody. And I's didn't wont dat ta happen jes 'cause I was sufferin' so.
So, I prayed dat da good Lord would see fit ta kill me and m'baby befo'
he let us be separated and sol' down da river and away from each otha.

I keept tellin' m'self dat dis was all jes a bad dream and dat it jes couldn'

be so but my ribs and m'sides tol' me dat dis won't no dream. Dis jes da

slavery m'Joseph tried so hard ta make me unnerstan' when I keept

sayin' no it jes cain't be. And den I ast m'self how da good Lord could let

dis be so when I knowed in m'heart dat he don't approve.

By dis time I's at da Reynold's Place and I figgers it mus' be close ta

midnight. And mas'r's words was still ringin' loud and clear. M'head and

m'face pounded from where I hit da parlor wall. But no sooner than I gits

back one a da hands I ast ta stand in fer me whilst I was gone tryna do

missy's biddin' say she been astin' fer me da entire time. Wel lnow, I do

declare, din m'heart and soul I's truly feel likes I had enough a white folk

ta last me a lifetime. And it seem like ev'rytime I tries ta he'p out in some

way dey acts da fool and worser than any ol' stubborn mule I's ever did

see so's I jes say dat it too late ta be callin' on anybody. But it seems dat

missy done left word dat no matta what times I's gits back she wanna

see me. So, I's ignores my betta senses and sneaks in da back door, in

case Mas'r Reynolds done stopped by ta visit. And a course he ain't so I

goes in and wakes missy ta see what all da fuss is about and what's so

impotent it cain't wait 'til t'morrow and when I steps in da door a her

bedroom and da fi'st thing dat hits me is da smell a bowels. Well, fact is

missy done los' so much much weight dat she almos' too weak ta stand

or use da outhouse wit'out some assistance and when she cain't hol' it

she has a tendency ta jes let it go right dere. And obviously ain't none

111

'round dere think enough a her or her husband ta make sho' she drown in her own feces or not and dis was jes da situation I come inta afta bein' bein' beaten half ta death by m'own saintly mas'r. I could feel m'eye swoll. And when I enetered dat room m'eye 'bout da size of a grapefruit and m'sides is feeling like pure mush but won't nothin' wrong wit' m'nose. And I jes about died from da stench of dat woman. And I's had ev'rything ta do ta keep from throwin' up what was left of m'insides right den and dere but I didn't want her ta feel bad. So, what I did was take a deep breath, hol' it, den smile and try ta comfort her and let her knowed dat it really won't all dat bad when it truth it were even worser. Dat's when dis heifer rose up offa her bed and commenced ta swearin' and hollerin' at me 'bout how long she been sittin' in her own feces whilst I's was probably out dered practicin' ta make some mo' younguns.

Well, Lord iffen dat ain't beat all. Dere was no doubt in m'mind dat she knowed where I was and what I was doin' 'cause we discussed it befo' I left. So, fer ta treat me so on her return was jes uncalled fer spcially since she ain't even bothered ta ast what happened. Well dis here was mo' than even a niggra slave could stomach so I turnt 'round wit' out even botherin' ta 'xplain and walkt away and left her ta set in her own filth.

April 9th

I don't know how many times missy done 'pologized ta me since last night. She mos'ly sleeps da day away now. Might be up'bout an hour or two at da mos' and den it's a spoon a laudenum and she gone ag'in. I' b'lieve I's done all I's ken fer but she ain't tryna help herself so ain't nothin' fer me ta do fo' her at dis point and it don't seem like nobody seem ta care.

Mas'r John come by one day dis week, lookt in on her but she ain't even knowed who he was and da laudanum done took hold so bad dat when she is woke she jes scream and scream and try ta brush whatever it is she think crawlin' on her off. Doctor say she schizo- somethin', which I guess means she thinks she gots bugs crawlin' on her but I know it ain't nothin' but dat laudenum drivin' her as crazy as a horse fly on a cow's tail. Dat laudenum done ate away at her brain but I's knowed dat it ain't nothin' but mens breakin' her heart dat is drivin' her mad. When mas'r come ta seed her in da condition she was in he didn't say a word he jes lookt one time time den tu'nt ta me and sayed. I don't b'lieve there's too much mo' you can do here Mary. Why the poor woman has gone quite mad. Start making arrangements for one of Master Reynolds hands to take over for you come the first of the week. Got a lot of work down on the lower fo'ty needs tendin' to wit' dis year's crop. He nebba lookt at me

113

though da whole time he was talkin' ta me and I's truly did not know dis man I called mas'r all m'life.

Dat was Monday and mas'r sayed he wanted me back on da next Monday which telled me dat nobody 'spected missy ta last da week. And Mas'r Reynolds took ta da bottle like dere was no t'morrow. He ain't even botha ta come home no mo'. Sayed da place smelled like death but it ain't smelt no worse than he did. He quit washin' and shavin' and spent all his time in whorehouses of Savannah. I knowed dis'cause every few days or so he'd send a niggra whore to da house wit' a note astin' fer a change of clothes and a draft so he could pay his bill at da whorehouse.

He telled da gals he sent ta give me da note 'cause I was da onliest one on da whole place what could read or write. Den I'd fill out da draft in da amount he sayed and give it ta da gal who not knowin' would take da draft to da bank and have it filled. Da man in da bank would put da money in da bag and tell da gal not to open it and dey would return to Mas'r Reynold's.

Everytime it was a different gal and in this way I's came to know a lot about Savannah and a bunch of otha thangs as well since mos' of dem gals was free.

By this time, almost all work had commenced. Niggras wasn't even t'inkin about plowin' or plantin' and each day that passed two or three niggras was slippin away under da cover of darkness. Da Reynolds'

114

Plantation already dang'ously low in hands, (which was why I was summoned in da first place), must of lost more dan fifty slaves an' he ain't had more than a hundred to begin with. Mos' a da one's dat did stick around didn't stick around 'cause of no loyalty to da Reynolds. Dey was jes too old ta run, too scared to run or believed dat de emancipation was right around da corner.

Dey say dat da emancipation be comin' any day and all da slaved be free den.

April 10th

Took Missy Reynold's laudanum and mixed it wit' some tobacco juice from da spittoon da way da Aunt Hattie told me too so ev'rytime missy drink from da bottle she throw up. It 'cause me a whole lot mo' work cleanin' up behind her three, fo' times a day but afta a day she already lookin' betta and ain't so quick ta drink no whole bottle up in a day. And no matta how mean dey are I cain't jes sit by and watch nobody kill deyselves. But on days like today when she cussin' and fussin' and git ta actin' ugly like a pure d fool I gives her jjes enough ta make her sleep

115

so I ken git my chores done and think about m'plan which I tries ta wo'k on a lil' bit each day.

April 11th

A real purty mulattoe gal ride up taday and woke me whilst I was catchin' a catnap on da veranda o'er lookin' da front porch. Dis here youngun' kicked me all night so I gots ta nap when I git a chance to. Kick like a mule too. B'lieve he gonna be a biggun jes like his daddy.

Anyways, dis gal come ridin' up astin' me iffen I's da niggra what ken read and write. Bein' dat I's didn't really know her I jes lookt at her and didn't say nothin' fer awhile but dat in no way stopped her and she say she gotta message from Mas'r Reynold's sayin' he need a hunnerd dollar draft and a change a clothes but bein' dat I jes nat'chally gots a suspicious nature I ast her how Mas'r Reynolds been farin'. And she say not too good since he eitha be drunk or sick mos' a da time she wit' him. Say he stay drunk mos' a da time.

I knowed dist ta be a fact but bein' dat I's still suspicious, I ast her fer da note and she showed me her pass which even though scribbled I still recognized as Mas'r Reynold's pen and his mark scratched at da bottom. Still, not thoroughly convinced I ast her what da note read and she admitted dat she couldn't read or write. So, I ast her for her otha note and she said dats all he gave her befo' tellin' her ta git.

116

I's still suspicious so I telled her he ain't got no hunnerd dollars. I tell her he done spent all but fifty dollars and when he gits dis last lil' bit dere ain't no mo' ta be had.

Dat way iffen he on a drunken binge like I 'spect den he won't have been keepin' track a da books which is what I was hopin' fer and iffen he was I 'spected him ta be showin' up mad as a wet hen in da next day or so. Anyway, she shake her head and say she would tell him jes dat but she gonna make sho she stand at da bottom a da stairs and yell dat part up ta him c'cause she got a fear a heights and didn't fancy rollin' down dem marble stairs. We both laughed at dis one. Now, I knowed even though I ain't checked his books but I don't wanna him ta wake up from his drunk and come a huntin' ta see what happened ta all his money den I know dat he purty far gone too.

Anyways, befo' dat ol' gal leave she say dis to me. She say, "You know you's a right handsome woman. Might think'bout gittin "inta da business afta ya has yo' youngun'. Might wanna head ta Natchez or Buloxi and stake ya a claim. Save up a little money den catch Mr. Reynold's when he all likkerd up and low on funds and get him ta sign da papers so's you's can buy your freedom. That's what I did. Went to Natchez worked fo a year...

All I heard was Natchez and my ears perked up like dat ol 'sorry hound Caesar what useta tag along behind Uncle Ben. "Did you say Natchez?" I ast searchin' fer da bill of sale I'd seed earlier wit' my Joesph's name on

117

it. Finding it faster than I's ever found in anything in my life I shoved it in fronf of her face. "Do you k now dis man?' I ast.

'Thought we been through this befo' honey. I's can't read.'

'Oh, da names of Franklin of da Franklin Plantation. Does you know him.'

'Of course, honey. Ev'rybody in Natchez knows da Franklin Place. One a da biggest slave holders in Natchez. Got mo' than a thousand slaves, he do.

"Tell me about 'em. Is he a fair man?'

"Well, now I never had da occasion ta havin' any business dealins with him otha than in the bedrooms,'she laughed. 'And there he was always fair. Won't nothin' like yo' mas'r here. M. Franklin. He strictly business.'

An hour later, amidst Missy Reynolds screamin' and bellowin' at da top of her lungs I hugs and kissed dat woman who tol' me anything and ev'ryting 'bout how ta put my plan inta action.

April 11th

Dey keep sayin' dat wars about ta break free da slaves and I's been waitin' da betta part of what seem like fo' ever so I's can put my plan inta action. I done already got word ta Aunt Hattie and Young Saul and tol' Aunt Hattie ta be ready but Aunt Hattie say she ain't decided yet.

April 12th

The war started today. I's ain't rightly sho' what dat means but niggras

run and jumpin' like its July 4th or somethin'. Dey say da war all about

freein' us but I ain't seed a niggra lookin' like dey free yet. Jes think its

anotha white folk's tricks ta keep 'em from runnin' away. So, many

slaves is runnin' and escapin' dat white folks is jes plain furious. Makin' it

real hard on dem dat's stayin' put. And da harder da white folk treat dere

niggas da more dey runnin'. It's all one big crazy mess. It's jes so many

crazy things, I jes don't unnerstan' and I feels jes like a chile when I ast

Aunt Hattie 'bout somethin'. Mos' ev'ry night I eitha goes o'er ta mas'r's

or Aunt Hatties come o'er here bein' dat Mas'r John's travelin' so much

dese days tryna drum up a army and enlist dese southern boys to join da

war when it do finally come.

Aunt Hattie says da North got way more boys than da South do and dey

is a standin' army which means dey is alla da time waitin' and ready ta

fight whereas da South ain't got nearly enough so' dat's why mas'r gotta

get out dere and round up da troops.

I sayed ta Saul and Aunt Hattie when we's speakin' about da war dat da

South's got enough niggras ta fight and dey always makin 'em do dey

dirty work I's right surprised dey ain't made 'em fight as well.

But Aunt Hattie says, de white slave owners what's all runnin' da war

effort for da Sout don't wont no niggras ta fight fer 'em on account dey ain't sho which way da niggras gonna point dem guns when dey tell 'em

ta aim at da enemies. We all laughed at dat one but truth is dey ain't

nebba gonna truss no niggras afta all dey done did ta 'em. Anyway, iffen

dey don't wont us ta fight dat's fine by me but I's still confused 'bout a

few things so I turns ta Aunt Hattie and says, 'What sense do it make fer

white folks ta get out dere and fight and die fer somebody dey says is

nothin'but a no good, lazy, shiftless, stupid, heathen. Don't seem like

much ta fight and die fer iffen ya ast me.'

'No gal, it sho' don't. But what dese boys is really mad 'bout is da fact

dat someone tryin' ta take somethin' what dey feel is legally and rightfully

deres. It's what dey refer ta as da principole of da thing. Dey simply

refuses ta let anybody tell 'em what ta do. Dat's all it really come down

ta.'

"So, let me git dis right auntie. Iffen da North win den alla us niggras be

free. Is dat what ya tellin' me Aunt Hattie? And iffen da South win, den

we still slaves?" I ast.

"Yes, chile. I'd say dat's 'bout da size of it."

"And in da meantime we's jes s'pozed ta sit back and wait and take care

of da homefront whilst we wait and see what's ta become a us. Plus

iffen da North win, what dey gonna do wit' us niggras den? Da North jes

gonna say we's free and take us home wit'em or is dey gonna leave us

here ta fend fo' ourselves afta dey done stirred up de ho'nets nest and

made dem boys madder than a cut bull in heat."

"Who you tellin' honey? Anything go wrong and dem fools git dem arm or leg blowed off defendin' you niggras from da freedom and abolitionists you sho'lly knows whose fault it gonna be, Mary."

"Of course I do, auntie. It's gonna be yours and mine. But I'll tell you dis much. I ain't settin' aroun' waitin' fer 'em ta come back. Win or lose it's always da same fer a niggra. Win or lose fer dem and it's always lose lose fer us. Eitha way dey ain't comin' back smilin'. Ya ken bet on dat. And Lord knows how long it gonna be fer dey gits done wit' fightin' each otha but I's sho ain't a sittin' here waitin' ta find out what da outcome gonna be. Since I's been o'er da Reynolds' Place I's been able ta see things a whole lot mo' clearer than I could when I was here and mos' a da things I see is jes likeyou said it was auntie. Now when I hears da thunder roar I don't wait fer da lightnin' ta strike. Now I got enough sense ta git out da way. No mo' do I has ta let da lightnin' strike."

Aunt Hattie jes laughed.

"Bout time you seed da light gal. I's was wonderin' when and iffen da dawn was gonna break fer ya, gal always walkin' round here talkin' 'bout mas'r sayed dis and mas'r sayed dat like somebody done appointed John Marshall yo' own p'sonal guiding light. I's useta pray dat one day you'd wake up and start ta see things fer what dey truly was and taday fer da fi'st time I b'lieves you is finally startin' ta see. Took Mas'r John and Mas'r Tom ta almos' kill ya fer ya ta see but at least ya startin' ta

121

see. And Lord chile you don't know how righ good dat dere makes me feel.

I had ta smile when I seed how happy Aunt Hattie was but I knowed it was no time ta be livin' in da past. Mas'r John be home befo' long and I 'spected me ta be comin' back from da Reynolds' Place in da next week. And iffen Mas'r Reynolds decided ta come outta his drunken stupor and return home he woulda swore da Union soldiers had already been through dere. Ev'ry slave dat could walk had already left fearin' his retu'n and dey'd already taken every piece of livestock dey could ta sustain 'em. Dere wasn't a chicken or goat left ta be had and aside from da cook and da butler da place had been all but abandoned. Course missy was in such a state a mind wit' da laudanum and all dat she hardly recognized what was goin' on even though it was happenin' right dere unda her nose.

Tall weeds now grew where missy's favorite flowerbed had been. Dere remained a few horses and a mule in da barn but wi' no one to feed or take care a dem or lead dem ta pasture dey'd grown gaunt and sickly. I knowed I was in no way responsiblefor dem folks leavin' but when dey gets da word 'bout da war it was like da Book of Exodus in da bible. Folks jes upped and left. Fact is dere ain't really no one ta blame but Mas'r Reynolds fo' his own negligence but I know he would hardly see it as such and there'd be hell ta pay fer anybody left. Dat was fo' sho. And it wouldn't matta who it was dat paid as long as somebody did.

122

April 13th

Lord have mercy. I swear white folk done gone plumb crazy wit' hate. Ev'rywhere you look niggras is payin' dearly fo dis war dey ain't had nothin' ta do wit' startin'. I swear I cain't r'memba dem astin' fer nobody ta pick up a gun and go **march**in' off ta fight. Mos' a us was mo' than content ta be slaves and those dat wasn't and won't scairt a gittin' whipped or worse, run. But ain't no niggras ast fer no war.

Young Saul and Aunt Hattie s'pozed ta stop by taday so's Saul ken take me inta Savannah and Aunt Hattie gonna keep an eye on missy whilst I's gone. But dey ain't showed as a yet and times a growin shorter and fo' ya know it mas'r gonna be back soon so I wisht dey hurry cause I ain't f'git what mas'r sayed about sellin' me and m'baby and I's ready ta put m'plan inta effect.

April 14th

Aunt Hattie and Young Saul arrived early dis mo'nin'. I's was nebba so glad ta see two people in all my life. Sayed ol' Sam wouldn't let 'em outta his site yestiddy. Dat's why dey ain't showed. Say he runnin' t'ings when mas'r gone da way a plantation s'pozed ta be run. Whipped

123

three field hands yestiddy and had ev'rybody jumpin'. He say mas'r too easy on da niggras and he could double da yield iffen he let him run t'ings da way dey was supposed ta be run. Say he whipped one young boy ta within a inch a his life. Dat was yesterday.

Say da Afreecans and some a da hands got together in da woods last night and held a meetin' concernin' ol' Sam da ova'seer.

Aunt Hattie sayed it was jes fer da field hands and den jes da men so she don't know all what happened but dis mo'nin' when she went down ta da lower forty same way she did ev'ry mo'nin' ev'rybody was out dere workin' as usual but dere was no Sam da ova'seer. When she ast 'around, ev'rybody smiled but nobody seemed to know.

A couple of dem young bucks dat Sam had whipped da day befo' sayed dat dey believed he done gone and joined da war and bust out laughin'.

Aunt Hattie b'lieves dat meetin' last night was a lynching and swers she heard screamin' all night long.

Times sho is gittin' bad.

April 13th/Early evening

124

Me and Young Saul done made it. I knowed Aunt Hattie didn't need ta be runnin' up and down no stairs at eighty ev'rytime missy gots a inkling fer a cold glass a water or a peach or someone ta wipe her butt 'cause she was too lazy ta get up so I's made her dose a laudenum a lil stronger than usual and she was still sleep when we gots back.

Ev'rything was moving 'cordin' ta plan. Ain't heared from Mas'r Reynolds so I guess he b'lieve that his account is empty.

Well, it shonuff is now. Wrote a draft fer three hunnerd dollars and had Saul take me into Savannah to Mas'r Reynolds' bank da same way those gals from da brothel does it ta cash it. Not knowing I's could read or write and seein' da same signature dey been seein' da same signature dey been seeing fer da last month I had no problems cashin' da draft and soon as we gits back ta da Reynolds I has Saul hitch up Mas'r John's hosses to Mas'r Reynolds carriage Aunt Hattie had Missy Reynolds bathed and dressed.

I still didn't have da whole plan work'd out as clearly as I wonted, but we had Missy Reynolds carriage and three fresh horses I had cashed da draft so we had enough money ta git a proper start once we got wherever it was we was going ta set up stakes and along wit' Mas'r Reynolds mulatto whore we had mapped out da whole way ta Natchez and da Franklin Plantation where we would pick up Joseph.

I's hoped dat da war would be o'er by dis time cause I's sho didn't have no money ta pay fer my Joseph's freedom but I sho couldn't

125

count on dat so's I figgered we jes' cross dat dere bridge when we come ta it but I's was ready as was Young Saul but I was even more ready than he was 'cause wit' alla Mas'r Reynolds savings under my petticoats and Mas'r John 'specting me back I's knowed dere was gonna be a heavy price ta pay.

I's still was purty uncertain 'bout a coupla thangs at dis point— like was Aunt Hattie comin' wit' us. I's really hopin' she would but she hadn't sayed one way or anotha nothin' more than she would t'ink about it and dat had been weeks ago.

But my main concern was Missy Reynolds. I's needed her ta go mo' than I's needed Saul or Aunt Hattie. Ya see iffen I hads missy along I's wouldn't had ta worry 'bout da slave catchers at all.

I'd already made up ar traveling passes statin' that two niggra slave nurses and one buck was ta accompany one Mrs. Thomas Reynolds ta da hospital in Natchez, Mississippi fer treatment fer a rare debilitatin' disease a da mind called dementia. Den I located and packed up all da medical books in Mas'r Reynolds library and placed dem in da carriage in full view and stored up all da laudanum I could lay my hands on and mixed it in equal parts wit' Mas'r Reynolds strongest corn likker. Dat way I's could keep her fairly well sedated durin' our trip.

But what scared me mos was da fact dat I's hadn't heard a peep outta Mas'r Reynolds. He hadn't sent fer no money and could be dryin' out and headin' back at any time and with or without I's wonted ta be a pretty fair piece ahead a him when he got ta lookin' fer his money and his carriage. Lord knowed he had enough ta worry about with da slaves and livestock gone and dere would be a fair amount of speculation when it came to both but dere was no speculatin' when it come ta his money. He knowed won't nobody capable a writing drafts but me.

Aunt Hattie had Missy Reynolds dressed so pretty and no one would a knowed ta see her that she was loony as a Betsy bug and I was glad fer dat and it was right dere at dat moment as me and Saul pulled in da front gates dat I made my decision.

' Saul', I sayed, 'Git missys trunk outta da barn. Dey be behind da second bale a hay ta da right. Tie dat spare horse ta da back a da carriage and be right quick about it. Ain't a second ta waste.

In da meantime, I he'ped Aunt Hattie git Missy and den Aunt Hattie up into da carriage.

"Who sayed I's gwine anywheres?" Aunt Hattie sayed smilin' dat lil ornery smile I had come to hate.

'Look a here auntie. I's unnerstands that you free in yo' heart and in yo' mind but I's truly b'lieves you needs a lil piece a soil of yo' own ta go wit' dat and I intends ta see dat you gits yo' own piece a land wit' some chickens and some pigs and all dat comes wit' it. 'Sides if I leaves you here mas'r gonna string you up fer sho' iffen you don't tell him where me and Saul done run off to so le's jes say I's doin' both you and me a favor.'

127

Aunt Hattie jes smiled and said, "You better git a movin' den, chile. Ain't no time ta be standin' around duckin' like an ol' hen."

I's glad she was wit' me and nebba loved nobody as much as I loved dat ol' woman then. Wit' ev'rybody tucked in and ready ta go I jumped in da front next to Young Saul who greeted me wit' da biggest smile I eva did see and fo' I could git set we was off at a gallop da carriage pitchin' dis way and dat 'til I started ta thinkin' dat if da slavecatchers didn't kill us Saul's drivin' probably would.

Seemed like we rode fer hours and we still hadn't come ta da end of Mas'r Reynold's Plantation. Da whole time my heart was in my mouth but towards early evening I knowed dat we'd come a fair piece and both plantations were a considerable ways behind us now. Ev'ryone was tired and I wondered if we should stop and rest awhile but dere was Aunt Hattie, always da voice of good sense statin' da obvious.

"You can arouse da curiosity of ev'ry slavecatcher in da country you tries to run dis white woman in dis carriage all night long, Mary. Needs ta give dis here child a double dose a dat dere medicine and find a inn so she can sleep through da night. We's can rise early in da mornin' and move on den. Is da papers in order?"

"Yas ma'am," I sayed.

"Well, then let's move on and boy..."

"Yas ma'am," Saul answered.

"Slow dis carriage down to a crawl at night. Don't wanna arouse no s'spicion. Da way you been drivin; people think you runnin' from somethin'" the old woman laughed.

And it seemed like no sooner had Aunt Hattie finished addressin' that matter than there was anotha, of no less serious content.

Asleep for close to nine hours. Missy Reynolds awoke stating that she needed to relieve herself which in itself was a blessing since up until recently she'd been content to simply go on herself and inform them afterwards which would have made things very difficult on a trip such as this but even Missy Reynolds seemed relieved to be leaving a place filled with so much pain and heartache.

"Where are you niggras takin' me," she asked as Aunt Hattie helped her back up into the carriage.

"Why to meet Mas'r John at da hospital in Natchez, missy. Say he wont to make sho ev'ryt'ing alright fo' he commence ta astin' fo' yo' hand. Oops, I b'lieves I's done let da cat out da bag. Lord mas'r gonna kill me now. Please say you won't tell him I let it slip. Oh, missy he gwine sho'-ly have me tarred and feathered now. Lord! Lord! Lord!"

The woman who had seldom been aware of anything over the last several months now seemed aware of everyone and everything around her. It was almost as if a burden had been lifted. No longer were there any clouds or cobwebs and these few words were all she needed to rejoin the fracas.

"Did John say that? Oh, Hattie tell me. Did he say that really? Oh, that man. And all this time he had me thinkin' that he didn't care. God, I felt so used. Oh, thank you Hattie. Thank you so much dear. Now, why are we stopped? Let's go. Mustn't waste a second . We cain't keep John waitin' now can we? Oh, Hattie it's seems like I've missed oh so much. Oh, Hattie you must fill me in on all the latest goings ons."

The flood gates had been opened and though Mary was glad to see missy regaining her faculties this was no time for missy to be opening Pandora's box that was her past and begin putting the pieces together. Forty-five minutes later she was talking away and Aunt Hattie tired of the questioning concerning the war and John Marshall administered a thimbleful of laudanum and she was fast asleep once more.

That was a tough call to make since Mary knew she'd soon need her once they found lodging. Chances were good that they'd need to her to gain admittance and Auntie bein' that she was close to eighty and had a touch of rheumatism could stay in the room with missy to tend to her needs whilst she and Young Saul would find the barn tend to the horses before making a couple of palettes out of straw and hay, catch a quick nap before continuing on their journey before the crack of dawn and before three niggras escortin' a sick white woman drew any concern.

But as evening quickly turned into night and they rode each with their own feras their worry grew. Slavers patrolled the highways relentlessly and in the days since the war had been declared there was even more commotion along the roads and highways than usual but up until now they hadn't run into anyone other than a farmer or two heading the opposite way to market.

Not accustomed to the ways of the road or the traveler, Mary had Young Saul pull to the side of the road each time someone approached and wait until they'd passed. But as it was getting late and Mary knew that if they didn't make haste and find lodging soon they would most certainly become suspect.

The panic growing, Mary said nothing as Young Saul whipped the two horses into a lather in an unconscious attempt to put some distance between himself and all that was wrong with the world.

Aunt Hattie was saying something now.

"Mary you best slow dat young buck down iffen ya expects ta make it outta da county by coach and not rope. Missy here say dere's an inn up da rode jest a piece. Sayed it ain't mo' n' a couple a miles. And I's gonna tell ya ag'in 'cause you and dat boy is hardheaded but all dat dere bumpin' and shakin' ain't good fer dat baby. Now ya ken mind me iffen ya wont ta but don't say nothin' iffen he come out here a bit touched in da head from all dat bouncin' along y'alls doin'.

No sooner had auntie pulled her head back inside the carriage window afta warnin' me and Saul 'bout dem hosses travelin' at such a speed than four horsemen appeared from a grove of trees on ar right.

131

Young Saul who was still purty much a novice in da handlin' a animals such as dese fine young Kentucky thoroughbreds had ev'rything he could do to bring dem two animals to a halt. Spooked by the sudden appearance of dem men he may very well have lost it altogether if not fo' da quick thinkin' of what appeared ta be da youngest of da four men, a boy not much older than Saul hisself but who unlike Saul was obviously no stranger to hosses. Riding up alongside of da skittish stallions , he placed a firm but gentle hand on da knape of of da young colt who bucked wildly den whispered somethin' in it's ear dat seemt ta have a mos' calming effect and settled him down immediately. Grabbing the reins da young man reeled the hosses in alongside his own then waited fo' de otha three in his party ta join him. Pulling up next ta da carriage now the eldest of da three and da one I presumed ta be da ringleader bent down as to view da occupants a da carriage and seein' Missyy Reynolds, tipped his hat and spoke.

"Evening ma'am."

Da carriage's sudden stop had already awakened da young woman who made a vain attept ta straighten da crumpled mess dat was her hair and fix her dress both a which was in utta disarray.

Meanwhile da otha three gentlemens sat high in da saddle waiting patiently ta see what would transpire next. All three sat in da path of da hosses so as ta make sure dat dey didn't bolt since dey still appeared uneasy and a might bit skittish, (as we all was), in da presence a da three strangers.

Me and Saul jes set dere waitin' patiently since we was purty much useta dis by now and even though we was nervous as a tick on a dogs hindquarters we ain't let it show and give off da impression dat was jes as calm and easy as a niggra could be considerin' da sit'chation.

"Beg yo' pardon, ma'am but we was wonderin' where you might be headin', ma'am?" the elderly gentleman ast missy who was not only havin' difficulty respondin' but keepin' awake as well.

She seemed bothered by da sudden intrusion inta her world a peace and melancholy which seemt ta only come when she was sleep and she seemt angered even mo' that dey had da audacity ta question her about her comings and goings.

"Excuse me sir, but I do not appreciate my carriage being stopped. And I do so hope you have a reasonable explanation."

"Yes ma'am. Jes tryin' ta do ar fair share on behalf of da Confederacy, ma'am. Wouldn't a stopped ya atall but y'all was goin' so fast we couldn't rightly see who was all in da carriage, ma'am. All we could see was dem dere niggras ridin' along wit' dis here fine lookin' carriage like dey was goin' ta a fire or something. Lookt mighty suspicious ta me ma'am. And as ya probably are aware of, wev'e had quite a problem wit' runaways since ar boys has gone off ta fight da Yankees. Yes ma'am, da war effort has taken quite a toll on maintainin' order. Dey say we're losin' somewhere's 'round seventy-five ta a hunnerd runaways a day since we declared war on da Yankees. So whilst mos' a da boys has gone off ta fight dem Yankee bastards—excuse m'French, ma'am—but like I said since mos' our boys is off fightin' we'rejes tryin' ta do ar part ta maintain law and order and what's rightfully ars 'ti they gits back home. LONG LIVE DIXIE!!" he shouted and was met wit' a few echoesand some blood curdling refrains from his men dat sent shivers through me. "Anyway, dat was all ma'am. Didn' mean ta delay ya atall. Now where was it ya sayed ya was headin'?"

"I didn't but if you must know we're presently looking for an inn in which to reside tonight and in the morning we shall be once again heading td

February 26th

A rida' come in taday from Mas' Reynold's place wit' da news dat Miisy Reynolds was ailin'. Well, she always been what ya might call sickly and I's guess I would be too iffen I was married to dat mean, ornery husband she got. But when masr John heared about Missy Reynolds getting' sickly you could jes look at his face and see how da news affected him.

I's truly do b'lieve he love dat woman more 'n he lettin' on to. But I's can rightly unnerstan' it. Missy Reynold's be one a da nicest misses you ever wanna come across. And I guess dat 'cause she always been so skinny and so sickly. Ain't nothin' mo' than skin and bones ta her. And she bein' all quiet and timid and da like; it jes hard not ta like her. Then when ya think about it and her bein' married ta da mos' meanest, mos' orneriest man in Georgia well ya jes kinda' feel like sorry for her. Anyways, I does personally.

Neither her nor Mas'r John likes what Mas'r Reynolds done

b'come o'er da years an iffen you ast me I's truly b'lieve dats exactly

what bringed Mas'r John and Missy Reynolds together.

Anyways, ya could see dat Mas'r John was powerful shook by da whole state of affairs but he jes couldn't go paradin' o'er dere ta Mas'r Reynolds 'cause dat in itself wouldn't be correct or gentlemanly.

Iffen Missy Charlotte was here she woulda been da one ta go o'er ta da Reynold's place but she ain't and Mas'r Reynolds won't lookin' for no sympathy. He was mainly lookin' fo' someone to come over and wait on her and make sho she was looked afta til she recovered her strength. And bein dat I's was gittin' bigga by da day ta da point dat I couldn't hardly do nothin' and wasn't much help 'round da place Mas'r john sent me ova ta da Reynold's so I could tend ta missy 'til she was back on her feets ag'in. Mas'r also sent Saul to 'company me so he could run up and down da stairs ta fetch things as was necessary since I's wasn't in too good a shape m'self and dis I much appreciated. But mos'ly I knowed he wanted me to keep a close watch on Young Saul and you could jes see how ev'rytime he looked a dat boy how he was calculatin' how much a big, strong buck like Saul would fetch him at da market right prior ta da plantin' season.

Anyways mas'r sent word word by dat dere rida' dat he be sendin' some mo' help since he knowed dat Mas'r Reynolds ain't had a hand ta spare wit' plantin' season right 'round da corner and him not bein' jes shorthanded but in ev'rybody's debt as well. Mas'r John say he jes a bad financial manager but I fo' one jes b'lieve he don't know how to calculate too good.

Well anyways, me and Saul gwine pack a few belongings and head on o'er to Mas'r

Reynold's fo' it gits too late. Ain't but a few miles and we mighta been dere fo' long but bein' dat ol' Ben ain't nebba bring da buckboard back Mas'r John ain't right p'ticular 'bout lettin' no mo buckboards go out so's we gots to git a move on fo' it gits late and da paddy rollas and slavecatchers comes out and wonders what da two us doin' out walkin' dis time a day.

I done heared mas'r say on mo' than one occasion dat you gots ta be mo afraid a da slavers than da abolitionists. He say dat dey da immediate threat. And it be knowed by mos' all a us dat da slave catchers and paddy rolla's along wit' da highwaymen dat be roamin' 'round at night is mo' of a threat ta kidnap dem po' devils than a dem escapin' on they own. And dat bein' sayed I's got ta rustle up Young Saul so's we can be on our way fo' night falls.

February 28th

Mas'r Reynolds da meanest man I ebba did see. He treat missy like she no betta than a slave. Even though she sick wit' da pneumonia he don't hardly pay her no mind 'cept ta yell 'bout her bein' well enough ta keep his books even though she be burnin' up wit' da fever.

Me? I jes did da best I could—bathin' her down—and feedin' her 'cause she too wek ta feed herself. Then when she ast me ta read da

143

bible ta her and I did. And dat's why I say he da meanest white man I's ebba seed. Like I sayed, my first day dere missy ast me ta read ta her from da bible which I was doin' when he walked in and slapped da Good Book from my hands and slapped me upside da head so hard it made ol' Sam's wallop feel like a love tap. I felled offa da stool I was sittin' on at da end a da bed and seed stars. I rolled up in a ball and covered up as well as I could to make sho' no harm would come ta my baby. Then he commenced ta kickin' and hittin' me wit' his ridin' crop like he was gonna make sho' no mo' niggras come inta his world. Missy Reynolds was screamin' and hollerin' da whole time and beggin' him ta stop but he won't listenin'. It was like da spirits had got a hol' of him and he was possessed by demons or somethin'. And all I was worried 'bout was him not hurtin' my baby. And alls I keeps hearin' is him sayin an astin' me, "Who teached ya ta read gal?" Over and over, dat's all I keep hearin' him ast me.

Then I hear dat door squeak open an who enter in butYoung Saul. Saul started movin' towards Mas'r Reynolds and I knew right den and dere from da look in Saul's eyes dat he had all intentions a killin' dat White man when he seed me lyin' dere on dat dere flo' wit Mas'r Reynolds standin' o'er me wit' dat dere ridin' crop but I grabbed his leg fo' he could do anything an held on wit' both arms 'til he couldn't move towards Mas'r Reynolds. Mas'r Reynols musta knowed what Saul had in mind 'cause dem demons eased up and he moved away from me and found his way out da door wit' da quickness. Later on I heared him ast one a his own who dat buck was referrin' ta Saul and I was glad when he sayed he belong ta Mas'r Johnson and was bein' loaned ta help ta him ta help wit' Missy Reynolds. Mas'r Reynolds woulda sho' nuff had Saul whipped or stringed up for bein' threatenin' and belligerent iffen it hadda been fo' da mere fact dat we belonged to Mas'r John. By da next day, me and Young Saul found ourselves bein' shipped back ta our plantation even though missy sho won't feelin' no betta.

March 1

Lawd knows I's always hearin' niggras complainin'. Dey always talkin' 'bout how bad things be and I always be quick ta yell'em dat things can be worser. But mos' a da time dey jes don't unnerstan. I tries ta tell 'em dat mas'r a good mas'r but dey don't see dat. I guess it's 'cause mos a dem ain't been wit' no otha mas'r so dey don't know. But truss' me I's knows. I goes ta Mas'r Reynolds fo' one day and he wanna whip me fo' somethin' Mas'r John allowed me ta do. And dat's read. Well, 'spite Mas'r Reynolds I's still glad I gots to go o'er ta da Reynold's place. Missy Reynolds was mo' then helpful when I tol' her about my Joseph and even went so far as to tell me where he been sol' and who buyed him. I's nebba heared of da Natchez, Mississippi but I show aims ta find it iffen m'Joseph be dere.

145

March 2

Mas'r John tried not ta let nobody but Aunt Hattie heared mas'r and some otha gentlemens in da parlor when dey brings Mas'r John da news. Seems dey found some ol' niggra 'bout eighty up in da mountains long side some ditch. Say da niggra still had mas'r tavelin' pass in his pocket. Say dey don't know who or why dey had kilt him but when dey found him he was deader than a doorknob. But from what dey could make out da pass sayed his name was Ben, gave his age as eighty even though he could have easily passed for sixty and sayin' dat he belonged ta Mas'r John Marshall a Savannah County... There was no buckboard and no hosses and dey sayed Ben was beaten so badly dat when dey found him dey say one side a his face was—how did Aunt Hattie say— oh yeah, almost unrecognizable. Dey was lookin' fo' a reward accordin' to Aunt Hattie but she say all Mas'r John do is slam his fist down so hard on da parlor table dat it shattered. Then he turned and he ast dem dere gentlemens wit' tears in his eyes, "Gentlemen, have you any idea how much I payed for those two horses and that buckboard?" The he bust out cryin' in earnest then...

March 3

Ev'ryday now I's beginnin' ta unnerstand m'Joseph and Aunt Hattie and Young Saul and da Afreecans mo' and mo'. I cried like I ain't nebba cried befo' when I heared da news 'bout ol' Ben. Ta me Ben was da closest thing I's ebba had ta a father figger I's ebba knowed.

When I was jes a lil gal I useta sit and watch and jes stare awhilst mas'r bounced his lil ones up and down on his knee on da front porch. Lil missy, she gon' now, she jes be laughin' and gigglin' and da like. She be lookin' like she was havin' so much fun dat I jes wanted ta run up ta mas'r and ast him ta bounce me up and down too but even den at such a young age I'd come ta know ma place. But ol' Ben—I useta call him Uncle Ben—he'd see da wanderlust in my eye and take me in da kitchen wit' Aunt Hattie and bounce me up–n-down on his knee da same way dat mas'r would do lil missy.

Otha times when he would seed me starin' whilst lil missy played wit' da new dolls mas'r would bring her back from N'Oleans and Macon and Charleston when he'd go away on da bizness Uncle Ben would grab ma hand and lead me away from watchin' lil missy. And 'til dis day I ain't nebba figgerd out exactly why. But a week or so later Uncle Ben would stop by Aunt Hattie's or takes me out ta da barn when we could both of us get away and have me look unda dat ol' hoss blanket and lo and behold I declare iffen dat man ain't seed fit ta find da time ta whittle me a whole family a dolls all brand new andpainted and shiny. And he telled me dat dese here dolls be fer' me and then he teeled me nots ta show

147

'em ta nobody. And da one time I did 'cause I's so proud aof 'em

don'tcha know missy went ta cryin' ta her pa, Mas'r John about 'em bein'

betta than hers, (which dey really was), and then mas'r he sayed, "Ben I

want you to make a set of those dolls for m'lil one here the same way

you did for Mary." And don'tcha know Ben did too. He make her a set

but dey won't no way as good as mine 'cause he put love and time and

tenderness in makin' mine and dat's cause he truly loved me like a fatha

loves a daughter. And now he gone. And all mas'r concerned 'bout is

his hosses and his raggedy ol' buckboard.

March 19

Well, plantin' season here so I's hardly got anytime atall ta

practicin' ma lettas and writin' an all. It seem like alla da work done

doubled and mas'r don't do nothin' but pick up supplies in town then stay

out in da fields 'til almost midnight rotatin' da crops and givin' orders ta ol'

Sam so he can give 'em ta da hands but bein' dat Sam ain't too

brightmas'r usually end up hollerin' at Sam and jes lettin' da hands know

directly what he want done hisself. Seemt ta me he could jes let Sam go

and commence ta tellin' 'em hisself and 'lleviate all dat extra

conversation. White folks sho' gotta funny way 'bout goin' 'bout things.

March 20

148

I's big as a house and tired all da time. I ain't sho' if it's dis baby or da fact dat mas'r stays up ta all times a da night workin' on his books and paperworks which mean either me or Aunt Hattie gots ta be 'round ta fetch him dis and dat as he see fit.

P'sonally, I's don't see what he doin' when he say he be keepin' da books so's me being of a curious nature and all I ast him. Dat's right I walked right up ta him and sayed, "Mas'r what is it dat you be doin' wit' dem books and paperworks ev'rynight?"

Mas'r him jes turnt ta me and laughed. Then he telled me dat I's wouldn't unnerstan' and I's says ta him, "Please 'splain it ta me Mas' John. I swears I don't wanna be a dumb nigga all m'life. And mas'r say ta me, "No I guess you don't wanna be in the dark your whole life."

Then mas'r he git ta tellin' me 'bout how he got ta balance da books so's he can can see jes how much he spendin' on seed and feed and how much he puttin' out on stuff like dat so's he knows jes how much profit he be makin' when he harves' and sell ev'rything in da fall. He say it very impotent dat he stay on top of things so he don't wind up in debt and losin' ev'rything like Mas'r Reynolds.

And I think about how Mas'r John been stayin' on top a Missy Reynolds da last few months and da way I figger it Mas'r Reynolds betta git ta work on his books fo' Mas'r John take ev'rything includin' Missy Reynolds.

149

But Lawd knows I don't rightly know why it's so impotent. Da way I see mas'r ain't really buyin' nothin'. All he doin' is usin' last years seeds along wit' dis years crop a niggas and ain't neitha one a dem costin' him a dime.

March 27

E'vrytime I see dat rida comin' in from o'er Mas'r Reynold's place I's gits a bad feelin' inside. I think a m'Joseph and how dat ol' mean Mas'r Reynolds tried ta stomp m'baby. I think 'bout how Mas'r be da main force behind Afreecan Jesse gittin' hunged. So, ev'rytime a rida come up from da Renold's place I jes git a bad feelin'. And it seems like Missy Reynolds done took a turn fo' da worse so I knows it's jes a matter a time 'til I'll be heading back dat way. And I'm sho' dis time won't be no diff'rent. Here come Mas'r John now and I already know what da verdict is from da look on his face. Seems Mas'r Reynolds say he need help carin' fo' her and I already know dat dat means Mas'r John gonna tell me ta go look afta her and though missy a good woman she still married ta da devil and as long as I's done carried dis here youngun' I's sho' don't won't wanna lose him now 'round no foolishness 'bout whether a niggra should read or write.

Aunt Hattie say dey don't wanna niggra ta read or write 'cause then he might find out dat he ain't stupid as mas'r would have him b'lieve. And maybe, jes maybe he gonna find out that he been put here

150

ta be more than jes a slave. She b'lieve dat too. She say dat she jes bein' held in bondage 'til Moses come ta let her peoples go. Like I sayed befo', I truly b'lieves dat age age is startin' ta sho itself where Aunt Hattie be concerned. She startin' ta speak real freely ta be Mas'r John's property. As good a man as Mas'r John may be he ain't gonna allow no slave ta jes talk any ol' kind a way. And ol' as Aunt Hattie be she sp'ozed ta know dat by now. And I fo' one know she do 'cause she useta stop me when I was a youngun' and gots ta sowin' my oats and would f'gits my place. But now it's like she still know but jes don't care no mo'. Like jes dis mornin' when I tells her ta hush 'cause mas'r ain't fond of his slaves talkin' like dat and she tell me dat she ain't nobody's slave and she freer than he'll ebba be. Well, dat's when I knowed the wheelbarrow won't entirely full but I ignores da remark and says ta her dat she a slave jes like da rest of us and she gits a right nasty attitude and says ta me dat she ain't nobody's slave and nebba has been nobody slave and ain't nebba gonna be nobody's slave. Dat's when I turnt ta her and says, 'Now Aunt Hattie, you been Mas'r John's prop'ty fo' mo' than seventy years has you tell it and now alla sudden you ain't nobody's slave.' Dat's when Aunt Hattie turn't ta me and sayed dat she been bought and held against her will but Mas'r John and no otha man alive could ebba enslave her unless she allowed 'em too.

Dat's when I lost it 'cause I knowed fo' a fact dat mas'r owned alla us and she was a slave jes like da rest a us. And ev'rybody else

151

knowed it too includin' Aunt Hattie and I' jes figgered she was gittin' closer ta her time and didn't want ta see herself in dat light no mo'.

Still, I's gotta admit she had me kinda worried. Her anUncle Ben was da closest thing I had ta family 'cept for dis youngun' I was carryin' and I done hes lost Ben and sho' didn't want to lose Aunt Hattie too. When I telled Young Saul what Aunt Hattie sayed he jes laugh. I telled him not to laugh at what Aunt Hattie sayed 'cause it was disrespectful but he telled me dat ain't laughin at Aunt Hattie he laughin' at me. When I ast him why he jes keep right on laughin'. Well, I ain't nebba taken lightly ta bein' teased and Saul seed my feathers was mo than a lil ruffled so he commence ta bein' somewhat and looks at me in a mos' curious fashion and say, "Miss Mary you really don't unnerstan' do you?" And I says, "Yes, I unnerstan' dat when peoples git ol' like Aunt Hattie dey minds start ta actin funny but Lawd knows I's woulda nebba expected nothin' like dat ta happen ta Aunt Hattie 'cause she always alla da time been so strong."

And do you know what Saul telled me?

He say dere ain't a thing da matta wit' Aunt Hattie mind. He sayed Aunt Hattie one a da few here on dis here place dat knowed from day one who she be and no matta what da white folk 'round here say or what dey might t'row her way she could nebba be no slave 'cause she always be free in her mind. Still, I let him know dat no matta how free she think she still be a slave in Mas' John's kitchen. Dat's when Saul

152

looked at me grinned and jes shook his head like he was right and I was

da one wit' da feeble mind and not Aunt Hattie. But I ain't sayin' nothin'

'cause I knowed dat Saul love Aunt Hattie much as I did. Plus dem

Afreecans had a tendency ta stick tagetha and all of 'em had funny

notions when it come ta slavery and admittin dat dey was slavery an

admittin' dat dat's what dey was. So's, instead a arguin' I jes let da

whole thang go.

March 28

Anyways mas'r come by dis evenin' ta tell me dat he

been informed dat Missy Reynolds won't farin' too well and he wonted

me ta ride over and look in on her 'til she feelin' betta. Sayed I needed ta

stay wit' her 'til she be up-n-about so I's should bring some things and be

quick about it.

I begged him to send somebody else 'cause Mas'r

Reynolds don't like me. But he sayed it won't me Mas'r Reynolds had a

dislikin' fer. He say it ain't nothin' personal. He say Mas'r Reynolds jes

peculiar is all and really don't like hisself. I's don't really know what dat

dere means 'cause sometimes he gots a right down funny way of

spressin' hisself but I begged him ta get somebody else ta take my

place. But he won't havin' it so I telled him dat I's scared bein' dat it

won't long befo'm'baby's due.

153

He jes look at me all strange like and sayed, "Mary tain't no reason ta be scared a Mas'r Reynolds." That's what he sayed ta me. He sayed I've known Tom Reynolds my whole life and he ain't nothin' ta be afraid of."

So I says, "Well, maybe not for you suh but maybe fer a niggra slave it's different."

Mas'r jes looks at me and sayed, "Mary, is there something you're not telling me?"

Well, I's been a slave and a niggra as long as I's can remember and certain things I jes knows. It's like dey jes comes nat'chal to a slave—almost like you was born with certain things you know dat you ain't s'posed to tell no white people. So, when Mas'r John ast me if it was somethin' I's wasn't sayin' I knowed right den and dere dat iffen I tells him I's may as well have tied m'self ta dat big oak m'self and put da whip in his hand. I knowed dis but I's figgered dat dat would still be betta than takin' a chance and lettin' Mas'r Reynolds kill me and my baby so I sayed, "Mas'r da last time I's o'er da Reynold's Place, Mas'r Reynolds beat me bad—real bad. Dat's all I sayed. And den I watched his face git all red like a beet before he say, "Why that low-down dirty bastard... Is he the one that give you that there shiner?

I nodded yes and when I seed dat he won't gonna hit me fo' tellin' on his friend, I tells him e'erything 'bout how Mas'r Reynolds stomped and kicked me fo' reading the Bible ta missy like she ast me to.

154

Fo' I thought about it good e'erything jes come rollin' out.

And I swear fo' God, I ain't nebba seed mas'r git so mad in all da time I's been wit' him. Al he sayed ta me was ta gits m'belongin's and git ready ta go. Then he says ta me dat he ain't got time fo' all dis here niggra foolishness and added dat when I's git back from da Reynolds Place he gonna deal wit' m'lyinn' ass.

Well, I knowed I was in fo' it den and da tears jes come a rollin' down dese here brown cheeks. And dat's when Saul come in ta see what all da ruckus was about. Dat's when I told him dat I be back in a few days jes a s soon as Missy Reynolds be back up-n-around and dat's when he start putting his stuff in a sack. Mas'r John jes look at him and say, "Boy, where in the hell do you think you're going?" ta which Saul replied.

Mas'r I though you sayed I was s'posed ta stay by Miss Mary's side like you telled me, suh?"

Mas'r say, "No boy, dis here is somethin' mary don't need no help with."

But instead a Saul jes noddin' in agreement and sayin' yassuh' dat Afreecan temperament come out and he sayed, "Beg your pardon mas'r suh but, you cain't send Miss Mary o'er dere ta da Reynold's place, suh. Iffen ya does chances are dat Mas'r Reynolds gonna kill her, suh."

155

Mas'r John stared at Saul a minute befo' he sayed anything. Then he lookt at Saul all serious like and sayed, "What the hell are you tryin' ta tell me? What are you talkin' about boy?"

Then Saul tell mas'r da exact same story what I jes telled him and mas'r now knowed dat I wasn't lyin'. But when Saul finished mas'r ain't say nothin'. He jes stand there and say nothin'. Then he tell me and Saul ta git' in da carriage. And da whole way ain't nobody sayed a word. Lawd knows by da time we gits ta da Reynold's place I's so scared I ain't know what to do.

Well, bay da time we gits dere Mas'r John still ain't sayed nothin' and I knowed dat all he's waitin' fo' is Masr Reynolds ta deny our claim so he can beat da tar outta us so I's jes sittin' dere shakin'. But when we gits dere mas'r ain't say nothin'. He jes leave us settin' dere and walk right up ta da big house wit' his riding crop and walk right inta da house wit'out walkin' or nothin'. Well, da next thang I knows, Mas'r Reynolds come a rollin' down da steps a da big house da same 'zact way I did when he was kickin' me all ova da place. And I could see he was doin' his best right through dere ta cover his head and all but won't nothin' he could do ta save hisself and I truly believed in my heart dat mas'r was gonna kill him. Still, won't nothin' I could do, in da condition I's was in and I ain't rightly sho' I would have even if I won't pregnant. 'Sides angry as mas'r was I was scairt dat he might jes turn and jump on me and say da whole dang affair was my fault. But even so

I jes kept my mouth shut and despite what Mr. Reynolds did ta me I couldn' he'p but feel sorry fo' him at dat point and I was halfway sad I'd sayed anything about it atall. But not Young Saul. He jes stand dere lookin' and trin' his best not too grin too much. And fo' da first time since I knowed him, he refused ta lissen ta me when I telled him ta pull Mas'r John offa Mas'r Reynolds befo' he killt him.

Now as y'all may very well know I ain't nebba had no love fo' dat dere man lyin' befo' me, face down in da dirt, blood all ova his hands and face but I prides m'self on bein' a Christian woman iffen I ain't nothin' else and I fo' one know da Good Lawd would not appreciate da way Mas'r John was actin' now. Besides mas'r was a Christian too and right through dere it was purty obvious dat da devil had got a hold a him in a big way and won't gonna let it go wit' out somebody interferin' directly. Sides dat, bein' dat dis here whole account was 'cause a me I knowed dat I's eitha gots ta git outta da carriage and stop mas'r or have dat dere killin' on m'conscience fo' da rest a m'natural born days and I knowed I could nebba live wit' dat.

By dis time ev'ry niggra on da Reynolds' Place was dere jes standin' dere lookin' on like dey was at a cockfight or somethin'. And ain't nary one a dem try ta step in and he'p dey mas'r out. And I's had ta wonder iffen dat had been Mas'r John in da same position would hissen niggras have come ta his aid and even though he dere mas'r I's purty sho one a dem would have. But not here. And I hadda think ta m'self dat dis here must be one purty evil man fo' nobody ta want ta he'p him not even his own ova'seer.

Still and all, I feel like it was m'fault and like I sayed I didn't won't nobody's death on m'head. So's I promptly gits down from da buckboard and walks o'er ta mas'r who by dis time done got down on one knee and is liftin' Mas'r Reynold's head head outta da dirt and den slammin' it back down wit' all da force a Zeus and it sho' appeared dat he was tryna kill him. Jes lookin' at dat man all covered wit' blood and leaves, bruises and cuts ev'ry inch I knowed then and dere dat it was my duty as a Christian woman ta stand up fo' righteousness and though da devil kept whispering dat dis won't none a my affair I's stood up against da odds and despite what dat man done ta me and come to his aid in his time a distress. I had ta. So I climbed down from m'perch on da carriage and went on ova ta Mas'r John expectin' fer him ta turn around and give me some a what he was givin' Mas'r Reynolds but by dis time it didn't much matta 'cause I knew it was m'Christian duty ta intervene and do m'part.

Besides and like I sayed, I knowed by now dat nobody else was gonna he'p dat man in his time a need and so's I went ova ta Mas'r John and whispered inta his ear those 'zact words Aunt Hattie been tellin' me all m'life when somebody do somethin' cruel to ya. I say, "Mas'r John remember what da good Lord say." Then I jes say, "Vengeance is mine sayith the Lawd". Then I backs up and braces

158

m'self and jes waited fo' him ta turn aroun' and slap me fo' causing all dis stress and ruckus. But when he ignored me I turnt ta him again and telled him he ain't handlin' thangs like a proper soldier in da Good Lawd's army. And ta m'surprise instead a turnin' and swingin' out at me he jes stopped. I'm sayin' jes like dat he stopped. It was almos' like da Good Lawd hisself come down and intervened and tol' him he won't actin' like a good Christian mas'r like we all knowed he was.

Me—well I jes felt real good and so r'lieved dat he didn't kill him. Not only that but I was also sho of one otha thang and of this I was certain. I was quite sho' I ain't haveta worry 'bout him botherin' me no more and no time soon even if he had a notion to bein' dat he won't in no shape afta dat whoppin' mas'r jes administered him. And then a funny thang occurred right afta I gits mas'r up offa him. When I turns ta head back ta da carriage ta gits m'belongins I notice dat dem very same niggras dat see me save Young Saul afta dey done hanged Afreecan Jesse was those very same niggras dat had been watchin' me silently and was grateful fo' me savin' one a dey own was damn near cussin' me now fo' not lettin' mas'r kill Mas'r Reynolds.

Even if he ain't killt him I was quite sho by dis time dat dey wouldn't have minded iffen I hadda let mas'r whoop on him jes a lil mo or at least til he got ta within an inch of his life. But I's da type dat don't care how bad a man aim ta be it don't warrant anotha man killin' him and Then havin' ta walk aroun' and shoulda da burden of takin' a life da rest a his days. And 'specially on my account. So's I stopped it and was content wit' mas'r jes lettin' him know dat he would finish da job iffen he eva again laid a hand on me or any a his prop'ty again. Then mas'r git ta talkin' 'bout how he gonna pull alla his notes iffen Mas'r Reynolds commence ta doin' any such a thang again. Mas'r say it loud enough fo' ev'rybody ta hear dat he da real sole and rightful owner of da Renold's Place anyway considerin' what Mas'r Reynold's owed him. He sayed iffen he didn't b'lieve it then all he hadda do was ta let him hear 'bout him layin' his hands on anotha niggra what ain't belongt ta him. Da minute he did he'd force him in ta handin' ova da deed ta da land and chase him clear outta Talladega County. Well, I ain't nebba been so proud a mas'r as I was dat day. Ta tell da truth, I could hardly speak and I do b'lieve I's even felt a tear a pride roll down m'cheek.

Then somethin' I heared catched m'ttention and I's eased up right close so as not ta miss a word and heared mas'r telled him how he done made it plain ta him dat he was to inform him befo' he sold da blacksmith—da blacksmith bein' m'Joseph. Anyway, mas'r say he had tol' him previously dat he was very much interested in in purchasin' and would buy him at a fair market price and despite Mas' Reynolds already in his debt but Mas'r Reynold's bein' stubborn and mean-spirited couldn't stand for his prized slave to bein' wit'in so close a proximity and him not bein' able ta afford him so he sol' him away anyway. Dat's when I got ta wonderin' why I hadn't let mas'r kill dat ol'

160

devil of a man and had ev'rything. I had ta do ev'rything I could do ta call on da Good Lawd ta give, me some mo' faith else ain't no tellin' what I's mighta done. Lawd knows I sho felt like pickin' up where mas'r left off.

And if dat ain't bad enough, Mas'r Reynolds layin' dere wit' in a inch a Kingdom Come mean as a backwoods black snake turnt and looked up at Mas'r John and sayed, "I'll be damned if you'll own ev'rything I have John Marshall," he sayed. "You already own damn near near half of Savannah County and if that not's enough you want my wife too. Jes how much is enough, you greedy bastard?"

By dis time Missy Reynolds who'd somehow found the strength to make it, downstairs and to the front door stepped out onto the front porch at jes about da time Mas'r Reynolds, his back ta her made his last remark before encountering the heel of Mas'r John's size twelve boot to his temple quiting him fo' da rest a da day.

Now, I's not too sho' iffen dat po' woman, who been through I don't know how much wit' dat crazy man was jes too weak dat she stumbled or iffen she fainted from havin' her most intimate business made public, (though we all know she and mas'r was beedin' down together long in advance a Mas'r Reynolds informin' da world). But anyways, she heared dat dere remark and come down dem steps in almos' da same fashion her husband did only a short time earlier.

Well, me and Saul bein' dat we was da closest ta her and da onliest ones who looked like we was willin' ta he'p dat po' woman

161

rushed ta her side whilst like I sayed mos a her very own hands acted as if dey didn't won't or didn't even see her and Lawd knowed when she fell it was in plain view a ev'rybody. But then soon as me and Saul gots her back on her feet I knowed why nobody stepped in ta he'p. Young Saul seein' dat da weight was too much fer me in m'condition and alla da time tryna he'p me in some fashion or anotha jes nat'chally grabbed missy up in his arms like she won't nothin' mo' n' a sack a potatoes. Then he proceeded ta take her inside accordin' ta m'directions when Mas'r Reynolds barely conscious now reared up and yelled, "Boy if you don't take yo' hands off that white woman I'll whip all the black off yo' sorry nigga ass."

Saul looked at me and then at Mas'r John. Mas'r John waved Saul on in da house befo' turning back ta Mas'r Reynolds dug his boot straight ta da side a his head putting him ta sleep fo' good. Saul stunned looked at me but I couldn't say nothin' bein' that I never expected nothin' like that eitha and Mas'r John pushed past me like I wasn't standin'dere and grabbed Missy Reynolds from Saul's arms and took her inta da house and up ta her room and informed missy dat I would be lookin' afta her jes as long as she needed me.

April 1

Now befo' I left ta go ta da Renold's Place Aunt Hattie had warned me 'bout reading and writin' whilst I's at da Reynolds.

162

Sayed Mas'r Reynolds don't takindly ta no niggra doin' no readin' and writin' ' he won't p'ticularly good at it hisself and won't p'ticularly disposed ta havin' neitha no smart nor no uppity niggra 'round him. She sayed it make him feel inferior. She sayed he don't won't no niggras who can see what he be doin'. But a niggra ain't gots ta be book smart ta da know dat Mas'r Reynolds is one evil man. Still, ain't no one seed or or heard from Mas'r Tom ta day though word is he done gone ta Savannah ta get likkered up and lick his wounds.

April 3

Whilst I's been here I stays in a empty shack right in da middle of da quarters even though missy gots a empty bedroom right next ta hers an ast Mas'r Reynolds iffen I could stay dere in case she git ta feeling bad in da middle a da night. She say dat way I can go and fetch her her medicine but he say no. Say he don't truss no niggra livin' unda da same roof wit' him. I tell you dat man sho' got a heap a problems. Ta tell da truth I don't see why my stayin' next ta missy would bother him so much since he always all da time down in da quarters at night anyway. It jes seems funny ta me dat as much as dat man hates niggras he sho do love stayin' down here in da quarters.

April 5

I ain't s'pozed ta be readin' or writin' but long as I stays up in da big house I can purty much write all I wont 'cause Mas'r Reynolds ain't nebba ebba here. Like I's told you previously he spend mos' all his time down in da bottoms or da quarters wit his niggras jes goin' from shack-to-shack. I's swear fo' God I ain't nebba seed nothin' like him and the worsest thing about the whole affair is dat he worser than even ol' Sam da ovaseer on Mas'r John's place and you's gots ta go a ways ta be worser than ol' Sam but I's swears Mas'r Reynolds gots Sam beat. Ta tell ya da truth, when it comes ta layin' down and propagatin wit' a niggra wench here and dere and propagatin' and nebba comin' home at night and showin sin' some respect for Missy Reynolds I don't think dat man give two bits ta how she feelin'. Funny thing is, I think she know it too. She jes done resigned herself to da fact dat she married herself to a good fo' nothin' sorry-assed polecat. I's tellin' you. Mas'r Reynolds is one sorry excuse fo' a man. Think dats why she done lost da will ta live. It's almos' like she done lost all her fight and da will to live. I guess she figgers since no one love her then what's da use. And fo' a while I knowed 'zactly where she be coming from. And since da man what s'pozed ta truly love her—dat would be my mas'r is already married or at least he ain't yet divorced—well she feel like she stuck in a lose lose sitchaation where dere jes ain't no help fo' a po' ol' sickly white woman like her. Now see, dat wouldn't be no niggra. I don't care. But white folks so worried 'bout keepin' up an air a

164

respectability dat dey sometimes f'gits what it takes ta be happy. I mean

we workin' wit' far less and fo' da mos' part we happy—at least happier

than dey are wit' dey money and big fine houses and all. Da way I sees

it dey jes a pitiful mess. And I cain't he'p but think a alla dese rich white

folks runnin' 'round here talkin' 'bout how bad it is and I'll be da first ta tell

ya—dese here white folks got it easy compared ta a niggra. Here dis

woman gots a big ol' fine house wit' so many servants I's cain't count 'em

all and ev'rything ya can possibly imagine and here she is da mos'

unhappiest person I's done ebba had da occasion a meetin'. And here I

is jes a po' slave gal who don't own nothin' and would die fo' what she

got and she got da nerve ta be sittin' here feelin' sorry fo' herself and

pinin' away ova some ol' sorry man. Here she sittin' fadin' away 'cause

da man she choosed in God's eyes ain't no damn good and da man dat

really do love her is already spoken fo'. Lawd! Lawd! Lawd! I do truly

b'lieve dat dey all crazy.

I b'lieve mas'r too embarrassed afta what Mas'r

Reynolds sayed about him wontin' ta own ev'rythang includin' his wife

'cause he ain't been around since I's been here. Still, he doin' ev'rything

else he can do to make sho' she git betta. He done sent fo' doctors from

as far away as Beaufort and New O'leans ta tend ta missy ta find out

what be ailin' her   But end da end dey all jes shakes their heads like dey

puzzled surrounding da mystery a her sickness. Then they tells Mas'r

John dat dey cain't find a thang wrong and iffen dere is somethin' wrong

165

it ain't in dere medical journals. Dey confused fo' da mos' part but I ain't. And iffen one a dem had stopped and ast me I's could tell 'em what's ailin' her right off. I 's could tell 'em what's got her witherin' on her deathbed but ain't nobody ast me.

One thing's fo' sho though and dat is da fact dat she is dyin'. She just a witherin' away like da leaves in winter on a weepin' willow. And what ailin' her cain't be cured wit' no laudanum likes dey keep prescribin'. Matta a fact iffen you ast me, I'd take her offa dat altogetha. Dat dere laudanum ain't doin' nothin' but makin' mattas worser. And right through here she done stopped almost completely.

April 7

Sent fo' mas'r taday. He need ta see missy iffen he care anything 'bout her 'cause I's can see she sufferin' from da same affliction dat had da grip on me not too long ago when dey sol' m'Joseph. Iffen mas'r come and spend some time time and tell missy he love her and wanna marry then I's almos' positive missy would be jes fine.

April 8

Mas'r ain't see fit ta come. I guess he don't figger m'request is serious enough ta warrant no c'sideration or otha wise he jes don't care. I's really beginnin' ta see anotha side a mas'r since I been away but anyway he send Aunt Hattie. And Saul in his stead. He

166

sent word dat his comin' would not be appropriate c'sidering what Mas'r Reynolds sayed 'bout him and him bein' a respectable gentleman and all in da planters community. I jes shaked m'head when Aunt Hattie telled me dis.

I's swear white folks always worried 'bout how something gonna appear. Here a woman lyin' here 'bout ta die and dey worried 'bout how it gonna appear iffen dey come ta see her. Lord, have mercy on dey mixed up souls. And dey gots da nerve ta tells us we dumb. He send Aunt Hattie wit' a couple a apple pies, some soup, and some orange marmalade and I guess dats s'pozed ta cure a broken heart. Well, I swears I cain't take no mo'. Here he got me doin' his job and settin' here waitin' fo' dis here good woman ta die and I guess it was mo than I could take. So, I jumped right on da back a dat dere buckboard and rides ova dere ta see and mas'r and telled him dat it won't nothin' wrong wit' missy 'ceptin' dat she outta her head wit' grief from missin' him so much and she done lost da will ta live. Well, I ain't had no problem wit' tellin' him dis since it was him dat was alla da time tellin' me dat da truth would set me free when he wonted ta know somethin' what was goin' on 'round da place so's I knowed dat he won't gonna have no problem wit'da truth now. And I's was certainly glad ta see dat he was deeply troubled when I telled him dis piece a info'mation and it occurred ta me dat he a in't changed atall and dat dere was still a good solid Christian man in dere despite how he go on tryna be tough when 'round ol' Sam and some a us more belligerent niggras who makes him act dat way. Now I can see dat dat ain't really how mas'r be. He jes very troubled was all.

Now I's glad I come and tol' him even though Aunt Hattie warned me against doin' so by telling' me ta stay outta white folks business. She say, "Mary you needs ta stay outta white folks business a da heart". Dats what she telled me but standing dere in front a mas'r at dat very moment I's was sho' glad I had intervened on behalf a both a dem. Yassuh, I was sho' glad I's hadn't tooken her advice this time. And mas'r—well he jes looked so sad. And I gotta tell ya. Dis was da first time in all da years dat I's known dat man dat he really and truly looked like he was ready ta shed a tear. Then he turnt away from me so's I couldn't see him cry but when he turnt back 'round ta face me I feelt like I was facin' Lucifa hisself. Looked jes like da devil hisself had taken ova Mas'r John. Dat's when he turnt ta me and sayed,

"Gal, I don't know where you get the unmitigated gall, and the audacity to come here with the idea in that nigga head a yours ta approach me, a white man, thinkin' you can advise me on how to run my own goddamn affairs but you are completely outta line and if you don't get your fat , black ass outta my sight immediately I'm gonna hog tie you and that bastard baby you're carryin' and whip yo ta the blood drips from yo' nigga ass so help me God. Yo' lil lyin asses make me think that Tom Reynolds might not have been wrong in whippin' yo' uppity ass. I'm of a

168

right mind to do it myself right now. I swear I don't rightly know what's come ova some of you niggras. He may jes be right about all that book learnin' goin' to your head. All that book learnin' do is make a nigga dumber than he already is. Make 'em uppity and think they is. Make 'em uppity and think they is good as white folks and make 'em think they can talk to white folks any kinda way. Well, gal I'm here to tell you that you can't and so help me God if you ever approach me and tell me how to run my affairs or ive me your opinion without me giving it to you first I'll hog tie, whip you and sell your yella ass down the river so fast it'll make your head spin. If it's one thing I can't stand it's an uppity nigga that don't know her place. Ain't nothin' worser. Now git! Do you hear me? Git!

Well, I couldn't hardly b'lieve mas'r was speakin' ta me in such gruff terms like I's was some ol' common good fo' nuthin' field hand or somethin' so I jes stood dere and stared at him. Here I is tryna he'p him and Missy Reynolds who he s'posed ta care so much about from da broken hearts and he threatenin' ta sell me down da riva. I jes couldn't unnerstan' so I stood dere wonderin' when I guess I's shoulda been movin' 'cause masr'r did somethin' he ain't nebba done since I's been unda his care. He grabbed me by m'neck and threw me up against da parlor wall jes as hard as he could jes like I's was a common fiel' hand. Thinkin' about it now I's still havin' a hard time comprehendin'. My head hit dat wall so hard I's sho he done jarred somethin' loose and all I's

169

sedd was white spots fadin' in an out. Iknowed I was gonna faint so I grabbed da corner a da fireplace ta keep m'self from fallin' as da tears jes busted out from da pain. I's tried ta gatha m'self and make m'way outta da room but m'legs acted like dey didn't wanna hol' me and fo' I knowed it I's was on da flo' and feelin' dis bu'nin' sensation in m'side right above m'hip where mas'r kicked me and was windin' up ta kick me ag'in. And all da while he jes rantin' and ravin' 'bout me bein' one uppity nigga and not knowin' m'place and I's knowed right den and dere dat whatever it was dat was botherin' him at da moment ain't had nothin' ta do wit' me but dat thought ain't cared no mo' about me than Mas'r Reynolds. Onliest difference dis time was dat won't nobody dere ta stop him or pull him offa me. He still rantin' and ravin' and cussin' 'bout how all da niggas in da world couldn't measure up ta da worst a po' Georgia white trash. Then he went on 'bout how he wished now he had followed his daddy's advice and been a lawyer 'stead a bein' in da nigga business. Sayed he jes wisht he could sell da whole damn lot a us worthless, no account, meddlin', shiftless niggas and be done wit' da whole kitten caboodle once and for all. And 'specially me fo' contributin' tta his losin' his wife and best friend. Dat's what mas'r say and all da time tryna find da strength ta lay his boot inta me agi'n. He sayed soon as dat baby a mine was born he was gonna sell both a us jes as far away as he could. Talk 'bout bein' shocked. I's couldn't b'lieve m'own ears. Dis mas'r dat I's done served so faithfully all dese years sayed he

170

was gonna sell both me and m'baby far away from da onliest home I's ebba knowed jes like I's one a dem common fiel' hands what constantly runnin' and causin' him so much problems. Dis da very same man dat give me his word dat he would nebba sell me or mine and now he jes gonna go back on his word. Now fo' da first time in my entire life, I wisht dat dat man and all those like him would feel da wrath a da Lawd and da Lawd would send down a plague a locusts, or a bolt a thunda, and strike 'em all dead.

It was at dat very moment dat I unnerstood why none a dem slave hands, at da Reynolds Place, went ta helps Mas'r Reynolds when Mas'r John was so set on sendin' him ta Zion. Guess Aunt Hattie knowed what she was talkin' 'bout when she telled me 'bout not meddlin' in white folks affairs.

I's begged fo' mercy and I ain't rightly sho' iffen mas'r heared or he jes git tired or iffen it won't da good Lawd who stepped in and stopped him from me but he stopped kickin' me and jes went ova, fetched hisself some brandy and set down and steered at me befo' tellin' me ta git m'ass up outta dere and carry m'self back ta da Reynolds.

I's won't sho' dat I could walk but I got up outta dere da best way I knowed how which meant crawlin' on m'hands and knees 'til I got outta his sight and then I checked ta see how bad I's was hu't. Bein' dat I ain't feelin' nothin' feel like it was broke I jes prayed dat he ain't hu't

171

m'baby. Da whole time I tried ta keep m'stomach covered and balled up in ta da tightest little ball I could and then I prayed. And I's says tat a m'self. Iffen dis here youngun' survives dis here he gonna be one strong man.

Dat night as I walked dem seven or eight miles back ta da Reynolds, I prayed. I mean I prayed da whole entire way. I prayed fo' m'baby and I prayed dat da Lawd would kill Mas'r John and iffen he couldn't see ta do it then he jes give me da power ta do it m'self. Dat's what I prays fo'. I prays dat he let me kill dat man befo' he has a chance ta sell m'baby away from me, like dey sellt me. I prays fo' a end ta alla dis here slav'ry and alla dis mean-spiritedness but mos' of all I prayed dat da Lawd give ma da strength ta kill him. Then as I finally come in ta view a da Reynold's Place and afta comin' up wit' a sho' fire way ta kill mas'r it come ta me dat whoebba takes mas'r was jes as likely ta be even worser and dey probably mas'rs place was jes as likely ta be even worse and dey probably would sell ev'rybody. And I's didn't wont dat ta happen jes 'cause I was sufferin' so. So, I prayed dat da good Lawd would see fit ta kill me and m'baby befo' he let us be separated and sol' down da river and away from each otha. I kept tellin' m'self dat dis was all jes a bad dream and dat it jes couldn't be so but my ribs and m'sides dat dis won't no dream. Dis jes da slavery m'Joseph tried so hard ta make me unnerstan' when I kept sayin' no it jes cain't be. And then I ast m'self how da good Lawd could let dis be so when I knowed in m'heart dat he don't approve.

By dis time I's at da Reynold's Place and I figgers it must be close ta midnight. And mas'r's words was still ringin' in m'ears loud and clear. M'head and m'face pounded from where mas'r hit me and I hit da wall. But no sooner than I gits back one a da hands I ast ta stand in fo' me whilst I was gone tryna do missys' biddin' say she been astin' fo' me da entire time. Well now, I do declare, dat in m'heart and soul I's truly feel likes I had enough a while folks ta last me a lifetime. And it seem like ev'rytime I tries ta he'p one a dem out in some way or anotha dey always acts da fool. Dey worser than any ol' stubborn mule I's eva seed so in m'mind I jes comes ta da realization dat ain't hardly no hope fo' none a dem.

Anyways when I's gits back, I figgers it's too late fo' anybody ta be callin' on anybody but missy done lef' word wit' one a da hands dat she wanna see me right directly soon as I arrives. Now I has all intentions a pretendin' ta miss dat message but I ignores m'betta sense and sneaks in da back do', in case Mas'r Reynolds done stopped by ta visit. And of course he ain't so I goes in and wakes missy ta see what all da fuss is about and so all-fire impotent dat it cain't wait until tomorrow. Well, let me tell ya. When I opens da do' ta her room da smell a bowels hit me so hard dat I doubled ova and started gaggin'. Da smell of bowels hit me like nothin' I ain't neva knowed befo' in m'life and

173

da woman looked like pure hell. In all m'born days I ain't neva seen a niggra or a white change so much in less than a week. She had los' so much weight it was hard ta even recognize the po' soul and she was so weak she could no longer stand or walk on her own. She was just downright pitiful. And whoeva was s'pozed ta be carin' fo' her didn't care iffen she drowned in her own feces or not.

It was a sad day 'round da Reynold's Place and I's found myself grievin' fo' dem as well as m'self but dat didn't last long atall 'cause I hadn't even got in da room good when missy reared up in da bed and commenced ta swearin' and cussin' like I's neva heard befo' from what s'pozed ta be a Christian lady a virtue 'bout me leavin' her ta sit in her own filth.

April 9

Missy 'pologized ta me I don't know how many times dis mornin'. Now she mostly sleeps da day away. She might be up a couple a hours here and dere but mos' a da time da laudanum she be takin' keeps her sleepin' like a baby.

Me? Well I's done all I can fo' her but she ain't tryin' ta help herself so ain't nothin' I can do fo' her at dis point and nobody seems ta care. Mas'r John broke down and came ta look in on her but she ain't even know who he was and da laudanum done took hold so bad dat when she awake she jes scream and scream fo' mo. She don't

174

seem ta care about nothin' but more laudanum and I's scared dat she really gone be somethin' if we runs out. Da doctor say it done ate away her brain but we all knowed dat she went mad 'cause fo' no otha reason than her broke and not her brain. Ain't nothin' mo' than dat. Dey white folks wit' all dey medical knowledge cain't even figger somethin' as simple as dat out. When mas'r seed her in da condition she was in he didn't sat a word ta her. He jes turn't ta me and whispered, "Don't believe there's much you can do for her Mary. Why the po' woman's gone quite mad. Start makin' arrangements for one of Mas'r Reynolds hands to take over for you starting the beginning of next week. We've got a lot of work needs done at home and Aunt Hattie cain't do it all on her own anymore."

Mas'r nebba looked directly at me da whole entire time he was talkin' ta me and I truly didn't recognize dis cold man I'd addressed as mas'r all my life.

Dat was a Monday and mas'r say he wonted me back by da next Monday which only verified my m'own suspicions dat nobody s'pected missy ta even last da week through. And Mas'r Reynolds seein' da state she was in took ta da bottle like dere was no tomorrow. He ain't even botha ta come home no mo'. Jes' sayed da place smell't like death but I'll tell you it ain't smell't no worser than he did. He quit washin' and shavin' and spent his ev'ry wakin' hour in da whorehoses down Savannah way. I knowed dist a be a fact 'cause ev'ry fo' or fi' days he'd

175

send a niggra 'ho wit' a note astin' fo' a change a clothes and a draft so he could pay his note down at da 'ho house.

He would tell dem gals ta give me da note 'cause I's was da onliest one dat could read and write. Then I'd fill out da draft and give it ta da gal who not knowin' would take da draft ta da bank fo' cash. Da man in da bank would put da money in da bag and tell da gal not to open it but ta give it directly ta Mas'r Reynolds and nobody else.

Now mos' a dem gals had by dis time bought dere own freedom and not nary one was whatcha might call dumb and in talkin' ta dem I not only come ta know a lot about dem but I got ta know a lot 'bout Savannah and a lot a otha things too dat I knew would seve me down da road, By dis time almost all work on the Reynold's Place had commenced. Niggras wasn't even thinkin' plowin' or plantin' and each day dat passed saw anotha two or three niggras slip away unda da cova a darkness. Da Reynold's Place already desperately low on hands which is why I was summoned in the first place must a los' mo' than fifty slaves and he ain't had more than a hunnerd ta begin wit'. Mos' a da one's dat did stick around didn't stick around 'cause a no loyalty ta da Reynolds. Dey was jes' eitha too old ta run, to scared to run or b'lieved dat wit' all da talk a freedom comin' it didn't make no sense ta take a chance runnin'.

April 10

176

Took Missy Reynold's laudanum and mixed it wit' tobacco juice from da spittoon da way Aunt Hattie telled me ta do so ev'rytime missy drinkt from da bottle she throwed up. It costed me a whole lot mo' work cleaning up behind her three sometimes fo' times a day but afta a day or two she already lookin' betta if ya ast me and she ain't so quick ta try and drank da whole dat burn bottle in a day.

No matta how mean and connivin' white folks is I jes cain't sit by and watch 'em jes kill demselves. Still, and all on days like dese when she cussin' and fussin' and git ta actin' like a pure-d-fool and gittin' all ugly I gives her jes' enough ta quiet her down and make her sleepy so's I can go about m'own plans which I works on a lil' bit each and ev'ry day.

April 11

A pretty mulatto gal woke me whilst I was nappin' on da back porch taday. Dis here baby kickt me all-night so sleep didn't come easy and b'twee missy and dis here baby I do declare dat I's ain't neva been so tired. So, I gotta nap when I can. He kick like a mule too. B'lieve he gonna be big and strong jes like his daddy.

Anyways dis here gal come astin' me if I'm da niggra what could read and write. I tells her, "Yes ma'm dat would be me." And she says she gots a letter from Mas'r Reynolds she need me ta look at sayin' he need a hunnerd dollar draft and a change a clothes but I's

177

suspicious so I ast her how Mas'r Reynolds been farin' and she tell me dat he ain't doin' too good since he eitha drankin' or sick from drankin' mos' a da time. And he ain't took a break from drankin' in ova a week now. Still, fo' some reason I's real suspicious. Anyways, I ast her fo' her note and she showed me her pass which even though torn and dirty I could barely make out his mark since I was so useta seein' it by now. Still, there was somethin' different 'bout this here gal so I ast her what da note sayed but it soon became obvious ta me dat da gal couldn't read a lick but I still ast her for her other note and she said dat's all he gave her befo' tellin' her ta git.

"Well", I tells her, "he ain't got no hunnerd left. All he gots is dis here fifty and once he gits here dere ain't no mo'."

She shake her head and sayed she'd tell him jes' dat but she gonna make sho' she stand at da bottom of da stairs and yell it up to him 'cause she got a fear a heights and fallin'. We both laughed 'cause we knowed dat fool won't in his right mind. Fact of the matta was though dat I ain't even checkedhis books but I's don't want him ta wake up outta his drunk and come a huntin' me like I done gone out and tied one on and spent up all his money so I only writes a draft fo' fifty. Plus if he don't come a huntin' fo' me ta see what happened ta all his money I know jes how far gone he is. And dat fifty should hold him a good week and allow me to do what I's gonna do befo' he eitha come home or send home fo' anotha draft.

178

Ol' gal took the draft and turnt ta leave but befo' she did she lookt me up and down befo' she say dist a me. She sayed, Ya know, you's a right handsome woman. Might wanna think 'bout gittin' inta da business afta ya has yo' youngin'. Might consider headin' ta Natchez or Biloxi ta stake yo claim. Gotta beat slavin' fo Mas'r Reynolds. He gots ta be da cruelest white man I's ever laid eyes on. I started ta tell her dat I wasn't none a Mas'r Reynold's possession but I thought it best ta listen right den and dere. And m'mas'r wasn't no betta. Yeah, no need ta say nothin'. Better jes ta listen so I listen ta what she sayed and I learned a lil somethin' dat day.

She telled me dat if I was smart I'd sve up a lil money den ketch Mas'r Reynolds jes like he is now—all likkered up til' where he cain't see straight, don't know his own name and low on funds. Then jes git him ta sign da papers so's you can buy yo' freedom. That's what I did. I went ta Natchez, worked fo' damn near two years and buyed my own freedom.

All I heared was Natchez and m'ears perked up like Caesar dat ol' sorry hound hounddog what useta tag along behind Uncle ben, bless his soul. "Did you say Natchez?" I ast searchin' fo' da bill of sale I seed earlier with m'Joseph's name on it. I found it faster than anything I's ever found in my life. I shoved dat bill a sale in front a her face. "Do you kow dis man?" I ast.

179

"Thought we been through dis befo' honey. I can't make out a word a dat. Tol' you I's cain't read."

Oh, anyway da name I's lookin' for is Franklin a da famous Franklin Plantation. Say it's one a da largest plantations in Natchez. Does you know him?"

"Course I do honey! Ev'rybody dats eva been in Natchez knows da Franklin Plantation. It one a da largest best known plantations in Mississippi." She saiyed ta me. Mr. Franklin one a da biggest slaveholders in Mississippi. Some say he gots more than two thousand slaves. It takes mo' n' three fo' days jes to cross the place. Say Mr. Franklin eitha da second or third richest man in Mississippi. That's what dey tell me."

"Tell me about dis Mr. Franklin. Is he a fair man?"

"Well dey say he is. Me, m'self well I ain't really had da occasion a doin' any p'sonal bizness wit' him 'cause dey say he a very pious and religious man and m'bizness don't readily lend itself to those type men but word has it dat he a purty fair and just man. At least dats what I heared. From all accounts he a fairly good white man as far as dey go. Ain't nothin' compare to yo' mas'r right here though. He da meaniest, nastiest, orneriest, critter I's evea come ta know. If I's was you I'd had ta run a long time ago."

An hour later, an amidst missy's screamin' and bellowin' at da top of her lungs I hugged and kissed dat woman fo' givin' me hope

180

dat m'Joseph was in good hands and fo tellin' me da best way ta put
m'plan in action.

April 11

Evr'body keeps talkin' 'bout war b'tween da states. Dat's
all you hear 'bout nowadays. All da white folk are all caught and worried
'bout how dey gonna be able ta survive and keep on makin' dey money
and how it gonna affect dey way a life. And da more dey talk about it da
worser it gits fo' us niggras. Ev'rybody actin' like it's our fault when we
ain't done nothin' but do what we's tol' ta do. I still don't see how it
bacomed our fault but dey say it is and keep on blamin' us and Lord
knows dey angry and upset and well—not that it's eva been good—but
right now ain't da best times fo' a niggra. That I will tell ya. Me, m'self
was hopin' for da war ta break out not jes' so's us niggras could be freed
but so's I could put m'plan inta action but dis might jes be anotha one a
dem thangs ta git us ta work even harder by sayin' if we do then we will
be let go but I don't know so's I jes telled Aunt hattie and Young Saul to
stay alert and be ready. But Aunt Hattie tell me dat she ain't rightly
decided yet.

April 12

The war started today. I ain't rightly sho what dat means
but niggras is runnin' and jumpin' and celebratin' anywheres dere mas'r

cain't see 'em. It's like one big ol' jubilee everwhere you look down in da quarters. Dey keep sayin' da war is all 'bout freein' us slaves but I ain't seen a niggra lookin' any mo' freer than befo' da war started. Like I sayed befo' I's don't b'lieve it's no mo' than anotha white folks trick ta keep us from runnin' away. So many slaves has been runnin' an escapin' dat I b'lieve white folks will do anything ta keep us from runnin'. Dey say da highways is bad and da paddy rollas and slavecatchers is out jes waitin' ta snatch us up and sell us down riva. Plus da Union Army intent on killin' alla us runaways for bein' part of a 'spiracy. Dats what dey do. Usin' all dem high-falutin' words a niggra cain't unnerstand jest a keep da wool pulled ova are eyes. Say we better stay put so's dey can protect us. Well, dis here niggra don't b'lieve nary a word of it. Me, m'self been beat da last two weeks by da same mens claimin' dey wonts ta protect me so I don't take no stock in nothin' dey gots ta say no mo'. And what's mo' when da word come down dat war's gittin' ready ta break out all hell breaked loose down here and slaves really got ta runnin' makin' it really hard on us dat stayed close ta home. And white fols was jes gittin' more and more furious about da whole situation and of course we was da ones dat took da blame even though we ain't had nothin' atall ta do wit' any a da decision-makin'.

If ya ast me it's one big ol' crazy mess. Dere's jes so many thangs I's jes don't unnerstan' an alla da time I jes feels like a chile when I ast Aunt Hattie somethin'. Mos ev'ry night I ends up walkin' da

182

seven or eight miles back ta Mas'r John's Place ta see Aunt Hattie ta talk 'bout dis here whole situation or ta jes go ova are plans. And wit Mas'r John travelin' so much on behalf of da war effort wes slaves can move pretty freely. All he tryna do is git some a dese here southern boys ta sign up and enlist.

Anyway, Aunt Hattie keep me informed of da war effort and she sayed da North gots way mo' soldiers and dey ready ta go ta war at anytime. Dey gots what called a standin' army which means all dey do is stand aroun' and wait for a war ta happen whereas da South ain't gots no army standin' and waitin' ta fight somebody so Mas'r john and hissen friends gotta 'round up a lotta po' white trash dat ain't workin', ain't got no land, or no skills and get dem ta fight for little or no pay ta make sho Mas'r John don't lose all his land and his holdins'. What su'prised me though is why Mas'r John and hissen friends like Mas'r Reynolds jes didn' come ta us and git us ta do da dirty work da way dey always do when it's somethin' dey ain't fond a doin'. But Aunt Hattie she jes laugh and telled me dat da white slaveowners don't trust us in da war effort. Don't think we can conduct ourselves and sho' as hell don't won't no niggra wit' a gun bringin' up da rear. She say, "Picture dat. An abolitionist in da front and a slave in da rear. Wonda who gonna get caught in the cross-fire?" Then she laughed.

"Well, dat's fine by me. Su'prised dey ain't got us out dere bathin' 'em and feedin' 'em or somethin' anotha. Freedom or no freedom, dis here war may be a godsend. I ain't nebba had so much downtime and dey ain't ereally started fightin' hard yet." We both laughed and I had ta admit it felt good to be back in Aunt Hattie's comp'ny again.

I was still puzzled 'bout a few thangs so I asts Aunt Hattie what musta seemed pretty obvious but still had me a might confused.

"Tell me somethin' Aunt Hattie. What is it dat make white folks go out dere and give dere lives fo' a no-good, lazy, shiftless, heathen? Dat don't seem much worth fightin' fo' iffen ya ast me."

Aunt Hattie laughed again.

"No gal, it sho don't make no sense but what dese boys is really fightin' mad about is da fact dat someone is tryna take away what dey considers legally and rightfully deres. It's what white folks calls da principle of da thang. Dey don't b'lieve dere's a soul on dis here God's green earth dat should be able ta tell 'em what's right and wrong and what dey can and cannot do. Dat's all dere is to it sweetheart. Dey done decided dat we is dere property ta be used anyways dey see fit and dey willin' ta die ta protect dere property."

"So's let me git dis right auntie. So, den iffen da North win and lill all dese here good southern gentlemen den da lot a us is free? But iffen da South win den we still slaves?"

"I'd say dat's da long and sho't of it Mary."

"And in da meantime we's jes s'pozed ta sit around and wait and take care of da place and see who win and who lose like dat's are job ta take care of dem so dey can fight ta keep us slaves and den come home and whip us anytimes dey git da notion. And iffen da No'th win den what we s'pozed ta do or betta yet what dey fitten ta do wit' us? What dey gonna do once dey set us free? Dey gonna wrap us all up in swathing and takes us home wit' dem or dey gonna leave us here ta fend fo' ourselves afta dey done to'e up da entire South and made dese here boys madda than a cut bull."

"Who you tellin', honey! Anything go wrong and dem fools git dere arms and legs blowed off defendin' y'all from freedom and dem abolitionists hopesy'all knows whose fault it's gonna be."

"Of course I know. It gonna be yo's and mine, Aunt Hattie. Always is. But I'll tells ya what Aunt Hattie. Dis time gonna be diff'rent than times past. Dis time Mary ain't jes gonna sit around and wait fo' 'em ta come back. Win or lose dey ain't gonna come back smilin' I may not know muc but iffen I do know somethin' I know dey ain't gonna come back smilin'. Dat I do know. Don't knows how long it gonna be fo' dey gits done killin' each otha but I's sho ain't gonna sit here waitin' ta tell me what da outcome gonna be and what dey got planned fo' me next. No suh. Whateva dey got planned one thang I knows. I know it ain't gonna be in Mary's best interest. Dat's one thang I knows fo' sho'. Since I's been ova at Mas'r Reynolds place I's been able ta see a whole

185

lot mo' clearer than when I was here. Now when I hears da thunder roar one thang I's come ta realize that I jes a matta a time befo' lightnin' gonna strike. I ain't gotta sees it or feels it ta know what's comin' next."

Aunt Hattie laughed.

"Bout time you saw da light, gal. I's was really wonderin' iffen or how long it was gonna take fo' you to smell the rain and see the light. Wondered jes how long it was gonna take fo' da dawn to wake you up. Always walkin' 'round here talkin' 'bout mas'r sayed dis and mas'r sayed dat like someone done appointed John Marshall yo' guiding light. Like he da messiah hisself. I swear fo' God I useta pray dat one day you'd wake up and truly see thangs fo' what dey really was and now fo' da fi'st time you is really beginning ta see thangs fo' what dey really are and not what dey seems ta be. Took Mas'r John and Mas'r Reynolds ta damn near kill ya ta open yo eyes but at least now ya startin' ta see 'em fo' what dey worth and b'tween da two of 'em dey ain't worth no mo more than cow manure. But you startin ta see and Lawd knows child, ya don't know how good dat makes me feel."

Aunt Hattie was beamin' wit' pride.

"I's had to smile. Even though times was hard for a niggra slave and right now mos' a us was in limbo when it come to are part in da war or even if we had a part in da war. Truth of da matta was we slaves wasn't even sho' if we should stay put or leave or where it was we was s'pozed ta go iffen freedom really did come. We jes ain't have no idea. Noone knowed what we was gonna do or what da future wouture would bring but fo'da fi'st time it seemt like us niggras had some choice in are lives and are futures. Still, I had ta smile lookin' at Aunt Hattie who had a new bounce in her step and looked like a lil school gal ready to jump da broom. Still, in da back a m'mind I knowed dat dere was no time ta be livin' in da past. Mas'r John would be comin' home soon from tryin' ta 'round up troops and he'd be 'spectin' me back from da Reynold's Place when he got back. And iffen Mas'r Reynolds decided to come outta his drunken stupor and come back home he'd swear da Union Army had already been through dere. Ev'ry slave dat could walk had walked fearin' his return and dey'd taken ev'ry chicken, pig and cow dey could take ta sustain 'em durin' dere journey. By da time all was said and done dere wasn't a chicken, goat left ta be had and aside from da cook and da butler da place had been all but abandoned.

Weeds now grew where Missy Reynolds favorite flower bed had been. Dere still remained a few horses and a mule left in da barn but wit' no one to feed 'em or lead dem to pasture dey too had growed gaunt and thin.

Mary knew dat she was in no way responsible for the mass exodus. In fact there was no one to blame 'cept fo' Tom Reynolds himself for his own negligence but he would hardly see it as such and there would be certainly be hell to pay. And it wouldn't really matter who paid as long as someone did.

187

April 13

White fols done gone plumb crazy wit' hate. Ev'rywhere you look niggras slavehands is payin' wit' dere lives fo' dis here war b'tween da states. It's sad 'cause I ain't nebba heard nary one ast for dis war. Sho' dey wanted ta be free but dey sho' ain't ast fo' dist a be da way ta freedom. All dis here killin' and spillin' a blood jes don't make no sense. Dere has gots ta be a betta way. Dere jes has ta be. Mos' a us was jes content ta be slaves. Well, maybe we wasn't content. It was mo like we jes didn't know no betta. Those dat wasn't content ta be slaves and wasn't scared a gittin' whipped run or tried ta escape but ain't nobody ast fo' dis here war. Niggras ain't even no da meannin' a war til' white folks gone and got demselves involved.

Young Saul and Aunt Hattie s'posed ta stop by taday. Saul was s'pozed ta come so he could take me inta Savannah whilst Aunt Hattie watch Missy Reynolds durin' da time we be gone but dey ain't showed yet. I's worried 'cause dis da fi'st part of my plan and time is growin'. Each day day dat passes is a day closa ta mas'r comin' back and dere is absolutely no time ta waste.

April 14

Aunt hattie and Young Saul arrived early dis mo'nin' and I's was nebba so glad ta see two people in all m'life as I was glad ta see

188

dem two dis mo'nin'. Dey telled me dat Ol' Sam wouldn't let 'em outta his site yestiddy. He say he runnin' da plantation da way a plantation s'poze ta be run whilst mas'r away. He say mas'r jes too daggone easy on his niggas and he coulda doubled da field yield iffen mas'r would jes let him run thangs like dey was s'pozed ta be run. Den he whipt one boy wit'in an ich of his life ta show dem no-account, lazy, shiftless niggas dat he won't playin'. And dey says he whippin' ev'ry hand dat scratch his head wrong. Dey say he so jumpy 'bout his hands runnin' dat he watchin' ev'rybody and one or two still manage to escape in da wee hours a da mo'nin'. Po' man drivin' his self plumb crazy tryna stay up all night and den manage da fields in da daytime too. But he tryin' too. And still he losin' hands right and left. Sayed he cain't even chase da runaways like he useta for fear dat if he leave dese here to go off and chase a runner when he git back won't be nobody lef'. From what dey tell me, Ol' Sam really lookin' ol' now. All I's could do was laugh. Say he whipt three hands yestiddy fo' lookin' like dey wanted to run. And since nobody knowed what kinda look dat was and ev'rybody feelin' like dey want ta run ev'body just walkin' 'round staring at dey feet fearin' ta look up at all.

Aunt Hattiesayed Sam only makin' thangs worser and dat da Afreecans gots tagetha last night in da woods palaverin' 'round what deys gonna do on account of da way ol' Sam been treatin' 'em. Aunt Hattie sayed it was only da Afreecans and den only da men and jes da field hands. Sayed she don't know what all went on but dis mo'nin when she went down ta da fields ta brang ol' Sam his breakfast ev'rybody seemt ta be workin' hard as usual but dere was no Sam ta be found. When she commenced ta astin' around, ev'rybody smiled but nobody seemt ta know. A couple of dem young bucks dat Sam had whipped da day befo' sayed dat he musta gone and joint da wore and den jes busted out laughin'. Aunt Hattie b'lieves dat meetin' last night was a lynchin' and swears she heard screamin' all night long. Much as I's dislike Sam and what he did ta me I's still a Christian woman and cain't agree wit' no lynchin' whether he be white or niggra 'spite what he done did ta deserve it. Lawd times sho' is gittin bad. Now niggras is lynchin' white folks.

April 13

Early Evenin'

Me and Young Saul done made it. I knowed Aunt Hattie ain't need ta be runnin' up and down no stairs at her age ev'rytime missy get a whim an a inklin' for a cold glass a water, or a peach or someone ta wipe her butt 'cause she was too dang lazy to get up so I made her dose a laudanum a might bit stronga so she would sleeps 'til we got back.

Ev'rythang was movin' right enuff an accordin' ta plan. An ain't nobody heared from Mas'r Reynolds so I guess he do b'live his account is empty. An iffen it wasn't it shonuff is now. I writes a draft fo' almost fo' hunnerd dollas and had Saul takes me inta Savannah ta Mas'r

Reynolds bank ta cash it da same way da gal from da ho'house telled me to. "Course da man at da bank dat waited ain't no I's could read and write and so da only problem was makin' sho' we ain't bump into Mas'r Reynolds. And bein' dat da bank was useta seein' da same handwritin fo' da last month ev'rythang worked out jes fine.

Soon as me and Saul gits back ta da Reynolds Place I has Saul hitch up Mas'r John's hosses ta Reynolds's carriage. Aunt Hattie already had missy bathed an I had already stocked up enuff laudanum to last her a month a Sundays so I's s'poze we was ready as we ebba be even though I still aint had da whole plan workt out as clearly as I wonted but we had Mas'r Reynolds and three fresh horses Saul had been fattenin' up ova da last two months. I had cashed da draft and so we had enough money ta git a propa start. And accordin' ta what ol' gal tol' me 'bout Natchez and m'calculations I b'lieves we even had enough ta set up stakes. And dis was all planned out by one shiftless, young Afreecan, one ol' lazy, fat, black heifer wit' not enough brains and far too much mouth and one uppity, mullatto, wench who thought cause she was high yalla dat she was betta den otha niggras. Between da three of us we had mapped out da best way ta git ta Natchez ta pick up m' Joseph and keept right on goin' til we reached Mexico or da West dependin' on da outcome a da war.

I prayed dat da war wouldn't be too long in bein' ova 'cause I's sho ain't had enough ta pay fo' m'Josephs freedom but since I

191

couldn't count on dat I fiiggered we jes have ta cross dat dere bridge when we git to it but Lawd knows I 's was ready to go no matta what fate bringed us and so was Young Saul. I b'lieve I's was even mo' ready than he was 'cause wit' alla Mas'r Reynolds savings tuckt neatly unda m'petticoats and Mas'r John 'spectin' me back taday I knowed dere was gonna be a heavy price ta pay. Still, I figgered wit' alla da commotion wit' da war, and Sam's disappearance and all da slaves runnin' now dat Sam was gone, and jes da general state of da place wit' noone ta watch ova it mas'r would have his hands too full to make us his numba one prior'ty. Least dat's what I's be hopin'.

But won't no time ta be hopin'. Alla us knowed dat iffen eitha a those two men happened ta return home early we was done fo'. Still, I was purty uncertain 'bout a couple a thangs at dis point but I didn't let on. Ain't won't noone else ta worry mo' den dey already was. But I's still ain't know whether Aunt Hattie had made up her mind 'bout comin' wit'us. She kept goin' back and forth da whole week and I's wasn't fo' sho' sho where she really stood even now. I's really hopin' she would. Her knowledge 'bout certain stuff and her clear thinkin' was really needed but she still hadn't said no mo' than she'd thank 'bout it and dat had been weeks ago. Still and all, much as I needed Aunt Hattie won't nothin' gonna stop me from goin'. Cleanin' out Mas'r Reynolds's savin' had committed me so even if I's had a change a heart I ain't had no choice but ta gio now. No, m'main concern was Missy Reynolds. I

192

needed her ta go even mo' than I needed Saul an Aunt Hattie. Ya see, iffen I hads missy along I wouldn't have ta worry 'bout da slavecatcha's atall.

I'd already made up are travelin' passes da same way Mas'r John showed me only dese stated dat two niggra slaves actin' as nu'ses to accompany one Mrs. Thomas Reynolds ta da hospital for da mentally insane in Natchez, Mississippi for treatment of a rare debilitatin' disease a da mind called dementia. Mos' a dat info'mation I got from da notes da doctor had left fo' Mas'r Reynolds info'min' him bout his wife's condition since he wouldn't nebba be dere when da doctor come-a-callin'. Then I packed up alla da medical books in Mas'r Reynolds's study and placed dem in da carriage in plain view and placed da laudanum right next ta 'em. I'd already mixed da laudanum in equal parts wit' Mas'r R'eynolds's strongest, mos' powerful co'n likker ta stretch it even mo' since I's won't rightly sho how long it was gonna take us. Dat way I's could keep her purty much sedated durin' are journey. But what mos' scared me though was dat I ain't heard a peep concernin' Mas'r Reynolds. He usually ast fo' at least a hunnerd dollas and would had sent somebody by now and dis time he only had fifty and dere wasn't a peep outta him. Onliest thang I's could think was dat he must be somewhere dryin' out and dat would mean he be returnin' anytime now. Me. I 's wonted ta be a purty fair piece b'tween me and him when he come home ta find he broke, his carriage gone and so is hissens wife though I's don't rightly think he worried too much 'bout da latter.

Lawd knows he had enuff ta worry 'bout wit' alla his slaves and livestock gone and I's sho' dat dere would be a fair amount a speculation when it come ta his money bein' gone as well. He knowed won't nobody capable a writin' drafts but me. His own wife couldn't even write.

Aunt Hattie had dressed missy so purty dat noone woulda knowed seein' her dat she was loony as a betsy bug an we was all glad fo' dat and it was right dere at dat point as me and Saul pulled in ta da front gates dat I made m'decision.

"Saul," I sayed, "Git missy's trunk outta da barn. Dey both be behin' da second bale a hay on da right. When you's gits finish wit' dat den tie da spare hoss ta da back a da carriae be right quick about it. Ain't nary a secon' ta waste young man."

In da meantime I he'ped Aunt hattie git missy and den Aunt Hattie up inta da carriage. Da decision fo' Aunt Hattie to come along was made by me afta she took so long in deciding and I jes had her wash her white kitchen outfits along wit' mine so we could use 'em ta show we was nu'ses and since nu'ses and cooks wo'e da same white outfits it would make it even easier to pass as nu'ses. When I seed Aunt Hattie in hers I knew she was comin' along as well. I knowed are chances a makin' it had jes got better and I had ta smile.

"Who sayed I's goin' anywheres?" Aunt Hattie sayed grinning dat lil ornery smile a hers I had so come ta love and hate all at da same time.

"Look a here auntie. I unnerstan's dat you free in both yo' heart an yo' soul but I's truly b'lieves you needs a lil piece a soil of yo' own ta go wit' dat an I intends ta git you yo' own piece a land wit' some pigs and chickens and all dat comes wit' it. Dat's m'promise ta you. 'Sides iffen I leaves you here mas'r sho'nuff gonna string yo' round, brown bottom up ta da closest tree he see iffen you don't tell him where me and Saul done run off to and I's don't want dat on m'conscious. So le's jes say I's doin' both you and me a favor.

"Well you betta git a movin' den chile. Ain't no time ta be standin' around cluckin' like a hen. Let's git a move on fo' one a dem decides ta retu'n home and see how you done cleaned 'em out.

I's was nebba so happy in m'life. Not once did I's have mixed emotions 'bout leavin' da closest thang ta a home I's ebba known. No, m'home was wit Aunt Hattie and Young Saul, who wouldn't let me lift anything, and m' Joseph who I's was goin' ta see. Dat was m'home an Aunt Hattie had jes made ev'rythang right when I seed her in her white uniform carrying her tiny bundle and ready ta travel. I was truly happy she was wit' us and nebba loved nobody much as I loved dat woman at dat moment—well 'cept fo' maybe m'Joseph.

195

Wit' ev'rybody now tucked in and ready ta go I jumped up in da front next ta Young Saul who greeted me wit' da biggest grin you'd ebba wanna see and fo' I's could get set good we was off wit' a gallop da carriage pitchin' dis way and dat I started ta thinkin' dat iffen da slavecatchas didn't kill us den Young Saul's drivin' probably would. Lo and behold we was on are way ta join da Freedom Train.

Seemt like we rode fo' hours and we still hadn' come ta da end a da Reynolds's Place. Da whole entire time m'heart was in m'mouth. Aunt Hattie sayed dis was da mos' dangerous and mos' impotent part a da trip. I knowed she was tellin' da truth but t'wards evenin' we had come a fair piece and put some distance b'tween us and both places so I 's feel a lil mo comfortable now. Well, least as comfortable as a runaway slave can feel afta runnin' away wit' mas'rs best hosses, his money, livestock and his carriage. Wit' some distance behind us now we slowed da hosses and let 'em drink from a runnin' stream and fed 'em some oats. Dey was mighty fine hosses but at dis pace dey wouldn't last longa than a couple days at best. Ev'ryone was tired and I wondered iffen we should stop and rest awhile but dere was Aunt Hattie—always da voice of reason statin' da obvious, sensible thang ta do.

"Y'all gonna arouse da suspicions of ev'ry slavecatcha in dis here county iffen you try ta transpo't dis here white woman in dis here carriage all night long, Mary. And ya needs ta give missy a double dose a dat dere medicine and find an inn where she can sleep through da night. 'Sides too much shakin' and bouncin' ain't gonna do dat baby a yours much good eitha. We jes gotta pray dat Mas'r John and Mas'r Reynolds ain't arrive home yet and iffen dey did dey is so overwhelmed by da state a thangs dat dey ain't fixin' ta come out ta hunt fo' us fo' da next day or two. 'Sides dey gots mo' n' jes us ta chase. Dey done lost damn near all dey prop'ty. Onliest diff'rence b'tween us and da rest a da hands is dere here white woman and dat money you done stole but iffen he in a drunken stupor like you say it gonna take him awhile ta get hisself in good 'nuff shape ta chase down some runaways dat don't wanna be caught. Now let's find dis here woman a place ta rest herself and you can rest dat baby. We's can rise early befo' daybreak and move on den. Is all da papers in o'der?"

"Yes mam, dey in order."

"Good now slow dis carriage down ta a crawl at night. We don't wanna raise no s'picions. Da way you been drivin' people gonna sho' nuff think we's runnin' from somethin'." Aunt Hattie laughed.

"I could unnerstan' you rushin' ta get offa da Reynolds's place but now ya out in da open so's ya gots ta acts no'mal like you jes carryin' dis here woman ta da hospital like da pass say not like ya runnin' from da devil hisself." Aunt Hattie said laughin' again.

"But I is," I sayed and we both fell out laughin'.

197

I wonder iffen Aunt Hattie recognized jes how much trouble we was in or iffen she was jes actin' like dat ta keep me from panikin'. Whe I lookt ova at Saul he seemt ta be jes as unburdened by da sitch'ation as Aunt Hattie. And here I is ready ta pee at da fi'st sight a white folks. Boy dem Afreecans sho'nuff is some strange folk. I's don't ebba think I'll unnerstan' dem.

Aunt Hattie finished addressin' da matta and went on ta some othas which turnt out ta be no less impotent. I lissened and befo' we knowed it we fount us a inn and afta payin' and gittin' missy bedded down we made are way ta da barn where Saul had mad palletes outta hay fo' me and Aunt Hattie.

Alla us sleept 'til close ta nine o'clock da next mo'nin' so tired was we and we still had ta wake missy up who fo' da fi'st time in I's don't know how long she sayed she had ta relieve herself which in itself was a blessin'. Up 'til then she'd simply been content ta go on herself, inform us afterwards and have one a us change her. Dat alone would have slowed us down a whole lot and been very inconvenient and made things very difficult on a journey such as dis where time was of da essence. Guess even Missy Reynolds was relieved ta be leavin' a place filled wit' so much pain and heartache.

She was a lil mo' clearer thinkin' than I'd seed her in weeks and after several miles a ridin' I heared her ast Aunt Hattie.

"Where is y'all niggras takin' me?"

198

"Why ta meet Mas'r John at da hospital in Natchez," I heared Aunt Hattie say.

"Say, he won't ta make sho ev'rythang okay befo' he commence ta astin' fo' ya hand in sacred matrimonys. Oh my, I b'lieves I's done let da cat out da bag. Lawd mas'r sho' nuff gonna kill me now. Oh, missy please don't tells him I done tol'you. Oh, missy he sho'lly gonna have me tarred and feathered now. Lawd, Lawd, Lawd I's sho' nuff one foolish ol' niggra. All dese years on God's green earth and Hattie Mae still ain't gots da sense she was bo'n with. I do declare. Please excuse dis here niggra fo' bein' so dumb, missy." I heared Aunt Hattie say.

Missy who ain't been aware a too much ova da last several weeks alla a sudden seemt ta be aware a ev'rthang and evr'yone 'round her now. It was almost like a weight had been lifted. No longa were dere any clouds or cobwebs hangin' 'round and Aunt Hattie's words seemt ta bring her right back in ta da whole scheme a thangs.

"Did m' Johnny say dat? Oh Hattie, tell me ag'in. Did m'Jonny really say dat? Oh, dat man. And all da time he had me thinkin' he didn't really care. Goodness! And here I was feelin' oh so used. Oh, thank you so much Hattie Mae. Thank you dear. Now don'tcha go worryin' yo' lil niggra head ova nothin' I wouldn't bit mo' say you mentioned anything atall. 'Sides I won'ts him ta tell me hisself.

199

Now would one a you darkies please tell me why we're stopped. Let's go! Mustn't waste a second. Why we cain't keep Mas'r John waitin' now can we? Oh Hattie you must fill me in on all da details and all da latest goins ons. I feel like I's missed so much"

Aunt Hattie had sho' nuff opened da floodgates and at fi'st I's won't 'zactly sho' iffen dis was a good thang or not and though I's was glad ta see missy regain her faculties I's wont so sho' openin' Pandoras Box was goin' ta be a good thang or not. "Specially iffen she started puttin' the pieces together. Forty-five minutes later she was still babblin' on about John Marshall and her upcomin' weddin' b'tween da two. Aunt Hattie whose patience ran lower and lower as she growed older now tired of all da idle chatter concernining her John and da war administer a thimbleful of laudanum and in a matta a minutes Missy Reynolds was asleep once mo'. Administerin' da laudanum was a tough call ta make since we all knowed dat we was gonna need missy as it was gittin' dark once ag'in and had ta seek lodgin'. Dey would need her to gain admittance and wit' her claimin' dat we was her nu'ses chances was good dat me and Aunt Hattie would has some shelter too. At worst Aunt Hattie could stay wit' her bein' dat she was close ta eighty or thereabouts and someone would sho'lly need ta tend ta her needs 'specially iffen she was ta wake up and git ta shoutin' and screamin' and fussin'. Me? Well, it won't really all dat necessary dat I be indoors though Aunt Hattie b'lieved it tabe bein' dat I was in a family way but den ag'in I figgered I'd be best helpin' Saul feed and bed down da hosses and lookin' ova da map and well jes gittin' ready fo' da upcomin' day. A pallete would do me fine. 'Sides, by dis time and afta sev'ral weeks at da Reynolds Place I done had quite enough a Missy Reynolds and her antics.

As evening turnt ta night we rode on, each wit' our own fears a what da darkness would bring and ev'rybody grew quiet. You could jes feel da worry amongst us mountin'. Slavas patrolled da roads constantly and in da days since da war had been declared there was even mo' commotion than usual. C'federate soldiers now joined the ranks of da slavers and as always dere was da highwaymen who aint care if ya was niggra or white rich or po' he was gonna rob ya iffen he could. Up 'til now though we'd been mighty lucky ain't run in ta nothin' but a few niggras like us travelin' dis way and dat and some ol' po' dirt farmers carrying what lil dey had to and from da marketplace.

Now I won't what you might call a traveler. Fact a da matta is I ain't been offa da Marshall Plantation mo' than a handful a times in my whole entire life and dat includes da Reynolds's Place but I's got enuff sense ta know ta pull ta da side a da road when anybody approaches from da front or da rear and even wit' missy we's da ones drivin' so we's still gotta give white folks da right-a-way. But now it was gittin' late and I knowed dat iffen we didn't make haste and find us some lodgin' soon we gonna mos certainly become suspect so I takes da reins from Saul and lash dem hosses ta wit'in a inch a dey lives. We rode dis way at a steady pace 'til both my arms was weary and sore. Then I hands 'em ova ta Saul who feelin' m'impatience whipped dem hosses into a lather in an unconscious attempt ta put some distance b'tween hisself and all dat was wrong wit' da world. By now, I had drifted off from pure fatigue when I heared da sound of Aunt Hattie's voice from da back.

"Mary, you best slow dat young buck down iffen ya expects ta make it through this here county by coach and not by rope. Missy say dere's a inn jes up da road apiece. Sayed it ain't no mo' n' a mile or two. Alla dat shakin' and bouncin' ain't no good fo' dat youngun a yo's anyway. B'lieve I told ya dat befo'. Betta stop bein' so hardheaded gal."

No sooner had Aunt Hattie whispered those words than four horsemen appeared out of a grove of walnut trees alongside of da road before Young Saul could bring da horses to a stop almost runnin' one of da men ova. Young Saul, still a novice in the handling of animals such as these finely bred Kentucky thoroughbreds had ev'rything he could do to bring the animals to a halt. Spooked by the sudden appearance of the four men Saul may have lost control altogetha if it hadn't been for the quick thinkin' of da youngest of the four who rode up alongside da lead horse and reined him in wit' no problem. Grabbing the reins and whispering into its ear as he rode alongside da young colt da horse settled down and came to a walk and then a complete stop. Da young man stood patiently waiting for da other three to join him. Pulling up alongside the carriage the ringleader bent down to see the occupants. Seeing Missy Reynolds, he tipped his hat, "Evening ma'am."

The carriage's sudden stop had awakened the young woman who made a vain attempt to straighten her hair and fix her dress both of which were in utter disarray. Meanwhile, the other three riders sat in the path of the horses so as to assure that they didn't bolt since they still appeared uneasy and a little skittish in da presence of da three strangers.

Both Saul and Mary waited patiently and though nervous gave the impression of being both calm and easy in the presence of the impending danger.

"Beg your pardon ma'am but we was wondering where you were heading ma'am?" the eldest asked missy who was not only having difficulty responding but keeping awake as well.

Missy seemt bothered that they'd been stopped and angered even mo' that she'd been questioned about her comings and goins'.

"Excuse me suh but I do not appreciate y'all stoppin' m'carriage. I do so hope you have a reasonable explanation."

"Jes tryin' ta do our fair share fo' da Confederacy. Couldn't rightly see who was all in da carriage ma'am. All we could see from this vantage point was them three niggas ridin' along in this fine lookin' carriage and as you probably know we've had quite a problem with runaways since our boys here have gone off to join the war effort. They say we're losin' between fifty and seventy five a day since the Confederacy declared war on the Yankees so whilst our boys is away we're just tryin' to do our part to keep everything in order 'til they get back. That's all ma'am. Didn't mean to delay you at all.

"War sir? What war?"

Da men looked at each other then back at missy. It was hard ta be a southerner and not know there was a war goin' on. Even us slaves knew dat and we was s'poze ta be da dumbest of God's creations dis side of a mule. Matta-a-fact it was hard fo' anyone no matta where you was from not ta know dere was a war goin' on. It was da biggest talk of da day, da only talk dese days. Da oldest of da four men who had been quiet up 'til dis point—just takin' ev'rythang in then drew his hoss closer to da carriage in order ta git a closa look at missy who knowed nothin' of da Confederacy's rally to arms but missy was already fadin' back into her menagerie of dreams enhanced by da laudanum not long ago administered by Aunt Hattie.

"Ma'am," he started ta speak but missy was well off inta one a da those deep sleeps we had b'come so used to. It was Aunt Hattie who spoke ta da men now.

"Beg yo' pardon suh, but please unnerstand, m'missus is sufferin' form both illness and exhaustion and dis here medicine she be takin' have a mos'powerful affec' on her as well, suh. Right now all we's doin' is tryin' are best ta find a place fo' her ta rest her head fo' da night, suh. She telled us dat dere's an inn up da road a fair piece and we's jes tryna git her dere as sonn as we can. Dat's why we be rushin' suh. It's a might bit easier ta bed her down when she be awake then haveta carry her wit' me bein' ol' and m'dauhta bein' in a family way an all, suh."

"Don't b'lieve I was talkin' ta ya, ol'woman" da man sayed hissen eyes still fixed on Missy Reynolds.

"Yas suh. Jes tryna he'p suh."

Da man ignored Aunt Hattie.

"Y'all gots travelin' passes?"

"Yassuh we sho do. Mary dis gentleman want dem travelin' passes Mas'r John give you. Be quick about it gal. Whiite folks ain't got time ta be waitin' on you."

"Yas ma'm, Is those those papers he give me ta show da white folks when we gits stopped?"

"Yas those be da ones. Now be quick about it gal. Lawd, I's sho wish missy was up so she could handle dis here sitcho'ation. Here she done gone and passt out a'gin. Lawd if we don't hurry and git her ta dat hospital in Natchez I's don't b'lieve she gonna make it wit' alla dese spells takin' hol' a her like dey is."

I located da passes and handed dem ta da elderly gentleman who be eyein' me da way ol" Sam useta do and I knowed dis won't no good thang.

"What dem papers say Jeffries he ast passin' da papers ta da man next ta him."

"You know I cain't read no book writin'", da man replied.

"Well, pass 'em here then ya ignorant bastard," da ringleader sayed.

"What it say, Morris?" Jeffries ast still eyein' me up n' down.

"Ev'rything seems to be in proper order 'ceptin' I cain't see why dis here Marshall fella' gonna send dese here three niggas all da way ta Natchez when we gots perfectly good hospitals right here in South Carolina. Somethin's a might strange 'bout that iffen ya ast me."

"Same thang I's sayed, suh. 'Specially wit' me bein' in a family way and all, suh. I jes prays he ain't sendin' me down riva ta have missy sell us off. Mas' wouldn't do dat ta us would he, suh?" I feeled da tears well up in m'eyes and could see I's had him thinkin' now. Course he say da hospital in Natchez be da best hospital in alla da land fo' what ails his lady. Say he want da best dat money can buy fo' da woman he gonna marry."

"Well, dere you have it," Jeffries said turning his hoss and pullin' back on da reins so da hoss reared straight up and turnt completely around. It was all quite a show and I took a deep breath knowin' dat we had passt are fi'st test but da older man was hardly satisfied and lookt intent on findin' somethin' wrong, someway, somehow.

"Hol' on Jeffries. We need ta be thorough about this. Whole lotta boys is losin' their lives so we can hol' on ta what we done built up here. Cain't jes let no niggas jes slip through our fingas. Gotta make sho' dis ain't no abolitionist or nigga shenanigans goin' on here. Now let me see dat pass one mo time 'cause ta me somethin' seem ta be outta kilter iffen ya ast me."

Aunt Hattie and me was both thinkin' da same thang and was mo' worried 'bout missy wakin' up than anything else. Certainly didn't need her babblin' away 'bout anything right thru here wit' her crazy self. She was liable ta git us all hung wit' her crazy self.

"Who you say yo mas'r was gal?"

"Why, m'masr's name be Marshall. Mas'r John Marshall, suh." I answered.

The man smiled.

Oh, okay no wonder. I know John. Knowed him fo' as far back as I can rememba. Good man too. Kinda peculiar in his ways. 'Specially when it comes ta handlin' his niggras but what can I say, still and all he a good man. You know John, Jeffries. He's one a da largest landholders dis side a Savannah, you know da one dat hired us two ketch those two bucks awhile back. I heared he had a public hanging

207

right afta we turnt dem ova ta him. Jes wish I coulda been dere." He sayed smiling.

Jeffries payed lil attention ta da older man's words as he steadied his hoss and kept a watchful eye on me.

"Say Morris," he said, "you don't see no problem iffen I take dis here filly and bed her down fo' a few does ya?"

"Know I ain't got no problem wit' dat but Missy Reynolds jes might. You do recognize dat dat gal's wit' chile don'tcha boy?"

"Dat ain't no problem. Flip her ova on her stomach and you'd nebba know. She's a right nice lookin' mixed blood. I might jes ride along wit' her for a few 'til I gits my fill a dis here one."

"Then again," the older one they called Morris said, "That might not be such a good idea. If you know John Marshall likes I know John Marshall then you know he mighty p'ticular 'bout his niggas and da way his niggas be treated. Might wanna hold off on dis here one fo' now. And da fact dat he let her make dis trip and da way she carry herself I's got a feeling dat she might be hissen p'sonal stuff and b'lieves you me you don't wanna cross John Marshall. 'Sides soon as we makes sho' dis here woman gits settled in good I's figger we might jes could mosey on ova ta da Fox and Boar and grab us a wench or two and maybe some grog."

"Sounds good ta me boss," Jeffries said befo' turnin' back ta me. "May see yo' black ass down da road a piece, gal," he sayed ta me.

I's knowed not ta answer and kept starin' at da ground da whole time he was talkin' 'cause I knowed deep in m'heart dat iffen I had lookt up and he had seed da hatred in m'eyes he woulda shot and killted me right dere on da spot. B'live you me I seen it happen. Plus I knowed he won't jokin' about seein' us down da road a piece but as God is m'witness da next time I sees him I'll be ready.

April 31

Ain't had no time fo' no writin' or no correspondence. Ev'ryday we be up at da crack a dawn pushin' on and ev'ryday we git a lil closa ta Natchez and a lil farther away from da plantation. And it's funny but in da beginning I thought I's gonna miss it but now dat we travelin' and I ain't got nobody ova m'back or tellin' me what ta do and makin' m'own decision 'bout lil thangs like do I wanna stop or push on or eat or pee I jes feels good 'bout me and ev'rythang.

Fo da fi'st time in m'life I can see da grass, and hear da birds sing and ev'rythang looks so diff'rent whan you on yo' own and gots a taste a da freedom. Mos' a da time I feels like a lil chile like when all I had ta do was run and jump and wait fo' Uncle Ben ta bring me somethin' from faraway places. Dat's how I feels now and Lawd knows

I's older but it sho feel good ta be or at least ta feel free ag'n.

Guess dat's part a da reason I ain't been writin'. I's jes been enjoyin' dis here freedom.

Must say though, we made a good choice in bringin' dis white woman along. I's don't know how many times da slava done stopped us but she alla time be tellin' 'em dat she headed ta meet her fiancée and ain't gots no time ta be foolin' 'round wit' no slavas. She tell 'em it's a ugly business what dey do; alla time tryna ketch po' defenseless niggras who ain't wanna be ketched so's dey can profit 'stead a finding some real honest work like real southern gentlemens do. Sometimes, crazy as she is she do me proud.

But sometimes she lights inta 'em so bad dat Aunt Hattie gots ta calm her down so's she don't say somethin' she ain't s'poze ta say. In da meantime I jes grin and bear it 'til she gets ta point of tellin' 'em how dey is da lowest form of human beins and how dey is and won't nebba be nothin' mo' than what dey is and what dey is is po' white trash. Den she tell 'em dat all dey doin' is given da South a bad name wit' dere drunken, heathen ways. She say dat mos' a dem ain't nothin' but pure 'D' scoundrels and failed farmers, lower than any niggra slavehand she ebba come across. And though m'head be down and m'eyes be focused on m'feet when she go off on one a her mad spells likedat I be grinnin' on da inside and be sayin' 'Yes Lawdy! You sho' is right missy. Nothin' but lowdown heathen scoundrels... all of 'em.' Tickles me da way she

210

lose her mind ev'ry time dey stop us. She tell 'em dat dey make dey livin' by bringin' hardship ta othas less fortunate but it puzzles me dat she cain't see dat both men she loved is da whole reason dese here slavcatchas got a job atall. Guess love makes ya blind 'cause it don't appear she see dat at all and from m'point a view john Marshall done brought mo' hardship on mo' people than a slava could ebba brang.

And all a da time Missy Reynolds be sayin' dese here thangs Aunt Hattie scairt dat one a those slavecatchas gonna f'git his manners and take offense and do somethin' bad ta missy and when she gone dey gonna sell us right on down da riva wit'out so much as a second thought. And I think she done growed attached ta missy in a way dat she really don't wanna seed nothin' bad happen ta her. She won't say but I think dat means as much ta her as missy jes bein' are key ta freedom.

Ya see even though Aunt Hattie like da res' a us say dat missy is quite mad, da truth is in my opinion dat she got mo' sense than mos' any white folk I's ebba knowed. I jes b'lieves dat she been hu't so much in her short time on dis here earth dat her brain done made a decision ta see only what it choose ta see and block out ev'rythang else dat might prove hurtful. But now thanks ta us and bein' away from her crazy husband and Mas'r John who she really and truly love and who don't give two cents about her ya can jes see her pullin' out of it a lil bit and her heart startin' ta heal just a bit.

211

I do b'lieve dis ta be da case. Jes da fact dat she don't nebba ebba mention da fact dat she married ta da meanest, cruelest man ebba ta walk da face a da earth. She don't nebba mention his name. Not once durin' are journey has I heard her mention his name and we been travelin' fo' what seem like forevea. No, dat's jes somethin' she ain't care ta remember, I recollect. But when one a us bring up Mas'r John's name—well lo and behold—she get ta carryin' on like da Jubilee Sistas on a Sunday mo'nin'. Her eyes gits ta sparklin' and glistenin' like it be da Second Coming or somethin'. Then all she wanna know is why Young Saul cain't push dis here buggy no fasta ta gits where we gots ta go. By da same token she don't nebba mention da fact dat she an Mas'r Reynolds is still married. She don't even entertain da idea. Dat's why we know she's quite mad. Ya see she be livin' in a fairy tale world she done concocted on her own where da only thangs dat exist are what she won't ta exist. She don't even ast da plain and simple like why ain't none a Mas'r Reynolds's slaves accompany her on dis journey. Simple lil thangs like dat dat a sane person would wonda about. And dat's why Aunt Hattie tell me dat missy done los' her mind 'cause even though she go in an out fo' da mos' part da woman ain't in touch wit' reality.

I tell Auntie Hattie dat ifffen losin' a man is all it take ta lose her mind she would have nebba made it as a niggra much hell as we goes through. Auntie Hattie jes say we built diff'rent. We stronger 'cause we from betta stock. I don't know iffen alla dat's true but I's sho' I ain't gonna lose m'mind ova losin' no man. And dat I do know. And like I sayed befo' iffen a niggra can keep his mind and not lose it wit' all he gotta go through ev'ryday den it's jes hard fo' me ta b'lieve dat white folks wit' all dey got cain't hol' on ta dey minds. Heck, and iffen dey losin' dey minds I's s'prised dey ain't got no niggras hol'in' on to 'em fo' 'em jes fo' safe measure.

I thinkt about what Aunt Hattie sayed 'bout missy though an I's jes cain't b'lieve dat dere's anything truly wrong wit' her otha than she jes useta havin' ev'rything done fo' her. She so useta hain' ev'rythang done fo' her. She useta havin' her clothes laid out and her hair did. She useta havin' her trips planned and her thinkin' done fo' her so won't nothin' diff'rent in da way she appeared ta me and prob'bly won't no diff'rent in da way thangs appeared ta her.

Onliest thang dat really appeared odd ta me is da way missy acted when around dem slavecatchas. Ya see, whetha white folk wanna admit it or not dere ain't but one king in all da land and dat was da mas'r. Now iffen ya don't b'lieve dat all ya gots ta do jes take a ride up inta mountains a Tennessee and I reckon you can find out from dat lil, skinny, pinched-face heifer Mas'r John useta be married to if ya wanna know who runs thangs. And Missy Reynolds jes shoulda knowed afta residin' wit' da devil hisself. But it's almost like we freed her 'stead a her

213

helpin' ta free us. It's almost like a weight been lifted off dat po' woman's head and in a way I guess it has.

Da way I sees it, missy in a 'bout da same boat as us niggras when it come down ta da way she s'pozed ta act when mas'rs gentlemen friends be around. Missy had ta be all prim and proper like she was at a cotillion ev'rytime menfolks was around like she was alla da time tryna sell herself off wit' alla da firtin' and what not jest ta hold dem otha gentlemens attentions. She was s'pozed ta act like she wanted alla dem ta bed down wit' her even though she only loved her man but still dat's da way she hadda act. Amost like she was a prize bull or somethin' at da county fair. Dat's what mas'r called genteel. And jes like us she won't allowed ta have no opinion or say much a nothin' iffen it wasn't cute or what's da word…I b'lieves white folks call it witty. Anyways, even though she mighta had somethin' ta say she won't allowed to say nothin' or do nothin' but look purty. Dat's why Missy Marshall back in Tennessee now and Missy Reynold's done los' her mind. Well, Mas'r John's wife shoulda knowed neva ta speak 'cause she ain't had much goin' in da way a looks eitha. She was jes too blame ugly and too blame ornery ta same somethin' cute.

Aunt Hattie say dat's da way southern men set it up wit' dem bein' in charge. She telled me dat da only power da women had

214

was in da bedroom and she best be good in dere cause iffen she wasn't no good in da bedroom then she ain't had no power atall. Well, I's speculatin' but I guess dat when somebody like missy do git fed up wit' all da genteel and git loose a dere own shackles once and fo' all, then chances are she ain't nebba gonna let nobody treat her like dat ag'in in life. And not only dat, missy was comin' from one a dem New England families that ain't much approved a slavery and I's don't think she took a likin' ta it eitha. Matta a fact da way she talk ta dem slavecatchas I knowed she hated it. Have her tell it she always had a hard time wit' da idea a one man makin' anotha man a slave.

Well she ain't had ta say no mo'. Dat's all Aunt Hattie had ta hear. She and Aunt Hattie become da best a friends afta dat. Although she nebba would say she agree wit' missy, Aunt Hattie agreed wit' ev'rythang da woman sayed. Slavecatcha, ovaseer—to Aunt Hattie dey was all da same but she could'nt unnastand how missy could leave out da slavemasta who was da beginnin' and da end a da whole thang. And like I sayed, she nebba mentioned it or anything else about da whole slavery affair but I knowed it was on her mind. Still, like I sayed she and Aunt Hattie become da best a friends—well—at least when she was appearin' ta be in her right mind. And it was during dese times dat Aunt Hattie tried to 'splain ta missy dat she couldn' jes go off spoutin' off what she feel 'cause she ain't only gonna git herself killt but us as well 'specially durin' dese times when ev'rybody was so tense and angry 'bout da war b'tween da states.

Aunt Hattie tried to tell her that anybody sayin anything about da South or slavery be lookt at like dey was eitha a traitor or an abolitionist. And dem southern boys ain't had no conscience 'bout gittin' rid a those raisin' up against dere 'cause and takin us slaves as booty.

But Missy Reynolds sayed dat's what was wrong wit' dis country now. She sayed it took us way too long to stand up and fight back and sooner or later somebody gotta take a stand against dis here evil but Lord knows she ain't big as a firefly and she talkin' 'bout standin' up to dese mens whats gots rifles and shotguns.

Well Aunit Hattie and me gits ta laughin' and all 'cause fo'da first time we heard white folks sayin' jes what it is we been feelin' alla dis time. Aunt Hattie sayed it jes da laudanum makin' her true feelin's come out.

Young Saul, who don't hardly nebba say nothin; sayed dat a whole lotta folks in da land ta da north feel da same way dat dis here white woman feel and is dyin' ta prove it but me—well—I's ain't 'bout dyin' tryin' to prove nothin' and I's gittin' like Aunt Hattie, right through here and wish missy would tone it down jes a might fo' she draw too much attention and git us all strung up from some tree.

I b'lieve Young Saul mus' agree wit' us 'cause he done become a first-rate top-notch driver ova da last few weeks. He say all he

216

truly int'rested in is puttin' as much distance as he can between him and da Marshall Plantation. He say da mo' miles we travel and da mo' days we be gone da less chance a us gittin' caught long as we can keep missy from 'causin' too much commotion.

Young Saul, done become jes like a son ta me or least ways he act like da way I want mine own son to act. Ain't nothin' he won't do fer me and iffen it even look like I's gonna do somethin' in da form a labor he done beat me ta it gonna do somethin' in da form a labor he done beat me ta it everytime. Say it's his job ta take care a me and da baby. When we first started out I's afraid he was afta mo' than jes bein' helpful since he happened along an seed me naked when I goes ta freshen up down at dis spring awhile back when we first started out and he seent me completely naked but he ain't nebba mentioned it or said nothin' about it. And den I's noticed dat he afforded Aunt Hattie da same respect he give me.

Aunt Hattie say dat honor and respect is big wit' da Afreecans and he'll always remember da one who saved his life plus he a lot older than his years. But whateva it was I jes thanks da Lawd he here fo' us now. Sometimes though I's sees him peekin' out da coner a his eye and I's gots ta admit dat fo' da life a me I cain't figger out what be goin' on in dat Afreecan's head.but all he did is look away wit'out so much as utterin' a word. But like I say, dat dere Saul is a good boy and I would jes feel terrible iffen somethin' would happen ta him on account a

217

me takin' him away. He so very good ta us dat I don't know what we'd do wit'out him. He won't allow me or Aunt Hattie do no manual labor and do all da heavy liftin', takes care a da hosses and all da repairs on da carriage hisself. He what white folks calls an asset. And I don't think we would have made it dis far wit'out him. Funny thing 'bout him though is dat as mindful as he is ta me an Aunt Hattie; he won't lift a hand tell he'p missy in any way. Not a hand... And he won't do a dat blame thang missy ast him ta do. He jes openly defiant and when I tells him he need to so's and dat we's a team and she a impotent part a da team and us makin' it depends on us workin' fo and wit' each otha he say unnerstan' and den go right on ignorin' her.

Well, we's pullin' inta what 'ppears to be a right sized little town wit' a good many folks so I's best put dis away for now. I don't know when I's gonna git da next chance ta correspond but I's prayin' it will be soon.

May 11

Glory be!! Seed our first blue coats today an Lawd knows dey was a sight ta see. I swears dey was da sorriest lookin'bunch a rag-tag, stragglers and hobos pretendin' ta be a army dat I's ebba layed eyes on. I's was so disappointed afta all da talk a Union soldiers bein' ten foot tall in shiny blue uniforms comin' ta are rescue and den ta see dis rag-tag crew a misfits. Lawdy! Lawdy! Lawdy! I telled Auntie

Hattie and Saul dat iffen dis is what dey sent ta free us then we in one sorry predicament alright. Aunt Hattie jes laugh. She reminds me dat we jes useta seein' those southern boys and truth be told dey lookin' worse fo' da wear as well. Aunt Hattie say she don't care how none a dem look she p'suing her own freedom and ain't d'pendin' on nobody freein' her. All in all, it don't look like dere gonna be no winna in dis here war.

May 12

Anotha' bunch a soldiers come by taday wit' da Union Army and dey seemt ta fare a might betta den those boys we seent yesterday.

Big ol' white man sittin' way up high on da biggest durn hoss I ebba did see tipped his hat ta me—a niggra wench and I swears I felt somethin' go through me dat made me tingle all ova. Aunt Hattie sayed she ain't feel nothin' but it might jes be da tingle a freedom or maybe it was m'body tellin' me it was time fo some good lovin'. She say da body don't know da diff'rence in southerners, northerners, black foks and whites. Say da onliest thang a body know is when it's time fo' some good love. But as I loves m'Joseph I don't b'lieve it's quite as simple as dat.

It was mo' ta do wit how he jes a sittin' up dere lookin' so fine in dat blue uniform wit' all dem shiny gold buttoms jes a gleamin' in

219

da aftanoon sunlight. I's thinkin' dat he must be da general a al da Union Armies and den I heared someone say he General Franklin while someone else say he General Sherman. I don't know and don't really care but what I do knows is dat he coulda been da president of dese whole United States da way he sat up dere on top of dat brown and white speckled stallion. I ain't feel half bad 'bout are chances then. Anyways, we was forced off da road by da army who was at da quick step and wasn't 'bout ta make no 'llowances for three niggras and some ol' crazy white woman. What su'prized me most though was dat at da end a da army procession was two or three hunnerd niggras followin' close behind. Aunt Hattie suggested we follow da procession 'stead a pushin' on and windin' up in some lil village or town what might not be to hospitable afta bein' ravaged by da boys in blue. But whilst Aunt Hattie and Saul proceeded ta make camp I moved back up outta da gully and stood dere by da edge a da road and jes watched da soldiers march on and lissened ta da local niggras dat was joinin' da march cheer dem bluecoats on. I watched and watched and when dat drummer and dat bugler finally come up da road dat chile a mine liked ta jump right outta my stomach. I don't rightly know how long I stayed dere watchin' but it was long afta dark and dere was still anotha comin' ta join da two I had jes seen. Anyway like I sayed befo' it was long afta dark fo' I got back ta camp and then it took me mo' n' anotha hour befo' I could find Aunt Hattie, Saul and missy so many niggras and soldiers was dere. Some

220

say dere was fifty thousand soldiers alone and had ta be a couple thousand niggtas in attendance as well. I don't know but there was sho' nuff enuff folks dere ta let me know dat freedom was are's fo' sho'. By da time I did find 'em ev'yone one was bedded down and settled in good

Young Saul had already fed and rubbed down da hosses and was 'bout to join Aunt Hattie and missy when he saw me approachin'. He run up ta me like he ain't seed me in a month a Sundays. At fi'st I thought somethin' was wrong but when I seed his face I knowed dat he had finally achieved all dat he'd wanted since bein' brought ta da Marshall Plantation. Fo' da fi'st time in years he was finally free ag'in. And I swears dat in all da time I's knowed dat boy I ain't nebba seed him as happy as I did right den and dere.

"Miss Mary, Miss Mary! Da soldiers says we is free jes as long as we is wit' dem. Dat's what da army man telled Aunt Hattie and da rest a da niggras and her say it be true. Can ya b'lieve it Miss Mary? We's free! We is truly free! Then jes like dat he went skippin' away jes a hoopin' and hollerin' 'bout how he goin' home, home ta Afrika and all like dat. And though I feeled real good 'bout da news it come ta me right den and dere dat I had no home ta go to. I knowed nothin' but da Marshall Plantation and iffen I's couldn't find m'Joseph I ain't had nowhere ta go. I went ta find Aunt Hattie and watcht as niggras ev'rywhere celebrated da news. It didn't mean da war was ova or dat iffen you was anywhere away from da Union Army dat you was free. It

221

just meant that if you were wit' da army you'd be protected. Now iffen dey happen ta lose da battle and da C'federates captured a niggra you can best b'live it was gonna go far harder on a niggra than it woulda a Union soldier but for right now dis lil bit a freedom dey was administerin' was far more than any a us had ever knowed so niggras was jubilant and gonna make sho' dey could do ev'rythang dey could do ta help da war effort and help demselves as well.

Onliest thang I's didn't unnerstand was why President Lincoln ain't won't niggras ta fight. If anybody woulda fought hard ta stop slavery it woulda been us. We would have been on da front line da minute he gave da word and nobody woulda fought harder ta end slavery than a niggra who had been out in dem Georgia fields in July jes so dey wouldn't had ta go back ta dem fields.

Alla dese here thangs puzzled me. Here I was fo' da fi'st time eba in m'life able ta sit and relax wit'out havin' ta wonda when Mas'r John or Ol'Sam da ovseer was gonna swoop down and decide dey wonted me fo' dere pleasure dat p'ticular night. Dis was da fi't time I's didn't have ta whispa and watch what I had ta say or if mas'r or missy was in da next room or comin' round da corna. I's didn't have ta be stringed up ta no tree ta let da otha niggras dat I wasn't nothin' special and could be whipped jes as easy as they could jes so mas'r could make an example a me his prize niggra. I's ain't had ta worry 'bout none a dat now but here I was not five minutes afta dey tell me I's freer than I's eva was worryin' about why iffen we was free why we couldn't fight for own freedom and why I's didn't feel all dat jubilation like ev'rybody else when I heared 'bout m'freedom. Seemt ta me when da North sayed we couldn't fight but could use us fo' ev'rythang else includin' takin' care a da hosses and takin' care a da wounded and diggin' ditches I's jes figgered we was tradin' in one mas'r for a new one. Dat's what I figgered and won't no need fo' niggas ta be gittin' all jubilant and happy until ev'rythang played out once and for all.

Talkin' ta Aunt Hattie and missy put ev'rthang I's was thinkin' in propa perspective in a hurry. Of course iffen anybody could set thangs straigt it was Aunt Hattie but on dis day it won't Aunt Hattie who let me know what time it was. It was missy who telled us all right directly dat couldn't no Union Army emancipate no niggras and den tell 'em dey was only emancipated when we was in dey company.

"Dat ain't no goddamn emancipation," she screamed. "And y'all niggas responsible fo' gittin' me ta Natchez fo' me ta be wed. And as long as y'all niggas is bought and paid fo' by Mas'r John Marshall of Savannah, Georgia den dat's exactly what y'all niggas is gonna do. And iffen y'all think dat jes 'cause some goddamn Yankee soldiers done showed up ya ain't goin' to why I'll have all da black stripped off a alla y'all. Yankee soldiers don't mean a goddamn thang ta me and you don't carry out yo' orders I promise all three a ya niggas dat I'll have ya whipped da same way da South gonna whip da No'th."

223

Aunt Hattie who had taken dis woman inta her confidence and made a friend had let us all know what was really on her mind. I lookt at Aunt Hattie and she retu'ned my look but sayed nothin'. She didn't have ta. I jes dropped m'head. Dis was da second time I had ta wonda iffen Aunt Hattie and da Afreecans hadn't ta been right all along. Dis here white woman who professed ta bein' a Northern Christian, an a Quaker an hatin' slavery and da cruel treatment associated wit' slavery stood fo' was soundin' mo' and mo' like her slaveholder husband by da minute. And I's really wodered iffen those slaves dat had run North had run all da way up dere jest a run inta da sme thang dey had here. I's couldn't sees no diff'rence and da way some a dem Union soldiers treated us coloreds made me wonda iffen I wouldn't had been betta off stayin' right dere unda Mas'r John's watch.

Maybe m'Joseph and Aunt Hattie had been right all along. No, dey wasn't no Christians and neitha was dey civilized even though they seemt ta unnerstan' da ways a civilized Christians dey won't no betta than me.

Lata dat evenin', Saul made a small fire and we roasted two small pheasants he brought in and Aunt Hattie seasoned it ta p'fection and informed Saul a missy's conversation wit' us and da Union officer. Neitha seemt overly concerned wit' her remarks but I's could tell dey was wonderin' what affect it had on me so 'stead a keepin' 'em guessin' and since dey was da closest thang I had ta family I figgered dey deserved ta know straight off. So, I telled 'em dat no maybe I ain't expect missy ta come out wit' nothin' like dat 'specially afta I's been cleanin' her butt fo' damn near two months now and maybe dey right about white folk jes bein' evil ta da core but dat ain't gots nothin' ta do wit' where we be now. And all I promised 'em was safe passage and since dey was safe now and dey had da army ta protect 'em den dey could purty much do as dey pleased and go dey separate ways in so much as dey had an inkling to do. Dat's what dey could do. Dey was free and didn't need me no mo'. Da Union Army promise 'em safe passage and declared 'em free and me—well—I couldn't do neitha. And I tol' 'em so.

May 14

Well, dere's one good thang ta say 'bout freedom if dis is freedom and dat's da fact dat I's can feel free ta write when I wants and ain't got ta hide or git up in da wee hours in da mornin' ta scribble somethin' down by candlelight. But I's still made a mistake by bein' so open about it. Now I's got lines from mo'nin' til night wit' folks, white folks and niggras, soldiers and slaves, lined up ta eitha right a letta or read a letta from dey loved ones and families at home. Aunt Hattie s'ggested I charge 'em a small fee and nobody yet done complained and we buildin' quite a lil nest egg fo' da next part a are journey.

May 15

I knowed Aunt Hattie was hopin dat when da Yankees sayed we was free I would give up dat ol' crazy idea about headin' ta Natchez ta find m'Joseph and go wit' da Yankees instead. But a baby needs a father and dem few times I spent with Joseph only let's me know dat I really and truly needs a man.

No ma'm I sayed ta her followin' da Union is fine fo' y'all and I unnerstand it's safer than travelin' alone or wit' dis here crazy white woman but I's determined ta find m'man and da fatha a dis here chile and start a family. Now I knowed deys tired—'specially Aunt Hattie—but I don't wont ta git to useta havin' all dis so-called new found freedom 'cause I jes know dat I won't go iffen I git accustomed ta all dis doin' as I pleases. One thang's fo sho though, we all is exhausted—well—'ceptin' fo' missy who ain't been doin' nothin' but sittin' on her hind parts takin' it all in and waitin' fo' us ta fetch her dis and dat and chatterin' away 'bout what kind of gown she gonna git when she git ta Natchez and whetha or not it would be appropriate iffen she wo'e white considerin'.

By now I come ta da point dat I knowed dat ev'rythang she sayed was jes like Aunt Hattie sayed. Won't nothin' but a lotta mumbo jumbo hogwash dat don't mount ta a hill a beans so I jes waited fo' her ta go ta bed 'til I got down ta any serious discussion 'bout are plans fo' da future. I knowed both Aunt Hattie and Saul was tired a runnin' and bad as it was in camp wit' da soldiers and alla time a lack a water or food or somethin' it was betta and safa than bein' out dere on our own. Say da war done made it so tough on ev'rybody white folks was robbin' white folks and niggras was bein' hung up by da bushels and robbed fo' da lil dey had as well but I's still ready to move on. We been on da road two full months almost all day ev'ryday and iffen it wont hard on Young Saul drivin' dem hosses I knowed it was doubly hard on Aunt Hattie at her age and wit' da added extra bu'den of havin' ta take care a missy who had gone back ta soilin' her clothes 'cause she was too lazy to git up. I knowed it was hard. I knowed 'cause it was hard on me and I's half Aunt Hattie's age. Anyways, I completely unnerstands 'em wantin' ta stay put and not worry 'bout da slavas or who Mas'John and Mas'r Reynolds got followin' us.

I unnerstan' alla dis and tol' 'em I did. Dat's why dere was so much in da way a happiness among da niggras gathered dere in da Union camp. No mo' did dey have ta worry. Aunt Hattie say it was 'cause dey finally had a taste a freedom and was finally findin' out how sweet it could be but us niggras bo'n to da slavemas'rs' whip ain't nebba had a clue a what it meant ta be free and dat's why dey da one's sittin' 'round here lookin' like dey lost. Dey ain't nebba knowed freedom and ta dem it's jes a word and don't mean hardly nothin'.

Young Saul—well—he won't grinnin' or smilin' afta I let him know my decision and when I's was finished he jes git up and walk away and started makin' his bed roll. It's kind harda tryna figger dat

227

boy's mind and I ain't try. I do know dat tonight was p'ticularly hard on alla us despite me an auntie tryna keep up appearances. We hugged fo' along time and I tol' her how much I loved her befo' makin' my pallet next ta missy's and lyin' down ta go ta sleep fo' da night.

First thang in the mo'nin' I got up alil sorrowful. I planned on leavin' da big charcoal gray bay wit' Saul so Aunt Hattie wouldn't have ta walk or ride on da back of one a dem Union buckboards but could'nt find him nowhere.

I thought back ta last night and it really and truly su'prised me dat Aunt Hattie ain't shed not nary a tear when I tol' her I's be pushin' on in da mo'nin'. Afta all dese years tagetha she ain't uttered a word about m'decision. And all I could thank was dat dem Afreecans sho gots some mighty p'culiar ways when it come to love. I don't know. Guess I's jes mo sentimental 'cause I's in a family way. I don't know but I sho' dropped a bucket full a tears jes thinkin' 'bout leavin' Saul an Aunt Hattie. It got so bad dat I figgered I's jes stay anotha day since dis might be da last time I might see eitha a dem dis lifetime.

Missy won't too happy though when I tol' her da change a plans and kept screamin' bout me makin' her John wait and how she was gonna have ta have me beat and hung out ta dry for bein' an insolent, arrogant, nigga who thinkin' she free now and jes as good as white folks. I had ta laugh when she sayed dat. It reminded me a da same thang Mas'r John had tol' me some time ago right before he beat me and it made me wonda if white folks was any diff'rent in da North than dey was in da South.

May 16

Saul waked me up at somewhere's around five in da mo'nin' and him an Aunt Hattie is already up. Da camp seem like it done doubled since I close my eyes a fortnight ago. Niggras from ev'rywhere is comin' in since dey hears dat da bluecoats is dolin' out protection and safe passage ta freedom. And mo' thana few is astin' ta sign up and fight and I must say I's right proud a dem boys fo' da courage dey been showin'. Jes wishes I could lend a hand and help out in someway but wit da war and folks movin' dis way and dat I's scaret dat iffen I's don't find m'Joseph soon I may jes lose him forever.

Aunt Hattie was good enough ta git missy dressed and load her inta da carriage fo' me but when I turnt ta give her and Saul a final farewell hug Saul turnt ta me and sayed, "We already an hour behind are normal schedule, Miss Mary. I b'lieve we need ta git a move on iffen we gonna make any kinda time taday."

Much as I couldn't b'lieve it my young Afreecan friend who so valued his freedom above all else in dis here world was ready to risk both his life and his freedom fo' me. Cain't tell you how dat boy made me feel right den but I's could feel da tears runnin' down m'cheeks as he stood dere jes a grinning' dat big ol' pearly white grin a his dat shone so brightly ag'inst his coal black face. Aunt Hattie turnt and lookt at me cryin' ag'in and shrugged it off while mentionin' somethin' 'bout m'baby havin' m'hormones all outta whack. And iffen it hadn't been fo' missy staggerin' all drunk-like, hair all matted down, and stuck ta da co'ners of her mouth yellin' fo' us ta git a move on and how Mas'r John don't like ta be kept waitin' and how she had a weddin' ta attend and such I's probably woulda been still standin' dere boo-hooin'.

"Y'all done already wasted a day here wit' yo' nigga family reunion. So's now dat y'all done had yo fun at my expense can we please git back ta da matta at hand. I's been too kind ta ya niggas as it is. Mr. Reynolds was sho' tellin' da truth when it comes ta y'all. Y'all ain't nothin' but some shiftless, lazy-ass heathens. Y'all don't respect nothin' but a swift kick and a whip iffen ya ast me. Now let's git a move on befo' I f'gits m'New England upbringin' and has all yo asses flogged for bein' belligerent. C'mon ol' woman and help me up and tell dat fool boy ta make haste and tellhim not to be no fool and run us into a gulley. Iffen he ain't noticed tell him Mary's wit' chile.

Well, now enough was enough and I's had ta do ev'rythang possible ta hold on ta m'Christianity at dat very moment. Dis woman who I done bathed and cleaned when she couldn't hardly pee offa herself good was callin' me a shiftless nigga who needs ta be whipped. Lawd please help me. Dis here woman who sometimes would be covered in her own feces and nebba even considered wiping herself.

230

Dis same woman who one day would be lucid and come ta da defense of us in front a da white slavas and championed our liberty then when tol' of our upcomin' emancipation reverted back to somethin' or someone I would have nebba imagined her bein'. By now, I was tired a her ol' crazy antics and moved ta take her right den and dere and put her ova m'knee and spank her ta she hushed dat crazy hollerin' but Aunt Hattie jumped b'tween us. Missy musta knowed what I had on m'mind 'cause somehow she managed ta jump clear a me and git up in dat carriage wit' no help whatsoeva. Aunt Hattie keept tellin' me ta be still but I done had enough and tried ta fight through her and Young Saul ta git me a pinch a dat wenches behind'. Dat's all I needed jest a git m'hands on her lil scrawny ass one time but Saul and Aunt Hattie were too much together and afta awhile a Aunt Hattie whisperin' 'bout me harmin' m'baby and tellin' me dat it was jes da laudanum talkin' I relaxed a bit but when I lookt up and seed dat heifer's face I went right back ta tryna git m'hands round her neck but Saul caught me jes in da nick a time or I woulda squeezed all dat sass and hatefulness right outta her.

"Look chile, I wantcha ta calm yo'self down right dis instant. Dat crazy white woman is yo' meal ticket so jes let her be. "Sides whatcha doin' ain't hardly da Christian thang ta do. "Sides she don't hardly know what she be sayin' and iffen she do it's da Lawd's job ta pass judgement not yo's. And rememba dat da Lawd said you reap what you sow so iffen she bein' ugly he will take care of it."

Now Aunt Hattie knowed me as well as anybody and I guess she figgered won't nobody gonna see no freedom on dis here earth iffen she left dat woman alone wit' me so she packed up her few belongin's and climbed up inta da carriage next ta missy and tol' Saul ta come on.

I gotta admit dat I's eternally grateful ta have m'family back in da fold and taday's journey been mighty won'erful so far even though Aunt Hattie keep sayin' dat da onliest reason she come is 'cause she ain't wanna see me go ta jail or hangin' from some tree on account a some crazy white woman. But I ain't one ta let 'em off dat easy so as soon as we gits up da road a fair piece and missy done settled in fo' her aftanoon nap I ast 'em. I says, "You Afreecans sho is some p'culiar people alright. Always talkin' 'bout freedom, freedom, freedom—like it's da best thang on God's green earth. Long as I's known you dat's all Iheared about. Cain't wait 'til I's be free or let freedom ring. Well back dere wit' da Union Army I heared da bell toll fo' freedom. I jes don't unnerstan'. Y'all laughed at me and says I don't unnerstan' 'cause I ain't Afreecan and ain't nebba had a taste a what it's like ta be free. Me— well—y'all know I's jes a dumb niggra not nearly half as smart as y'all Afreecans but when y'all gits da chance ta be free here y'all are followin' behind dis here dumb niggra back inta da jaws a da lion. And bein' dat I's ain't nearly as bright as y'all could eitha a y'all tell me why ya willing ta give up all dat beautiful freedom you always goin' on about?

232

I's jes cain't unnerstan' it. Dis here one done risked his life and come wit'in a hair a bein' strung up by Mas'r John an iffen I ain't come ta his rescue he wouldn't been no mo' than anotha piece a strange fruit danglin' from a tree dat don't bear fruit and yet when he git a chance ta be free here he is here wit'me. And for as long as I can rememba you's been sangin' and prayin' fo' freedom Aunt Hattie and here you is one day afta da Union done declared you free sittin' here wit' me. Please jes he'p me ta unnerstan. Must be you like stayin' one step ahead a da night ridas and patrollas and takin' orders from white folks like missy who don't hardly know where she is mos' a da time but can still recollect how ta say fetch me dis and fetch me dat nigga or fetch me a bucket fo' me ta piss in and den hol' it steady whilst I commece ta piss. Well I knows I's jes ain't dat bright bein jes a niggra an not no Afreecan but it sho' do puzzle me how y'all Afreecans wo got all da knowledge a da world and who invented civilization and built da Pyramids is followin' 'roound behind a pregnant niggra wench and a half-crazy white woman to who knows where when freedom's right dere at yo' fingertips. Yassuh, y'all intelligent Afreecans sho' do puzzle dis dumb ol' niggra gal I'll say dat fo' y'all."

I was teasin' 'em and really and truly glad fo' dere company but somethin' must have hit home 'cause both of 'em jes sit dere all grim-faced and tight-lipped and da way Saul come ta whippin' dem hosses inta a frenzy I's at once sorry I's sayed anything atall.

Wasn't 'til sometime lata dat evenin' when we'd made camp and was sittin' 'round a small fire dat Saul confessed dat da onliest reason he'd come along was 'cause he knowed I couldn't control dem ol' wil' hosses up fron't and dat ol' wil' heifer in da back at da same time. And no sooner had Saul sayed dat den Aunt Hattie chimed in sayin' how she won't worried 'bout eitha one a us crazy heifers she jes worried 'bout any harm comin'ta her baby.

I's was da one smilin' now 'cause I knowed why dey coma along now, no matta what dey say.

May 17

Ev'ry where we goes I sees niggras movin to and fro' oftentimes dey on dey own, carryin' all dey b'longins dey own. Mos' of 'em look plenty bad. Dere clothes ain't nothin' but rags tied tagetha ta hide their private parts and don't cova much else. Hardly any of 'em got shoes and mos' a da time dere be as many as nine or ten in a group pullin' a wagonful a lil ones and when dey see us dey jes gits ta jumpin' and squealin' like monkeys shoutin' dat dey's free. Ain't none of 'em goin' da direction we's goin'. All of 'em is headed North ta da land a milk and honey. Mos' a dem look like dey on dere last leg and I don't know how many times dey come up ta us beggin' fo' scraps. Aunt Hattie tries ta feed 'em all and I b'lieve iffen she ain't feed 'em dey'd all starve ta death but dey so happy jest ta have da yoke taken from 'round dere neck dat I don't reckon dey knowed dey was starvin'. Dey jes so happy dey free dat I truly hopes dis here freedom don't turn out to be a letdown and dat dey finds what it is dey is lookin' fo'. I swears I do.

Ain't much else happen on da road taday. Somebody sayed dat no news is good news afta some a da sites I's done seed so far. But anyways Aunt Hattie had missy ast some white folks how far we was from Natchez taday and from what dey tell us we ain't no mo' a week's ride which means at da rate we be travelin' Saul should have us dere in no mo' n' fo' or fi'e days which is a good thang 'cause dis here baby seem like he ready to jump outta me at anytime.

May 18

I's truly thought taday was gonna be da day. No matta what I did or tried ta do I couldn't git comfortable. No matta how I sit dat chile insisted on pressin' on m'bladder and along wit' all dat shakin' and rattlin' it got ta be a bit much. And wit' da weather borderin' on ninety degrees I 's was in pure agony. Made Saul pull ova six or seven times but Saul ain't nebba one ta complain and missy been quiet ebba since I tried ta choke da life outta her.

Aunt Hattie pushed missy up in a corner a da carriage and made me a bed so's I be mo' comfortable and administered missy and extra dose a laudanum ta keep her from sayin' anything so's I could sleep and dentook m'place up front wit' Saul but Aunt Hattie knows I's

235

strong and I's don't think she was was so much worried 'bout me restin' as she was concerned 'bout gittin' away from dat crazy white woman.

Lawd knows I's didn't want ta b'lieve autie when we fi'st set out but I's thoroughly convinced dat dis here chile is crazier than any a us would have ebba imagined settin' out. One minute she be strain' out da side window a da carriage lookin' at da po slaves passin' and she git ta cryin' and cussin up a storm 'bout how terrible and wrong it is in da Lawd's eyes fo'one man ta treat his brotha so wrong and den bust out in enough tears ta flood all da plains a Georgia and Mississippi together. Den a few minutes later a few stragglers from da Confederate come a limpin' downda road all hu't and wounded lookin' every bit as bad as dem po' niggras in dem rags she went on about and da next thing ya know dis fool done jumped clear up in da carriage hangin' her head and callin' us all dirty black bastards fer startin' dis war and bringin' all dis pain and heartache ta good decent white folk. Dat in turn would almost always be followed up by a scripture from da Good Book and usually revelations telling us how da world was comin' ta an end and da niggas what caused it would sho'lly bu'n in hell.

Dat's when I telled auntie dat I b'lieve I's had quite enough rest and she could have her mos' comf'table seat back and resume her discussion wit' her friend.

May 18th

236

We seed both Union and Confederate troops today and I know one thing fo sho now afta seein' um. Ain't no winners in war.

May 19th

Well, we is runnin' outta laudanum wit' all da fightin' and da killing and wounded soliders don't seem like our chances a getting' any is all too good. Stopped in a small town and was sent cross da tracks ta da Chinese part a town. Lord knows white folks treats dem worser than niggras. And though none a us speaks no Chinese Aunt Hattie managed to purchase somethin' called opium dat you s'poze ta mix wit tea. Well, auntie jes like da lil Chinaman tell her too and gave it to dis crazy heifer ta make her sleep but it had jes da opposite effect and she got ta screamin' so loud and causin' such a ruckus as we was leaving through town that I thought fo' sho dey was gonna lynch all us includin' her fer makin' all dat racket.

May 20nd

Missy Charlene see the Yankees marchin' with dere chin up- - all proud - - even if d'feat den she see da niggras fallin' in behin' em grinn' and laughin' - - ya know - - da way niggras do if ya ever been 'round niggras before. But when she see da Yankees wit' dat little extra pep in dey step - - she knows jes like da rest of us knows dat da Confederacy, (dat's what dey call da southern troops). Well, like I sayed

237

when she sees dem blue coats wit' dat lil' extra pep in dey step and a smile in dere face den she know, jes like da rest of us dat it's only a matta a time fo'ure gonna sees da Confederacy come stragglin' along all beat up and broken down beggin' fer somethin' ta eat and lookin' right pitiful dat it's only a matta a time befo' dey gots ta throw in da towel and admit dat deys been defeated.

When missy see 'em like dat she git all misty eyed like she know in her heart dat it's jes a matta a time fo' she ain't gonna be able ta tell niggra's ta do her biddin' fer her no more.

May 21st

Da war ain't jes makin' it hard on da white folk down south. It makin' it hard on ev'rybody us niggra's included. Everybody walkin' 'round hungry and da Union Army what's s'pozed to be freein' slaves and helpin' dem start a new life where dey's free ain't doin' nothin' but makin' it harder on 'em if ya ast me. Ev'rytime we passes a farm or a plantation where da Yankees been dey done took alla da livestock and what dey can carry of da crops fo' dey army which I s'poze is okay but den dey burns what's left so nobody else ken eat and ta me dis is terribly wrong. Dere be women's and children's on dem plantations, not ta mentions all da niggra slaves dey say dey tryin' to save from da slavery.

Well, iffen ya ast me I b'lieves dey is betta off wit' da slavery and bein' able ta eat than bein' free and starvin' ta but Aunt Hattie, she say dere gotta be a storm befo' da waters calm. She say

238

dat's jes how war's conducted but I's startin' to wonda iffen dere ain't a betta way but den ag'in who is we to question da ways a white folks.

Afta all dey is da one's dat saved me from dis sinful world and a life in da brothels a New Orleans and rescued auntie and millions of heat hen Afreecans from da pagan religions dat runs through da jungles a Afreecan ta have a betta life in dis here land a civilized livin' and Christianity. Guess auntie right again but somethin' sho' feel wrong wit' all dis death and starvation ev'rywhere ya turn ta look.

May 22nd

Well, me and Aunt Hattie been talkin' mo' and mo' ta Missy Reynolds ev'ryday. Her mood changes wit' da weather and I know her jes 'bout ta drive Aunt Hattie crazy wit' all her gripin' and mumblin' and all.

Sometimes, I jes sit up front wit' Saul and me grin and laugh at her ramblin's which covers ev'rything from abolition ta slavery and all da men dat useta come a callin' befo' Mas'r Reynolds latched onta her. I useta wonda what she seed in dat ol' mean ol' ornery Mas'r Reynolds but now I see what ol' Ben useta tell me about dem birds of a feather flockin' to'gether. Bein' dat both her and Mr. Reynolds is both loony as dey comes

We jes 'bout outta laudanum and was tryin' ta save it fer an emergency or when we run into some sho'nuff trouble so we havin' ta

239

real put up fer alla dat time she been sleep.

Anyway, I's been lettin' missy wear out my ear fer da past two days and I's gotta admit dat m'mind ain't nowhere's as strong as dat ol' woman. I hate to say it but it seem like dem Afreecans jes got a stronger tolerance than us niggras. Dey sho'nufff got mo' stamina when it come to workin' in da fields and da mo' I lissen ta 'em da mo' sense dey startin' to make. Dey still is black and ugly as hell but I wouldn't be an educated woman iffen I's didn't admit dat a soul ken learn somethin' from most anybody even iffen dey be Afreecan.

May 23rd

Well, today is a very, sad day, and ev'ryone is quiet. Young Saul is always quiet but today he even more somber than usual.

Ya see, we run into da patrollers last nigh and dey was goin' 'bout dey usual routine a harrassin' every niggra dey see dat appears to be movin' on dere own and checkin' fer abolitions and Union spies all at da same time. Well, bein' dat I's big as a house wit' dis here chile and Aunt Hattie 'bout da same size wit' no youngun we don't attract much attention ta speak of.

And bein' dat mos'a da night riders that ast to see— papers can't read no way—all dey really doin' is checkin' ta see iffen we has 'em and dey official. A lotta da time dey pertends like dey can read 'em but half da time dey jes tryna show dat deys betta than us niggras

240

'cause I notices dat da papers be upside down when dey s'pozed ta be readin'

Tickles me but I don't dare crack a smile 'cause mos' a dem dat's paradin' as slave catchers and patrollers is no mo' than drunken bands a po' white trash dat's got mo' anger and hatred inside of 'em than a coon in a corner. A lot of 'em done lost dey land and ev'rything dey owned 'cause a da war. But mo' and mo' deys jes bands of men's all likkerd up lookin' ta out da fear a God in a niggra and let him know dat dere ain't nebba gonna be no freedom for a niggra.

Dese da one's what calls demselves nightriders and comes ridin' up a hoopin' and a hollerin' and shootin' and scarin' a niggra inta doin' somethin' stupid so deys ken jump on 'em. But da times dey done run up on us Aunt Hattie tells us ta jes stop and set dere 'til dey blows off alla da steam and devilment up inside of 'em.

And den when dey see missy sittin' back dere sleepin' dey jes moves on. I's mo' scairt of dem makin' all dat noise and wakin' her ol' crazy self up than I is of dem. Ain't no tellin' what gonna come outta her mouf.

And don't cha know dat's exactly what we been tellin' her all along. Aunt Hattie and me both been tellin' her right along dat she needs ta not let dem git ta her 'cause it ain't helpin' her state-o-mind none and mos' a dese fools out here has gone plumb crazy wit' losin' ev'rything in da war and all and she need to know her place 'cause ya

241

cain't talk jes anyway ta southern gentlemens dat jes lost everythin. We tried hard ta tell her and make her unnerstand but missy say she don't care but afta last night I do b'lieve she care a whole lot mo'

Ya see, last night we was all feelin' kinda restless and on edge. We kept gittin' conflictin' stories 'bout how far Natchez be. Two, three days ago, when we was campt wit' da Union Army we was tol' dat Natchez won't no mo' thean a week at best. And since den we been declined lodgin' 'cause da last two inns has been full of wounded soldiers so dey tell us dey concerns lie wit' da war efforts and dey ain't had no time nor space fo'no crazy woman.

So, we ain't had no choice but ta push on. Den when we come ta inquire 'bout how far we is from Natchez we's tol' everything from a week ta two weeks 'til we git ta what's left of it. Dey say Sherman burned it ta da ground and I knows auntie and Saul probably thinkin' I's done led 'em smack dab inta da jaws a da lion and for what when dey coulda been jes dat closer to Canada and freedom iffen dey had jes stuck wit' da Yankees. And dey ain't alone in havin' second thoughts right through here.

Wit slave catchers, patrollers and night riders stoppin' us almos' every night now and Natchez in flames it was da first time since we run dat I's start wonderin' if I's ever gonna see m' Joseph ag'in.

And I guess wit alla missy problems deep inside won't none a us no real comfo't to her either right thru here. I's kinda figgered

242

dat it was all gonna blow up sooner or later but I kept prayin' and tryin' to be strong fer everybody involved. And den I was hopin' too, dat dis baby would have da patience ta wait least 'til we git ta Natchez.

And den, like I's 'bout ta tell you it was like da walls a Jericho all come a tumblin' down at once. We was makin' purty fare time and evenin' was creepin' up on us and we had already begun lookin' fer an ol' abandoned farmhouse in plain view of da road so we could bed down fo' da night and missy could have some half decent 'ccomodations so we wouldn't have ta lissen ta her squawk all night 'bout how disgraceful it was fo' a fine southern lady like herself ta have ta sleep unda such conditions. We also had ta make sho' dere was a clear view a da road so we could see danger approachin' and like I sayed it was gittin' mo' n' mo' dangerous as da days went on.

We was hopin' ta find an inn or some folk desperate fo' a few dollas as I still had mos' a da money I got from da Reynold's Place. But up 'til now we hadn't even seed no travelers or nothin' what could even recommend no lodgin'' so we jes pushed on hopin' ta come ta a town wit' a inn or boardin' house fo' missy and a livery stable or barn fo' us and da hosses who by dis time was plumb wo'e out.

Bein' dat we wasn't havin' no such luck Aunt Hattie and Saul decided we ain't had no choice but ta keep movin'. By now it was quite late and still nothin' appeared 'ceptin' fo' a pack a dem devilish nightriders appearin' like ghosts from out da woods spookin' da hosses and all but scarin' dat youngun' right outta me.

Young Saul had ev'rythang ta do ta keep dem dat blamed hosses from tippin' da carriage ova on it's side but done become quite da hossman since we first started out and he somehow managed to keep us upright despite our bein' lodged ratha deeply in a drainage ditch long side a da main road we was on.

Well, I knowed right away dat dis band a misfits was a bad sort right from da outset. Like I sayed somethin' from da outset jes let me know dat it won't gonna be showin' 'em are passes and they'd let us pass and maybe tell us where we could find food and lodgin'. And though it won't mo' n' fo' or five a dem best won't hardly nothin' we could do in da way a resistin'.

At fi'st it didn't look lik e it was gonna go too bad on us an bein' dat we'd been through dis same o'deal so many times befo' we had gotten purty durn good at fashionin' our tales. In fact, we was so good by now dat iffen Aunt Hattie start a tale I could durn near finish it no matta where she left off. But dis time it was different. I twas obvious dat dey was all likkered up and dat in itself meant we was gonna be all kinds a niggas and porchmonkeys and thangs a dat sort and I knew it fo' sho when dey doused me and Saul wit likker and threatened to set me on fi'e fo' not being ready and bein' in a family way.

Anyways, me and Saul climbs down from da buggy like we was tol' and jes stand dere whilst dey calls us all kinds a names and I s'poze dis jes da way good, civilized, Christian white folk 'spresses demselves afta dey gits a little likker up n' 'em. I don't know but I learned so many new words I's was seriously considerin' makin' up my own po'backwoods, co'n likker drinkin' southern trash dictionary fo' all those who aspire ta be jes like dem iffen dere's anybody out dere dat really wanna be southern trash.

Well me and Saul got quite a tongue lashin' standin' dere our eyes firmly focused on da ground in front of our feet and I b'lieves I saw a slight grin on Saul's face as the man went on and on with his description of Saul, me an Aunt Hattie. I don't know but we purty much done got useta ta dat kind a treatment so it really don't strike a chord or pluck a nerve like it useta in any a us. 'Sides like Saul always say he knowed his parents and his daddy was an Afreecan king and his motha a queen so no matta how many bastards dey call him he know he a prince an iffen anybody be a bastard it's dem dat stole him away.

Well, when da nightriders in dem funny lookin' sheets and hoods couldn't get no rise outta me or Saul dey proceeded ta pull Aunt Hattie outta da carriage and heap insults on her callin' her among otha thangs a fat, black, ugly, heifer and cow and always ending ev'rythang wit' nigga which I guess was s'pozed ta be da ultimate insult but like ol' Ben useta tell me when I's growin' up. 'I heared nigga so many times when I's growing up I couldn't unnerstand why peoples kept callin' me Ben. I thought m'name was nigga. So, when dey called me by

245

any otha name but nigga I'd turn around ta see who dey was refeerin' to.'
We'd all laugh ev'rytime Ben would us his story but truth a da matta was
it ain't nebba botha'd nobody we was all so useta it.

And iffen da nightridas didn't know Aunt Hattie was fat 'til
den she sho' as hell was aware of it afta eighty some years of bein'
larger than life so dere insults was no revelation ta her and rolled offa her
back like water off a ducks. She jes stood dere next ta me and waited
mos' quiet like 'til dey had dere fun and da likker started ta wear off like
da res' da us so we could be on our way. White folks wit' a lil likker in
'em an nothin' ta do can be some a da meaniest orneriest folks dis side a
Hades so ya gotta be careful how you conduct yo'self 'round 'em or ya
just might find yo'self hanging fro da closest tree. In any case, da three
of us jes stands dere wit'out utterin' a single solitary word b'tween us.

Missy on da otha hand was sleepin' soundly afta runnin'
her trap da entire day 'bout how we shoulda been in Natchez and how
she couldn't and won't gonna go anotha day wit'out suitable lodgin'. Fo'
many a day I wondered how she could sleep in dat carriage wit' all it's
pitchin' back and forth. Still, it nebba waked her and I's jes prayed dat
she'd sleep through dis as well but wit' all da hoopin' and hollerin dem
dere nightridas was doin' dere won't no way she could sleep through all
dat. And when she waked up and saw us all standin' dere wit' dem
nightridas heapin' insults on us and dat one wheel stuck in dat dere
ditch—well—missy jes git beside herself. Now us, we was useta her

246

tantrums though dey slowed down considerably any time I was around but now dat we was low on laudanum she was startin' ta revert mo' n' mo' ta her ol' ways. Sometimes she would git ta rantin' and ravin' fo' da better parts of an hour and Lawd knows we would all see it comin' on. And we could sede it comin' now. Both Saul and Aunt Hattie lookt at me ta say somethin' but I's could have been blind ta see dat dere won't no reasoning' wit' dese crackers in dey condition jes like dere won't no talkin' ta missy when she was in dis condition. Didn't take much ta read eitha a dem and sho won't no reason ta whipt fo' eitha side. 'Sides me an Aunt Hattie done spoke ta her mo' than a few times 'bout how she need ta conduct herself in jes such sitcho'ations and she act like we ain't sayed nothin'. We done tol' her countless times dat she had ta curb her language and stop bein' so free wit' her speech 'specially wit' all dis war and peoples losin' dere homes and dey livelihoods in da midst of all dis unfortunate turmoils. People and 'specially white folks on da verge of losin' ev'rythang dey ebba owned didn't wanna be tol' nothin' atall 'bout da rightss and wrong a slavery right through here. Dis here war done made white folks on both sides so God awful angry and mean and bitter dat da best thing anybody could do was stay away from 'em if dat was all possible and iffen ya did have ta come inta contact da best thing ta do was say as lil' as possible and be on yer way.

Lawd knows we tried ta tell missy dat but her bein' from New England or maybe jes her gittin' away from up unda Mas'r

Reynold's hand or maybe it was jes da fact dat she was jes plain loco. At otha times we won't nothin' but some no-aacount, lazy shiftless niggras and I's only hoped she'd take dis tone right through here and maybe we could all walk away from here in one piece. But it jes won't no tellein' who would appear from da carriage.

But appear she did and da fi'st thang she sayed when she climbed down from da carriage was how dem goddamn slavas was delayin' her when she shoulda already been in Natchez. Not on the day she commenced ta changin' inta dat purty pink and floral sundress dat Aunt Hattie take from her ev'ryday to stop her from wearin' somethin' so revealin' wit' so many po' white trash around. Now it was on mo' than occasion Aunt Hattie had warned her 'bout how she gonna be da death a us wit' all dat cleavage showin'. But somehow shed found it and changed into it whilst dem nightridas was out here foolin' wit' us.

When I seed her climb down from da carriage I knowed it was ova fo' alla us and jes prayed ta da good Lawd above dat dem heathen crackas would at least have da decency ta see dat I was wit' chile or dat I's was jes too big and too fat ta want ta try and ride me tonight. Swear fo' God I's could nebba let dat happen and Saul wouldn't eitha. Lawd knows dey'd have ta kill both a us and of course ain't wantin' no screamin' fat woman around dey'd have ta kill Aunt Hattie too. Dat's jes da way it was and I's seed it play out jes dat way mo' times than I's liket ta remember.

But da ringleader su'prised us all by lissenin' ta missy befo' apologizin' ta missy by statin' dat his boys sho'lly ain't mean ta cause no delay ta da missus—dey was jes havin' a lil' fun wit' da niggas. We all breathed a deep sigh a relief hearin' dis and knowed dat we had once ag'in survived. And dis here woman dat cussed and fussed and blamed us fo' da war b'tween da states on her bad days sayin' how it caused ev'rythang from her husband's drankin' problems ta dere failed marriage ta man's fall from grace and da end a time as stated in The Book of Revelations. I mean missy tol' 'em ev'rythang includin' dat dey was a rag-tag bunch a misfits who ain't had da right ta tell her niggras what ta do. Then she telled 'em dat she hol' her niggras in da highest regard and it be a long time dat dere po' white asses could ebba hol' a candle ta her niggras. Well, by dis time missy had dere full attention and mines too. And it's my b'lief dat iffen she had let it go at dat point and jes acted like she had some sense—which she didn't—she coulda ast dem men right den and dere ta help git da buggy outta da ditch and dey still mighta done so. Dat's how much dey seemt ta be taken by her looks. And she was sho'lly one beautiful woman iffen ya didn't know she was crazy as a Betsy bug.

But missy nebba did unnerstan' da power a her beauty or her tongue or her place in da southern landscape so 'stead a usin' her attributes and actin' like a southern belle in distress she continued on like a goddamned nut and did ev'rythang we warned her 'bout givin' each a dem a pice a her feeble mind whilst runnin' down der family tree. "You ain't nothing' but a bunch a po'ass, thievin', incestuous, backwoods dirt farmers. Y'all so po' ya gotta wait fo' one a y'all ta go ta da bathroom befo' da next one a y'all can eat. And y'all got da nerve ta be out here harassin' m'po slaves. Da utter nerve a y'all."

At fir'st dey laughed at her spunk but afta awhile thangs musta got old and tired and ya could see dey was gittin' perturbed ta say da least a missy's lil' charade and I do b'lieve dey started ta realize somethin' was slightly amiss in da petite lil' fireball standin' in front a dem. Dis was usually da time I would jump in front a her and let whoeva she was cussin' and fussin at and let 'em know dat she was ill and ta pay no 'ttention ta da madness. But I's could see da venom in dere eyes and I knowed dis was not da time ta try and play peacemaker. She had put her foot in her mouth and bein' dat it was obvious dat dese was not whatcha might call ova'ly compassionate gentlemens I stayed put and hold m'tongue whilst Aunt Hattie hold m'hand makin' sho' I don't git involved. I heed her warning and jes sayed a prayer on missy's behalf dis time and jes stand by and watch missy dig her own grave.

Well, missy went right on ahead bein' missy and givin' dem nightridas da what fo' and it was purty obvious ta ev'rybody but missy dat dey was tired a her mouth by now and was growin' mo' n' mo' angry. All 'cept da ringleada anyway. I's couldn't really tell fo' sho wit dat hood coverin' his head but he seemt ta be older and whilst da rest

250

had tooken off dere hoods his remained on and you could hear him chucklin' ta himself as she continued spewin' insults at 'em. But da whole time he kept his eyes on me which made me a might uncomfortable ta say da least.

Anyways, We's all standin' here in dis here gully wishin' missy would cease heapin' alla dis abuse on des here men so's we can be on our way and can rest m'weary bones and I peaks ova at Aunt Hattie and she gots dat silly grin on her face dat I done come ta despise so much 'cause it mean she thinkin' some right devilish thoughts. Well, now hard as I's tried ta figger I ain't had no earthly idea what she be thinkin'. No, I ain't gots no clue as ta what she be thankin' but she gotta funny way a sensin' thangs and da next thang I knowed dem men gits offa dey mounts and stands right in front a missy and starts ta pass da moonshine back and fo'th in front a her and den one a dem grab missy by da hair tiltin' her head back and po'rs what seem like mo'n' half da bottle a moonshine down her throat whilst two othas hold her hands.

But what s'prised me mo' than anythang was dat Aunt Hattie was smilin' mo' n ebba and dat jes won't like her ta derive pleasure from someone elses pain. I turnt ta Saul and I seed dat faraway look he always has when white folks be around and da leader a dat roguish crew jes standin' dere leanin' against ta carriage puffin' on one a dem co'n cob pipes like won't nothin' wrong and ev'rythang in da world was right. Dat's when it seemt ta me dat ev'rybody present

251

includin' Young Saul knowed what was about ta commence 'ceptin' me. And den I heared missy scream some mo' 'bout dem bein' no mo' than backwoods filth dat was all related 'cause no one outside dey own clan was dumb enough ta bed down wit' 'em. Dis tickled Aunt Hattie ta no end and though ya couldn't tell from her facial 'spressions I knowed dat she was enjoyin' da hell outta missy right through here. I's really thought Aunt Hattie was gonna lose it right dere afta dat last remark and jes bust out laughin' and git us all killt. But it won't us who had ta worry and dat last remark was da one dat done it fo' missy. Dat's da one dat broke da camels back. And beefo' I knowed it one a dem picked missy up like won't nothin' mo' than a ol' rag doll and slung her ova his shoulda and went off tawards da woods wit her. Feelin' partly responsible I started ta go afta her wit' dat six shooter I purchased from a Union officer a few days prior but Aunt Hattie, her smile gone grabbed my arm and dat man what still had his hood on kept on watchin' m'ev'ry move ordered me ta set down and be still befo' I's be next.

I's did as I was told and set down promptly. In da distance I heared missy screamin, and den cussin' but she won't callin' no mo' names 'ceptin' fo' da good Lawds and I could tell she won't mad no mo' or call dem boys out dey name. A few minutes later, da fi'st one done come out da woods and da second one took his place. Dere won't no screams a pain dis time eitha and fo' da fi'st time in a long time missy was quiet. But by da time dat last man went inta dem dere woods missy

252

was cryin' like a newborn baby. As dey made dere way around da second and third times dere won't a peep outta her and I feared she must be dead and then I knowed she won't when one or anotha would git upp from sittin' around drankin' and wanda off inta da darkness ta visit her again. And den outta da blue black darkness you'd hear missy squeal like a stuck pig and you'd jes know dey was rippin' her insides ta shreds. At least when she screamed I knowed she was alive. Still, I ain't feel good in da knowledge dat I had been right and I knowed dat Aunt Hattie took no comfort in dat eitha and none a us spoke not a word da whole time those men kept missy penned down in those weeds.

In da mornin' dey was quite sober and it was den dat I ast da man I's presumed ta be dere leader to please he'p us git da buggy turnt upright and outta da gully which he promptly did. And to m'recollection he had nebba taken his hood off and nebba gone inta da woods wit da othas. And seein' how cooperative he'd been around honorin' m'first request I now felt da liberty a submittin' anotha an so's I ast him in quite a docile fashion iffen he minded iffen I fetched m'missus so's we could be on are way but he ignored m'second request totally and it was durin' dis time dat I noticed dat his men was still seekin' da pleasures a da forest. And so I's did da onliest thang a niggra could do and found me a seat on an ol' rotted out log next ta Aunt Hattie and Saul and continued ta wait.

It was at dis time dat I heared da sounds of a bugler in da distance and to m'relief he won't playin' no Dixieland eitha. None a us knew iffen missy was dead or not by dis time but no mo' screams were heard dis mo'nin' and I declare I won't rightly sho' iffen da Yankees was here had come ta he'p us niggras secure are freedom or not but one thang was fo' sho' dey certainly had secured dat white womans.

Why I ain' nebba seed white men git ta movin' dat fast in alla m'bo'n days a nd no soona did dey takes flight den da Bluecoats was dere and whilst Aunt Hattie tol' da officer in charge what happened den me and Saul went ta fetch what was left of Missy Reynolds who in spite of it all seemt not to be dat bad considerin' what she done been through fo' da past day and a half. Me and Aunt Hattie fount a stream not too far off and wit' da he'p a da Union soldiers carried here dear and cleant her up as best we could and rid a her blood soaked unda garments while Saul minded da hoss and buggy. By da time we finished wit' missy it was early aftanoon and when we returnt ta camp da army captain say dat a detachment had rounded up five a da six men based on Aunt Hattie's description and was holdin' 'em though he didn't know how long he could wit'out someone comin' forth and identifyin' 'em and testifyin' dat dese were da men dat had raped and sodomized missy. But missy wasn't in no kinda state ta be testifyin' and a niggras word ain't mount ta much 'gainst white folk so I figgered it best we jes git outta dere as soon as possible befo' dey decides to hunt us all down. Onliest one

254

day didn't ketch was da one wit' da hood.

Anyway, it's been a lot quieter since da episode wit' da night riders. N' don't onliest thing I heared missy say dis afta noon was dat dere was no accountin' fer people actions but iffen she done learnt anything it was ta be careful watcha say and who ya say it ta.

Den she say dere's good and bad in all races, which I have ta agree wit' but I b'lieve she be hard pressed ta find whie folks ta treat her as good as me and Aunt Hattie do. And much as I's confesses ta dislikin' dem Afreecans 'cause a da way dey looks wit dem big lips and wide noses. Even as black as dey is wit' dey nappyheaded selves and dere backwards ways, heathen religions and skin da color a coal—I's still gotta admit—dey always treated me good, wit' respect and awhole heap betta than dem dere whatcha might call civilized Christians. 'Course I's could nebba tell Aunt Hattie dat.

June 6

Aunt Hattie always telled me. Ebba since I was knee high ta a grasshopper she telled me ta nebba b'lieve whatcha hear. Dat's what she telled me. She say only b'lieve whatcha see wit' yo own eyes. Well, I's really started ta b'lieve dat dem same folks dat teached me ta b'lieve in da teachin's a da Good Book ain't took da time ta read it demselves.

And fo' da third day in a row we done come across niggras dat's been lynched. Dere was three of 'em hangin' from diff'rent limbs on one weepin' willow. On anotha da body been burnt so bad it was hard ta tell iffen it was a man or a woman but one thangs fo' sho'; it sho won't no white folk hangin' from dat tree.

Saul git so sick when he seed dat body all burnt and disfiggered hangin' dere fo' all da world ta see dat he stopped da buggy, git down, and commenced ta throwin' up all ova da side a da road somethin' awful. Didn't help dat da smoke could still be seed comin' from da body and oh dat smell. Only dead bodies have dat smell. I felt sorry fo dat po' chile and I guess da fact dat mos' a da time you sees a lynchin' it's a niggra man don't he'p Saul none too much eitha. I knowed he thiankin' 'bout how close he come and probably still worry 'bout da fact dat it can still happen at anytime. A wrong turn here or dere and da wrong white folk and he could sho' nuff be da next one. I tried ta comfort him by tellin' him dat as long as he b'lieved in da Good Lawd Jesus Christ won't no harm gonna come ta him and he sayed dis ta me.

"Miss Mary is you tryna tell me dat none a dese people I seed hangin' b'lieve in yo' Jesus?"

To which I replied, "No Saul I ain'y sayin' dat."

"Well den why is dey dead den?"

"I's cain't tell ya dat Saul"

256

"And white folk dat hang us niggras; tell me do dey b'lieve in yo' Jesus?"

"Ain't no tellin' I sayed ta Saul."

Missy Reynolds who was gittin' along fairly well considerin' her recent ordeal had come ta da decision dat she was soiled goods and couldn't marry John Marshall or an anybody else won't much betta than Saul when it come ta da hangins. And she had hardly get ova one when we'd run inta anotha one and missy would commence ta cryin' all ova again.

Me, well I kept my sights set on seein' m'Joe and away from da hangin's and kept m'ev'ry thought on gittin' ta Natchez and dat way dey didn'affect me so much but I's won't not seein' 'em. Jes made me question a lotta thangs mas'r had done tol' me 'bout southerners bein' good Christians and lovin' da good Lawd and alla da time hangin' niggras like dey wasn't people. It all jes made me thank and fo' da fi'st time I's really begun ta thank dat maybe m'Joseph an Aunt Hattie had been right all along when it come ta white folks and den jes like dat when I gits ready ta call 'em da devil some ol' white couple wit' a couple a acres and not much mo' than we got will feed us and 'llow us to stay wit' 'em fo a night or two when da slavas is hot on are heels. Jes cain't call it. Peoples is jes people I s'pose and I guess da truth is dere's good and bad on both sides though white folks got us far outnumbered when it comes ta brangin' pain, death, and heartache.

257

Now me and Aunt Hattie both done come ta da conclusion dat what dem nightridas did ta missy is equal ta any hangin' and iffen it had been me I'd a probably wish I hadda been hanged and jes put outta m'misery steada being' tortured like missy and lef' ta face anotha day. Truth of da matta it was downright shameful and we was both sorry it had happened but it did somethin' ta her dat all da talkin' and da preachin' in da world ain't been able ta do. And fo' da fi'st time she seem ta unnerstan' dat bad thangs do sometimes happen ta good peoples. And bein' aroun' us I think fo' da fi'st time she realize dat we ain't jes beasts a burden ta be used, abused and den throwed away or sold when are usefulness was done. I think she finally done realized dat even though we niggras we' gots feelins too.

We laugh and cry and hurt and love jes da way white folk do. Its jes dat we ain't 'llowed to show how we feel but da truth is we feels da same thangs she feels and I's really beginnin' ta thank she unnerstans a lil' betta what we goes through ev'ryday jes 'cause we's bo'n wit' a diff'rent birthright. I's truly b'lieves she comin' outta dat blindin' light dat been keepin' her so confused. Now she beginnin' ta see thangs dat ain't right befo' her. Aunt Hattie sayed she finally beginnin' ta use her mind's eye which is when you can see in da darkness and past da ovious.

Guess us niggras always been able ta see past da obvious 'cause we had ta. Ain't nothin' really what it appears to be in light

258

a da whole situation, jes like missy thankin' she betta than ev'rybody 'cause she from da New England and knowed thangs and thankin' she marryin' inta money. Dat's da way she seed thangs up 'til a few days ago and befo' dem nightridas got ta her. Here she gonna condemn dem fo' dealin' in da capture a human flesh but she don't see dat it wouldn't be no market fo' human flesh iffen people like those she love so much like Mas'r Reynolds and Mas'r John didn't have such a demand fo' niggra hands. Iffen dey ain't purchasin' some baby from its mama so's dey can have someone ta clean up afta her den dese slavas wouldn't even exist. Her and Mas'r Reynolds owns or at least dey useta owns mo' n' three hunnerd slaves alone and she fussin' at dem fo' traffickin' in flesh when she and him da main ones keepin' dem in business. Seem like she comin' 'round but Lawd knows she still got a far way ta go. Well, she ain't nearly so high and mighty now dat dem fellas brang her down a peg or two but like I says she still gots a ways ta go.

She telled me dat she ain't nebba really realized how bad it was fo' a nigga 'til Aunt Hattie telled her dat what happened ta her wit' dem nightridas happened ta her almost ev'ry week when she was younga or anytime da mas'r decided he was in da mood fo' a lil' dark meat. I's could see dat she lookt like she was ready ta cry but she held d tears back da best she could. Sayed Aunt Hattie birthed nineteen chi'dren but only fo' a which she could rightfully claim as hers and her husbands. Da rest of 'em were da mas'r's doin' and only two a which

259

she knew da whereabouts. Say her mas'r sell da rest of 'em off. Say sometimes when mas'r had male company mas'r would shoo her husband off and tell his gentlemen friends dat dey could use her as a bedwarmer fo' da night. Sayed any resistance by her or her husband and dey be whipped and she still end up havin' ta sleep wit' da gentlemens so afta awhile she jes went through wit' it wit'out a fight and save both her and her husband a good beatin'. Say dat's why she ain't mind gittin' ol' at all. Then she at least git some rest at night.

June 7

When we woke taday Missy was already up gittin' herself dressed and fixin' some breakfast. We was all stunned and even mo' stunned when she telled Aunt Hattie dat she ain't won't no mo'laudanum. Sayed she wanna be able ta see da world fo' what it was worth. Good or bad she wonted ta see. Den I heared her ast Aunt Hattie why we was so good ta her afta all da hateful thangs white folks had done ta us niggas. And I's still waitin' fo' auntie ta answer dat one but all she sayed was 'dat's a good question, missy.'

June 8

I's truly prayin' we reach Natchez in da next couple a days 'cause dis here is a heavy burden ta be totin' cross da country and I ain't jes talkin' 'bout dis here youngun dat gots m'belly all swolled up. No

260

suh! Jes havin' da responsibility a makin' sho nothin' happens ta nobody unda m'watch is one heavy load ta bear.

Aunt Hattie say I shouldn't feel like dis. She say dey had made da choice a dere own free will ta come. Still, dey da only real family I's ebba knowed ceptin' fo' m'Joseph and Uncle Ben and I swears I's don't know what I'd do iffen somthin' happened ta eitha one a dem and even Missy Reynolds at dis point.

June 9

We's stuck and in m'heart I jes feels like we ain't nebba gonna reach Natchez. From all accounts I estimates dat we somewhere b'tween a hunnerd and two hunnerd miles northeast of Vicksburg which ain't a far piece from Natchez but we cain't make no time wit' dis long procession a nigras in front a us tryna join up wit' General Grant's Army .

From what I heared, Genl. Grant done laid siege ta Vicksburg fo about a week now wit' his army standin' at da ready and wit' da Confederate Army unda constant artillery fire and hardly able to come up and catch a breath. Say he makin' dem rebel boys wish dey had nebba ebba considered secedin'. And even though I knows he fightin' on are account I's truly feel sorry fo' all dem boys a dyin' and da utta devastation and hardship dat done befallen dem po' people. It's almost like da good Lawd is havin' his own sorta retribution or payback on all dem dat's 'caused us so much pain and sorrow fo' so long.

261

June 10

Missy seem ta be comin' 'round mo'n'mo' which ain't necessarily a good thang bein' that she beginnin' ta ast a whole lotta questions dat let us knowed dat she gittin' betta but also disturbin' since some thangs ain't makin' much sense ta her like why Mas'r John wont ta meet her in Natchez of all places. Me and Aunt Hattie tries ta give her an aswer as best we could but its gittin' harder and harder as da days goes by.

July 12

Well, we's finally in Vicksburg. We attached ta Grant's Army and we ain't exactly receive da warmest a welcomes. Da hu't and wounded is evr'ywhere; walkin' 'round here wit' arms and legs severed and blowed off, and wit' holes in dey chests large enough ta put a small cannonball in. I cried da fi'st time I's seed da makeshift Union Hospital but Aunt Hattie put a end ta alla dat sayin' dat it won't no time ta cry. She say da Union soldiers is fightin' and dyin' on are behalf and dey ain't lookin' fo' no tears or sympathy on their behalf. What dey really want and need despite what President Lincoln sayed is fo'us ta ante up and throw in are lot and do are part fo' da Union. And dat's what we been doin' since we got here and I's got a feelin' we'll be doin' fo' da next couple a weeks.

Funny thang 'bout da whole situation is dat ev'rytime we seems ta gits a chance ta relax here come anotha group a casualties so bruised and toe up wit' limbs danglin' and hangin' dat dere ain't nothin' ta do but man up and git back ta work tryna save those boys so intent on savin' us dat dey riskin' dey very lives.

Somethin' else I's noticed since we been in Vicksburg amongst all dis here blood and pain and destruction and dat's dat missy don't hardly mentioned Mas'r John no mo'—almos' like she done reconciled herself ta da fact dat he dead or maybe he jes dead in her eyes. And in a way, I guess he is. She done seed so much lynchin' and bloodshed on both sides cause a dis here ol' senseless war b'tween da states she don't hardly mention nothin' when it come ta da war, or bein' married ta a slaveholda. Don't know if she finally come ta see da whole picture or she jes tired a wishin' and hopin'. I don't know but she jes resigned herself ta da task at hand. But right through here she jes fall in line like ev'rybody else and do all she can ta do her part.

July 13

Saul and missy and Aunt Hattie lef' me taday. Seem like dey done hadda meetin' or somethin' and agreed dat I didn't need ta be movin' or travelin' in m'condition and I b'lieve dat's why Aunt Hattie so persistent 'bout us stayin' on wit' Grant's Army right through here. 'Course dat don't seem ta stop her from assignin' me ev'ry kind a lil' duty

263

she can find ta keep me busy when it come ta aidin' da troops. But mos'ly da work she be assignin' me ain't hard atall. Mos'ly it be lil ' thangs like walkin' from here ta dere ta read a letter ta some a da troops dat cain't read or fetchin' linen and cuttin' it up inta strips fo' bandages. Or jes talkin' ta dem ta keep dey spirits high. She call it fo' morales sake whateva dat means but I does it ta keep from goin' stir crazy 'specially since I knows dat m'Joseph only a few miles away and I's cain't get ta him.

Aside from dat ain't nothin' really new and when I finished readin' fo' da troops and doin' da bandages I commenced ta sittin' around and jes wait for dere return at which time I pulls Aunt Hattie ta da side and discuss somethin' dat's been on m"mind fo' a couple a days now. Seems like we still gots a fair share a money left and afta countin' it I b'lieves we still got betta than two hunnerd and seventy-fi'e dollas left. But da word goin' 'round is dat da Confederacy is so far in debt dat purty soon it won't have no value atall. So, Aunt Hattie takes missy wit' her ta see iffen we can get us a fair price on anotha wagon some fresh hosses and some otha supplies. And when dey did come back. Dey come back wit' a buckboard and two young colts fo' less than forty dollas. Now dey was gone fo' mos' a da day and when dey gits back I knowed somethin' was wrong 'cause I ketched missy cryin' and I ain't seed her drop a tear in quite some time now.

Didn't seem like too much bothered Young Saul and wit' dem two fine lookin' young colts in his possession and unda his carehe seemt like he was in pure heaven since all he did from dat day out was groom dem colts. Sayed as soon as we git ta da freedom he gonna start breedin' 'em but iffen ya know Saul then ya know he ain't nebba one ta speak on anythang too much so's I knew he won't gonna be da one ta tell me nothin'. Still, aside from Saul I knowed dat whateva had happened musta been one frightful experience 'cause nobody includin' Saul sayed much-a-nothin' and dat sho won't like Aunt Hattie who usually had somethin' ta say jes 'bout alla da time. And it was da fi'st time since we set out dat dey didn't ast me nothin'. Dey didn't tell me nothin' and dey didn't ast me nothin'. Dey jes telled me dat we's couldn't stay dere unda General Grant's protection any longa. Dat's what dey decided. Say we needed ta pray a lot but dat we could make are way around Vicksburg but Aunt Hattie got da attitude and sayed she ain't care which way we took but she couldn't and wouldn't stay in Hades anotha day. She sayed da devil hisself had laid his imprint on dis here land. Now I's knowed Aunt Hattie fo' as long as I's can remember. She basically raised me and I's ain't nebba knowed her ta be afraid a nothin' in her life. And iffen ya know Aunt Hattie then ya know dat ain't nothin' much affect her but somethin' sho' 'nuff had affected her 'cause dis da fi'st time since we started dis journey where she ain't consulted me on nothin'. But here she was ready ta leave da security a Grant's Army and

265

take a chance movin' through or around Vicksburg despite da shellin' Grant's got it unda.

July14

No soona had we gotten undaway than da rains come, both hard and heavy. We rode on fo' what seemt like hours in da downpour alla da time tryna find shelta wit' nary a word bein' spoken. Ev'rythang was closed up tighta than a board and both small towns we come across reminded me a ghost towns I read about in dem dime books 'bout da ol' west. At least dere won't no menfolks present in dese towns and I's s'pose dat's 'cause mos' a dem is back in Vicksburg tryna hol' off Grant's army.

What few dat's lef' is eitha too young or too ol' ta fight so we ain't really had ta worry 'bout runnin' inta no real trouble 'cept fo' screamin' missus's blamin' us startin' dis war and havin' dere boys and husbands killt. But dat ain't nothin' new. We been hearin' dat since we done lef' Georgia. Ev'ry now and den some Confederate widow will commence ta callin' us ev'ry vile name unda da sun as we pass by her place. We even had one ol' woman come out da front door and fire a coupla loads a buckshot at us but fo' da mos' part it's been calm.

Nightridas and slavecatchas is rare ta see nowadays and Saul wanna keep pushin' on through the night whilst da goin' is good and make time whilst Grant gots dem southern boys preoccupied and

266

wit' da rain makin' sho nobody on da road lessen it be an emergency we coulda made good time but Aunt Hattie say no. She say it ain't good fo' me or da baby and wit' m'time bein' so near and ev'rythang I's ain't inclined ta disagree wit' nobody who done birthed nineteen younguns.

July 15

I's always professed ta bein' a good Christian woman wit' humility jes like mas'r teacht me ta be. You know in all m'days I ain't nebba really cusst or used da Lawds name in vain. And I ain't nebba had da occasion a takin' even a swallow ta drank. And I ain't nebba sayed what you might say was a negative word 'bout m'fellow man though Lawd knows I's wonted to from time-to-time but when I waked up dis mo'nin' wit' dat pain where in da same exact spot m'Joseph had made me feel so good dat I was travelin' cross country ta feel it all ova again I's must confess dat I's sayed some words I ain't even knowed I had in m'vocabulary. I cusst dat Afreecan til' m'mout went dry. Missy had ta come and give me some water jest ta dampen m'lips. Den when I's was finished drankin I started all ova from da beginnin' and cusst him ag'in fo' causin' me all dis pain. I ast m'self how in da hell I could let dis happen ta me afta all da years I spent he'pin' Aunt Hattie deliva younguns. How in da hell could I let dis happen ta me? Aunt Hattie sayed writin' would ease da pain and take m'mind ta anotha place but I's bout ta put dis here quill down 'cause ain't nothin' gonna ease dis here

267

pain and 'sides I b'lieves I's 'bout ta pass out.

July 16

Aunt Hattie sayed it was a fairly easy birth and I guess it was fo' her but dis here niggra took me through pure hell and won't nothin' easy 'bout it ta me. Imagine tryin' ta push eight pounds through a keyhole. Don't care if you Samson ain't nothin' easy 'bout dat. But I's gotta admit dat it ain't take me long and fo' I knowed it I was holdin' a big, strong, strappin' boy in m'arms. My anger subsided by dis time an I named him Joseph and iffen ya didn't knowed I was da mother you'd a swore fo' God hisself dat I ain't had nothin' ta do wit' dat boy. He lookt so much like his daddy dat it was downright scary. Aunt Hattie sayed won't no people wit' stronga genes than an Afreecan an afta lookin' at dat baby I's kinda inclined ta agree. Onliest thang I could see dat had some 'semblance ta me was his straight hair and Aunt Hattie say dat was a temporary thang and dat was gonna change in time as well.

I thank Saul was more elated than any of us and called him his lil' brotha and refused ta let anyone near him includin' me. He washed him, bathed him, sang ta him and rocked him ta sleep. Iffen I's didn't have ta feed him I's probably wouldn't have gotten ta touch him at all.

July 17

Da rain ova da past couple a days has cooled thangs down some and it ain't quite as hot as it has been and da dew dat covered da grass made a cool soft bed beside me. As da day went on I's feelin' all kinds a mixed emotions and diff'rent thangs I couldn't rightly put a finger on or git a grasp on. It was jes like a whole diff'rent bunch a emotions come rainin' down on me at da same time. I's was happy and sad at da same time. Den da next minute I's be cryin' fo' no reason atall. On da one hand I wisht I hadda stayed wit' da Union Army and moved North 'cause I was hatin' Joseph fo' havin' caused me alla dis pain and heartache and fo' makin' me love him so much dat he had me riskin' otha people's lives and not jes m'own. Then I's went back ta cryin' and carryin' on fo' no good reason. Feel like somethin' was bein' taken away from me or somethin' when I dropped dat dere youngun'. And even though he was sittin' right dere next ta me jes as big and beautiful in Saul's arms I still felt like I'd lost somethin' very dear and close ta me. Aunt Hattie sayed dat was normal ta feel da way I's do and dat in a day or so my emotions would all fall back in dey natc'chal place and I'd be m'normal evil self.

Moved 'bout a half a mile or so inland and found an ol' abandoned plantation smoldering from where da Union had burnt it down. We knowed den dat Grant's army was on da move. Well, Grant or Sherman's army I don't know but whoeva's army it was was rollin' through da South like it won't no tomorrow just wreckin' havoc ev'rywhere dey went. Dey was in front a us now and we felt safe—well as safe as a runaway slave can feel in Mississippi. Anyways, da barn was still intact but da army had cleant it out takin' all da livestock and anythang else of value not dat dat mattered much. We won't too much worried 'bout food since Aunt Hattie—in gittin' rid a dat Confederate paper—had purty much got us enough food and supplies ta tide us ova til' St. Peter come ta open da Pearly Gates. Anyways, she insisted dat we lay ova in dat barn fo'a day or two so as to let me rest up and git m'strength back alla dat hollerin' and screamin' I done did welcomin' Joseph inta da world. This was fine by me but I done come to know dat anytime da union army come sweepin' through a burnin' and lootin' dat afta da battle and even sometimes durin' da horror would make a lotta dem po'boys on both sides jes up and desert and come lookin' fo' jes such a place as dis ta hide out in. Ta tell ya da God's honest truth though I cain't blame 'em fo' desertin. I's remember we went up ta one a da highest bluffs ova lookin' Vicksburg 'cause Saul wanted ta see Grant's Army in actual battle. Well, up til' dat point dat's all Saul talkt about. Keept sayin'how he wisht he could fight fo' da Union and have da oppo'tunity ta meet Mas'r John or Mas'r Reynolds on da battlefield. Dat's all he talkt about. But Aunt Hattie was totally ag'inst it. Now don't get me wrong, she won't ag'inst Black folk wontin' sa sign up and fight fo'dere liberty. She was jes ag'inst her Saul signin' up. Didn't matta whether President Lincoln gave niggras da right ta sign up and fight or not dere was no place fo' her Saul in dis here war.

And standin' on dat bluff ovalookin' General Grant shellin' dem po' folks in Vicksburg hour afta hour, fo' days on end and watchin' dem po' folks down dere scurryin' like rats in a silo, all bloody and wounded wit' limbs contorted and hangin' I b'lieve Saul give up dat notion a wontin' ta join too. But what made da whole situation even worse and mo' dangerous was dat dem boys—wounded and othawise—dat did manage ta escape Grant's wrath was some a da mos' desperate men I's ebba seed. And if dey won't hurt real bad den mos' a da time dey was hungry and starvin' and posed da worst threat 'cause dey was both angry and desperate which made us da enemy and prime targets.

So, we had ta be very careful bein' dis far away from da Union Army 'specially afta dey done wreaked havoc on those southern boys.

Well, dat was da situation dat evening when we stopped at dat ol' burnt down plantation.

By dis time, we's was useta sleepin' in barns and places like dat—well, everyone dat is 'ceptin' fer missy but even missy was aware a da dangers da road presented us by now. And dats why I's purchased my derringer, (well, actually I stealed da derringer from Mas'r Reynold's study), but was mo' n grateful that I ain't nebber really had no occasion ta use it. (Da Colt 45 I buyed from da Union Army officer.) And da one time, I had even considered usin' it was da time dem mens was

271

rapin' Missy Reynolds but Aunt Hattie had warned me dat iffen I had it would mos' likely mean da death of us all. Aside from dat dere had really been no 'cause. Now dats not ta say dat iffen I hadn't been pregnant I wouldn't have been da subject of dem night riders but up 'til now no one had pursued. But no soona had I sayed dat den a rider approached an I had ta wonder iffen I hadn't jinxed us. Hangin' ta one side a his sorrel it was obvious dat he was wounded and da gray Confederate uniform was now a dirty brown or rust color, tattered wit' holes da size a buckshot.

We had jes got settled in when Saul noticed da stranger approachin' da barn. I flipped da tiny derringer ta Aunt Hattie, concealt da 45 in m'waistband, instructed Saul ta climb inta da loft and let missy do all da talkin'. Far more humble since her lil' incident, missy had flashes of madness but fear had pusht dat ta da backburner and now when anyone approached she was eitha silent or cordial as a southern belle servin' mint juleps. So's it was missy who approached our southern friend on dis day and dere was no doubt dat he was in sad shape and as he approached da barn door missy emerged su'prisin' da soldier who immediately straightened up in his saddle and pulled da revolva from his holster all in da same motion.

"Easy soldier noone mean ya know harm here. Ain't no need fo' no shootin'. We jes a few hongry travelas seekin' some shelta in dis here barn and outta harms way."

"Who's we missy. You and who else be stayin' here?" da soldier sayed wavin' his revolva in da area a da barn.

"Don't thank dat's none a yo' business, suh," I sayed steppin' out from da shadows fo'ty-five aimed squarely at his back.

No soona had he turnt and lookt into da barrel of m'pistol then Aunt Hattie cracked open da barn and sayed, "Pleae drop ya guns, suh. We sho' don't wont no trouble here. You drop that gun, suh and won't be no trouble."

Da soldier sat dere shocked.

"Well, I'll be damned, niggas wit' guns. What da hell is da world comin' to?" He said before fallin' from his horse.

Aunt Hattie and Saul dragged da man and his sorrel inta da barn and Aunt Hattie and missy begun strippin' his clothes b'fore sendin' Saul ta da well ta fetch some fresh water and start a small fire. Once dis was done missy and Aunt Hattie finished strippin' da man naked, bathed him down cleant and dresst his wounds. I, on da otha hand, secured his arms wit' some hemp I found lyin' 'round da barn and relieved him of his revolver which I give ta Saul jes in case. And jest ta make sho' he ain't git no funny ideas 'bout tryna git free and killin' us all I give him an extra strong dose a laudanum ta make sho' dat he rested and was free a pain but so's we could sleep trouble free and wit'out havin' ta worry 'bout him. Lookin' at him I noticed somethin' vaguely familiar although I couldn't rightly put my finga on it right den and dere.

273

Cleant up he lookt totally diff'rent than when I first layed eyes on him but there was something that struck me about him that sent shivas through me.

Afta a good meal prepared by Aunt Hattie we all nestled in fairly well and 'cept fo' gittin' up ta feed lil' Joseph I b'lieve ev'ryone sleept soundly.

July 18

Bein' dat we was only a day's ride no'th of Natchez I was su'prised dat I sleept atall da night b'fore. Jes thankin' 'bout seein' m'Joseph in a matta a hours had me moist in a way I ain't been since he left. Nobody—not missy—not dat cracka soldier—nobody could dampen my spirits or rain on m'parade taday cause taday I's was goin' ta see m'Joseph. Onliest thang dat really bothered me 'bout da whole situation was what we was gonna do wit' dis here Confederate soldier who seemt like he was jes hell-bent on makin' da last leg a are journey pure hell. And sick and lamed up as he was he ignored all dat me and Aunt Hattie had did for him and cursed us even as we changed his dressings that mornin' and tried ta make him as comfortable as possible. By da time Saul had finished saddlin' da hosses I's still ain't come ta know decision 'bout what we was gonna do wit' dis fool but we sho couldn't sit dere. We knowed da Confederates was in da area and won't no tellin' when da owners would be back

274

Aunt Hattie suggested we leave him right dere in da barn tied ta da post but I knowed dat iffen we did dat chances was good dat he'd eitha starve, be eaten by wild animals or be captured by da Confederates and hung for desertion or imprisoned by da Union boys. I didn't rightly give two shakes a da pecan tree what happened ta him but whateva happened I didn't wanna thank I had a hand in his death. Saul b'lieved and made it known dat he thought da man should be tooken prisoner and handed ova ta da Union Army but Aunt Hattie sayed no and da onliest thang I could thank of was dat dere man wasn' gonna do much a nobody no harm in his condition and wit' out no hoss could nebba catch up ta us iffen we put a fair amount a distance b'tween us so what I suggested was dat since I's was in da best position or da only position to stay wit' him and care for him befo' escapin'. Wit'missy bein' are pass to freedom and Saul bein' are driver and takin' care a da hosses won't nobody really left ta tend ta da soldier and then make a break from him when he was up and ready ta travel but me so I elected m'self. And though Aunt Hattie won't wit' da idea atall she knowed dat she won't capable and it would take a whole lot mo' than one soldier ta keep me from m'baby or seein' m'Joseph. Hell, I was jes too close. Fact of da matta was da whole Confederate army couldn't stop me iifen dey had wanted to. I was jes too close.

I watcht as the closest thang ta m'family pulled out of the barn and made their way down the dirt road and inta da distance. I watcht til' dey were all but tiny specks and wondered seriously iffen I would ebba set eyes on any a dem again. Walkin' back ta da barn I's kept astin' m'self what made me m'brothas keeper alla da time when m'brotha hated da fact dat we both were allowed ta walk God's green earth. Iffen he had had his way I's quite sho' he would have wiped me and those dat lookt like from da very face of da earth wit' no qualms about it. I wondered why I couldn't be jes like dat dere soldier so full a hate and venom dat even seein' him layin' dere half dyin' and hatin' me all da same simply because we was a diff'rent color he could jes walk away from me had it been a similar situation but not I from him.

I thought 'bout my Christian upbringin' and didn't regret a thang I'd been taught even though mos' a m'teachers ain't b'lieve and adhere ta dere own teachings. But I did and as I checked his wounds ta see iffen his bandages were secure it come ta me jes how I was gonna free him from da post wit'out him followin' us and bringin' da wrath a da Confederacy down 'round are necks and so I's quickly went about da task a buildin' a small fire and roastin' some potatoes, boilin' some water and fryin' apiece a salt po'k. Occasionally I's would glance ova at him and to m'surprise found dat he still hadn't awakened.

When he did wake up it won't nothin' purty wit' him callin' me half a porch money and a coon and I hasta admit that I was confused 'bout him callin' me an animal and not bein' able to decide whether I was a porchmonkey or a coon. And had ta admit that as long as I been on dis here earth I ain't nebba unnerstood white folks. Now here I is tryna save dis here po' fool from pushin' up daisies and he cussin' me like dere ain't no tomorrow and I keep havin' dem flashbacks of Mas'r Reynolds and Mas'r John beatin' da tar outta me and I'ma thinkin' dat I's let m'newborn go on wit' out me so's I's can he'p dis here fool who wanna keep me in bondage and dats when I started fingerin' dat Colt in m'waistband. Aunt Hattie won't here ta stop me and I's puttin' m'self in harms way. One mo' jungle bunny porch monkey and I's was gonna send him to meet his maker sooner den he eva' expected.

I pulled dat dere Colt out and aimed it right fo' dis peckerwoods head when I heared da sound of approachin' hosses and durn near wet m'self. Here I is 'bout ta be strung up on account a dis here no account cracka who hated me 'cause I was bo'n aniggra. It jes didn't make no sense. Pushin da barn door shut I left him right dere on da pallet in da middle a da barn and climbed up in the hayloft and hid behind some bales a hay. Not bein' able ta see nothin' I heared 'em when dey come in and discovered da soldier dere.

"Say boy what battalion you wit'?"

I still couldn't see and won't about to stick my head out when I heared da boy start ta cuss dem dat's askin' da questions.

"Ya damn Yankee soldiers! Ya can kill me right here but I ain't tellin' ya nothin'. Ya nigga lovin' Yankees!"

Made me feel a whole heap betta knowin' dat dem who had come upon us was Yankees but I knew too that dem boys had been away from home quite a spell to and bein' dat I wasn't in da family way anymo' I would make fo' some right good entertainment afta all dat soldierin' and killin' so I proceeded ta stay right where I was and not make a peep.

Anyways dat dere soldier was a namecallin' and seemt ta be even angrier and mo' disrespectful to dem Yankee soldiers den he been ta me and I gotta admit I's was kinda glad when dat dere seargeant took the rifle butt and knocked him clear outta his wickedness. I gots ta admit I felt a tingle inside and was jes glad dat I didn't have ta do it. He leaned back ta deliver anotha buttstroke dat would surely have put an end to da soldiers misery when a young lieutenant come in and demanded he stop talkin' all this mumbo jumbo 'bout some articles a war. White folks got some funny ideas when it come ta war dat I swears I don't unnerstand. Seem like a few minutes earlier dat dere Confederate soldier can set his sights on yu and shoot you but once you catch up wit' him you gots ta protect him and cain't seek no retribution accordin' ta da articles a war. Don't make no sense ta me and I guess it ain't make no sense ta dat dere seargeant who was going ta make short work a dat dere C'federate soldier. Anyways, dey handcuffed 'em and carried him outta dat barn and on away and I was jes glad dey ain't search 'cause not only would deay have found me but dey would have

278

found dat soldiers hoss as well as m'own which I promptly saddled. I used da soldiers for a pack animal and gathered all da supplies Aunt Hattie had left fo' me and da soldier and headed towards Natchez. I's figgered I couldn't be mo'n than a couple a hours behind dem and couldn't wait ta rejoin m'family. Wit' da road being crowded wit' all kinda travelers tryna flee Vicksburg it took me 'til noon ta catch up wit' 'em and I must admit dey was quite glad ta see me.

Dey say dat da Union Army laid siege to Vicksburg fo' mo' than a month but da word on da road was dat da people in Natchez won't hardly affected at all by da war 'cause mos' a dem was Yankees who jes come down there ta try dere hand at plantin' and ta make money offen da trade alonst da Mississippi so it was fair ta say dat m'Joseph was probably unharmed and ain't had da need ta take flight like mos' a dese here niggras.

I's was sho' hoping dis was da case but bein' dat I's won't in contact wit' m'Joseph fo' da past six months it won't really no way ta tell and bein' only a day or so outside a Natchez, (dependin' on who you ast), I was almighty anxious and scairt and it must have been obvious 'cause all Saul would keep tellin' me was 'it gonna be alright Miss Mary; ev'rythang gonna work out jes like you planned it'. I guess he be tellin' me dat 'cause ta him I was da svior and he probably mo den me wanted it ta work out.

Dat evenon' we found a few niggra slaves on a abandoned plantation who was mighty gracious and let us spend da night. Seem liked dey had been free fo' some time 'cause dey sho ain't act like no slaves I's ever come in contact wit. Dey was proud and sayed dat won't no reason fo' dem ta run North or no other place 'cause dis here was dey home and even though Mas'r had gone off ta join da C'federacy he won't no average mas'r. Seems he paid 'em fo' dere labors and give 'em a share a da what he made offa his harvest. A few of 'em had nice homes wit' flowers and gardens a dere own. Me and Aunt Hattie jes looked at each other but didn't say nothin'. I knew what she was thinkin' and bein' dat a few a dem spoke dat ol' Afreecan mumbo jumbo she was right content and I does b'lieve dat iffen it won' fo' me and da fact dat she done come all dis way and won'ted ta see how this thing were gonna all play out she mighta stayed right dere wit' dem niggras. Dere was a couple a old ladies dat she said she faintly remembered from da old country and I's swear I ain't nebba seen her so happy in all da years I knowed her.

Dem Afreecans made us mo'n comfortable and Saul was fit to be tied as he and the other young men his age talked and reminisced about the ol' country and the games they useta play as if it were yesterday. And despite ev'rythang that had happened ta us ova da last few months even Missy seemt at home in da comforts of an olda couples home where dey made ev'ry effort ta make her stay as

280

comfortable as could be. Missy just set there da ol' man's rockin' chair jes a rockin' in front of dem old folks' fireplace as quiet as a church mouse sippin' mint juleps made a co'n likker as if she was in da big house.

I guessin' I was da only one outta sorts and Aunt Hattie always havin' a inclination made it a point to leave her new friends and come set wit' me a spell and try to reckon wit' my fears.

"Chile I's only been wit' one man in m'life and dat was m'husband and Lawd knows I loved dat dere man dearly. But I's seent a heap a men come and go and iffen it's one thang I's knowed about when it comes ta men is dat dey cain't alla da time be trusted. And even iffen a man be in love he gots needs dat needs ta be met and iffen he cain't get his needs met by his love one he will find a way ta geit 'em met."

I ast her why she be tellin' me dis and she say dat as long and hard as I's worked tryna get ta m'Joseph I has ta know dat it been since Christmas and ain't hardly no man, no matter how good or how in love he be can go six months wit'out no woman ta warm his bed and meet his needs. And even tho' she don't know Joseph personally I's shouldn't be too upset iffen I travel all a dis way and find out he done taken anotha woman. Da thought ain't nebba occurred ta me but I jes knows dat iffen Mas'r Reynolds hadn't sold m'Joseph we would still be married now and ain't nutjin' changed in da way I feel so ain't nuthin' shoulda changed in da way he feel and even if he saw fit ta take up wit' anotha woman when he see me he gonna jes haveta turn her loose. Dat's what I was thinkin' but dats not 'xactly how I was feelin'. I won't entirely shod at he was da same lovin' type a niggra he useta be. Slavery can change a niggra quick and in a hurry from a downright lovin' individual ta almost an animal and it don't matta what side you on. I seed Mas'r John go from a gentle, lovin' mas'r ta da devil hisself in a matta a days. Dat's what scared me most and now here we was about ta see him on da very next day and ain't nobody knew what to expect and da anticipation was killing me so after bedding little Joseph down I took a swig a laudanum m'self and called it a day.

July 19

I'm guessin' ev'ryone kinda knew what was goin' on in my mind and figgered on

jes' lettin' me be alone wit' my thoughts 'cause nobody said too much to me as we headed into Natchez. Missy and Aunt Hattie fixed breakfast which consisted of bacon, eggs, grits and auntie's home made biscuits and though ya couldn't really compare auntie's breakfasts I ate little. When I finished feeding lil' Joseph Saul took the baby and handed me the reins. Now I done driven dem hosses at breakneck speed across fo' states but this mo'ning I let them dally along at an easy canter 'til missy started astin' Aunt Hattie if I was alright.

I'm certain Saul wondered too but not a one said nothin'. Reachin'
downtown Natchez Aunt Hattie ast some niggras she seent walkin' if
they knew where the plantation was and they seemt only too glad to
point the way.

'Jes keep straight through town it ain't but a mile or two on the oth other
side of town. Its da first plantation you'll hit when you leave town.'
By this time, I was not only anxious I was plumb scared but still had the
courage to ast 'em if they kney knew a Joseph M'butu.
"You mean Joe the blacksmith. Aunt Hattie seayed my face lit up like a
jack-o-lantern when she tells the story. I don't know. I don't know 'bout
him havin' no other lady. I don't know 'bout him gittin' bitter and mean. I
don't know nothin' but that he my Joseph and he gonna love me da way
only my Joseph can. I done come too far fo anything but that. Anyways
when I ast iffen dey knew where I could find him dey sayed he won't at
da Franklin Plantation no mo' and seemt like my heart jes fell right down
to my toes. Scairt ta ast where he go I jes sat there when Aunt Hattie
say 'well can you tell me where we could find 'em. Yes ma'm. Seem like
Joe "the blacksmith" and Mr. Franklin could see this war were gonna end
up wit' da Union winnin' and so Joe made him a proposition and Mr.
Franklin always the shrewd businessman took Joe up on it. Sayed if Mr.
Franklin give him da startup money and his freedom dat he would give
Mr. Franklin a share a his blacksmith shop and bein' dat dere won't no

blacksmith in Natchez and da closest one usta be in Vicksburg before da Union leveled Vicksburg Joe would have a right profitable business and get both the business from Natchez and Vicksburg. Both men had shook hands and that's how Joe the blacksmith was becoming one of the wealthiest men niggra or white in Natchez. Sayed he had more work den he could handle and d hired a couple a hands ta help him and still didn't have enough.

By this time I was fit ta be tied and I's swear I ain't need nobody ta tell me what Joseph could tell me hisself and so I cut Aunt Hattie and dem men short and ast where I could find him to which they replied. 'Ya can't miss him. He be in the center of town. Go 'bout five streets up and he on yo' right. Got a big sign up that say B-L-A-C-K-S-M-I-T-H, well that is if any y'all can read.' Won't no need ta answer dat and I thanked him and we was off dis time at a gallop and I heard missy say Lawdy me as her head hit the back of da carriage.

I's counted da streets and read da signs and still ain't seed no blacksmith when out da corner a my eye I seed da purtiest charcoal niggra crossin right in front a my carriage and I knew at dat very instant and he ain't had ta turn around or nothin' dat dere was my Joseph. And lo' and behold iffen it won't. I give da reigns ta Saul and jumped from da carriage and runs ta my man. Now I don't know iffen he thinks he havin' a nightmare and died or iffen he thinkin' he in a dream and died and gone ta heaven but he staood dere for I don't know how long just a starin' at me like I am somethin' out of a fairy tale and den he do something I ain't nebba seen dat big Afreecan do. He cry. Den I starts ta cry and befo' ya know it Saul, Aunt Hattie and even missy is all standing' in da middle a downtown Natchez jes a bawlin' ar eyes out.

M'Joseph was still my Joseph and for once I was glad that Aunt Hattie had been wrong. Won't no other gals in da picture and he had secured his freedom just as he said he would and had opened up his own business making him an impotent man in Natchez—and a man that both niggras and white folks depended on. And he didn't stay in no slave quarters neither. M'Joseph had built himself a big ol' fine house wit' an upstairs and downstairs and three bedrooms and one that he called da master's bedroom but it won't fo' no mas'r unless you thinkin' dat me and Joe's da mas'rs here. Got a bedroom for Aunt Hattie and one for Young Saul and dey just lovin' it. Missy say she won't him to build her a cottage on the lake and Joe sayed he would and I b'lieve he will to iffen for no reason otha than ta git dat white woman as far away from him as he can. He say Lil' Joe cain't be nobody's but his 'cause he gots Mandingo features. I don't know what dat all means but it don't matter. I's got my family all back and in one place.

Made in the USA
Charleston, SC
04 April 2013